PENGUIN BOOKS

# THE WIDOW AND HER HERO

Tom Keneally won the Booker Prize in 1982 with *Schindler's Ark*, later made into the Steven Spielberg Academy Award-winning film *Schindler's List*. His non-fiction includes the memoir *Searching for Schindler* and *Three Famines*, an *LA Times* Book of the Year, and the histories *The Commonwealth of Thieves*, *The Great Shame* and *American Scoundrel*. His fiction includes *Shame and the Captives*, *The Daughters of Mars* (long-listed for the Miles Franklin Award), *The Widow and Her Hero* (shortlisted for the Prime Minister's Literary Award), *An Angel in Australia* and *Bettany's Book*. His novels *The Chant of Jimmie Blacksmith*, *Gossip from the Forest* and *Confederates* were all shortlisted for the Booker Prize, while *Bring Larks and Heroes* and *Three Cheers for the Paraclete* won the Miles Franklin Award. *The People's Train* was longlisted for the Miles Franklin Award and shortlisted for the Commonwealth Writers Prize, South East Asia division. In 2022, his novel *Corporal Hitler's Pistol* won the ARA Historical Novel Prize.

# Also by Tom Keneally

*Fiction*

The Place at Whitton
The Fear
Bring Larks and Heroes
Three Cheers for the Paraclete
The Survivor
A Dutiful Daughter
The Chant of Jimmie Blacksmith
Blood Red, Sister Rose
Gossip from the Forest
Season in Purgatory
A Victim of the Aurora
Passenger
Confederates
The Cut-rate Kingdom
Schindler's Ark
A Family Madness
The Playmaker
Towards Asmara
By the Line
Flying Hero Class
Woman of the Inner Sea
Jacko
A River Town
Bettany's Book
An Angel in Australia
The Tyrant's Novel
The People's Train
The Daughters of Mars
Shame and the Captives
Napoleon's Last Island
Crimes of the Father
Two Old Men Dying
The Dickens Boy
Corporal Hitler's Pistol
Fanatic Heart

*Non-fiction*

Outback
The Place Where Souls Are Born
Now and in Time to Be: Ireland and the Irish
Memoirs from a Young Republic
Homebush Boy: A Memoir
The Great Shame
American Scoundrel
Lincoln
The Commonwealth of Thieves
Searching for Schindler
Three Famines
Australians (vols I, II and III)
A Country Too Far (ed. with Rosie Scott)
Australians: A Short History
A Bloody Good Rant

*For Children*

Ned Kelly and the City of Bees
Roos in Shoes

# THE WIDOW AND HER HERO

TOM KENEALLY

PENGUIN BOOKS

*To the Coverdales – Alex, Rory, Craig, Margaret.*
*With the author's love.*

PENGUIN BOOKS

UK | USA | Canada | Ireland | Australia
India | New Zealand | South Africa | China

Penguin Books is part of the Penguin Random House group of companies
whose addresses can be found at global.penguinrandomhouse.com

Penguin
Random House
Australia

First published in Australia by Doubleday in 2007
This edition published by Penguin Books in 2024



Cover photography by Tom Uhlenberg / Stocksy (centre palm trees); Sheralee Stoll / Alamy Stock Photo (tall palm trees); Kevin Griffin / Alamy Stock Photo (plane)
Cover design by Adam Laszczuk © Penguin Random House Australia Pty Ltd
Typeset in Sabon by Midland Typesetters, Australia

Printed and bound in Australia by Griffin Press, an accredited
ISO AS/NZS 14001 Environmental Management Systems printer

NATIONAL LIBRARY OF AUSTRALIA
A catalogue record for this book is available from the National Library of Australia

ISBN 978 1 76134 145 8

penguin.com.au

MIX
Paper | Supporting responsible forestry
FSC® C018684
FSC www.fsc.org

We at Penguin Random House Australia acknowledge that Aboriginal and Torres Strait Islander peoples are the Traditional Custodians and the first storytellers of the lands on which we live and work. We honour Aboriginal and Torres Strait Islander peoples' continuous connection to Country, waters, skies and communities. We celebrate Aboriginal and Torres Strait Islander stories, traditions and living cultures; and we pay our respects to Elders past and present.

# Author's Note

Incidents which occur in this tale bear a debt to two real wartime operations against Singapore, named Jaywick and Rimau. But, though the real issues of Operation Rimau and the beheading of its operatives provide a spark for this tale, this narrative is not meant to be a *roman à clef* of those times and characters.

The characters here presented, their motives and their inner souls, are, therefore, not meant to reflect the actions, motives and inner life of any person who lived or died. There was, for example, no World War body named IRD (though similar organisations did exist). Nor were any battalions of the Royal Ulster Fusiliers part of Singapore's garrison. And so on.

Just the same, for their depiction of secret operations from Australia at that time, I have a great debt to the following dedicated authors and sources:

Ronald McKie, *The Heroes*, Sydney 1989;
Lynette Ramsay Silver, *The Krait: The Fishing Boat That Went to War*, from the research of Major Tom Hall, Sydney 1992;
Lynette Ramsay Silver, *The Heroes of Rimau*, from the research of Major Tom Hall, Singapore 2001;
Peter Thompson and Robert Macklin, *Kill the Tiger, The Truth About Operation Rimau*, Sydney 2002;
The Transcript of the Trial of the Rimau men, Australian Archives, Victoria.

Other correspondence, including interrogation of the Japanese interpreter Furuta, and Special Reconnaissance Force documents and reports, can be found in the Australian Archives, Canberra.

Tom Keneally, 2007

Leo, as I dream of him. His last consciousness is written not on toilet paper supplied by Hidaka but on the yellow ether there, in Reformatory Road. He knows something enormous has fallen on his neck, but mercifully not much more, no focus, no subtle thought. So I'm assured. The subtlety is bleeding out of him. Perhaps he thinks of it as a bludgeon, a mallet, something ponderous. He had been expecting something more exact than that.

Had he remembered the hymn from our wedding? He chose it himself, you see. It was one he sang at idle seconds: oh Lord of all Being throned afar, thy glory flames from star to star, and so on.

So where are we? Pitiably undistinguished ground to which I have been once since, on a trip to Singapore, and hope never to see again. It is dead earth baked solid that has never been built on, perhaps for fear of spirits, I don't know. Near Reformatory Road. Scattered over with the tube-shaped weeds they call Dutchman's pipe. They eat insects, those weeds. I remember mites and flies stuck half digested in their mucus. Plants which grew all over this ground and came not from the hand of the God of mercy.

They picked this and that man up after unsuccessful blows. I know that. Those clumsy, effete swordsmen. They who postured about being knights of the blade! They had, engraven on the haft of the sword, a quotation-cum-prayer invoking the divine wind. No such wind honoured this. Yet at least one of the Outram Road samurais had done well, because Pat Bantry's head had rolled near Hidaka that day, and Hidaka claimed he could see some light still there.

Captain, said Pat Bantry's severed head, since the heads of the saints and martyrs certainly talk when sundered, and since the heads of priests and noble folk still spoke after decapitation in the French Revolution. Then, Mother of mine! he said.

Judicial Sergeant Abukara, however, was not a knight but a butcher. But at last he extinguished Leo Waterhouse. All confusion ceased. The cloud of unknowing came down for my beautiful captain, Leo. It was a lost mother's kiss.

As Leo quoted from *The Devil's Disciple: All I can tell you is that when it came to the point whether I could take my head out of the noose and put another man's into it, I could not do it.*

Lovely words make it just about OK, Leo wrote.

# One

I knew in general terms that I was marrying a hero. The burden lay lightly on Leo, and to be a hero's wife in times supposedly suited to the heroic caused a woman to swallow doubt or to understate her demands. Although, as much as women now, we suspected men might be childish or make mysterious decisions, it wasn't our place to say it for fear of damage to the fabric of what we had. The Japanese had barely been turned back and had not abandoned the field of ambition. It was heresy and unlucky to undermine young men at such a supreme hour.

But with the confidence of near-on nine decades I can talk about doubt now. I would at least ask, what is so precious about the heroic impulse? Why do ordinary lusty boys love it better in the end than lust itself, and better than love? Why did Leo – judging by his actions – love the Boss, Charlie Doucette, in a way that rose above love of any woman, me included?

There's a documentary on television every second night these days about the end of World War II and the kamikaze pilots, avatars of self-immolation. The voice-over commentators are bemused by it all, as if self-immolation were alien to us. And that annoys me. Because self-immolation was a respectable fashion with us too then, in the early 1940s. Every man and woman put their love on the altar of the war, and that's just the way it was. We didn't reflect on or criticise the impulse. We never really believed till it happened that it was our marriage which would be picked up and hurled into the fiery pit. We believed excessively in the fatherly wisdom of generals and statesmen. Every picture we saw and every song we sang approved of what was happening, approved of the risks, celebrated the immolations, and saw the hero return grinning and unaltered by the stress of events.

I believed I began to write this for the sake of my granddaughter Rachel, and for her daughters, but it grows to have a vaguer, more general audience than that. It is the manuscript I always fancied I could write. I am not averse to their finding it amongst what I leave behind, and I don't think anyone else but the girls would be interested. But the act of addressing one includes the vain ambition to address a million. And to address to the unheeding millions what Leo in his innocence and martial mode wrote of it all.

Anyhow, let me get down to the case. Leo Waterhouse was the most beautiful adult boy I have seen in nearly ninety years of life on earth. I first met him when my cousin Melbourne Duckworth brought him home on leave to the

New South Wales town of Braidwood in the warm December of 1942. My father came from Melbourne, like his brother, who had labelled his son with the city's name. My father had moved north of the Murray River for his career's sake and he was the Braidwood National Bank manager, which counted for a lot in a bush town at the end of a long drought, an endless succession of dry skies over eastern Australia. A bank manager's discretion with credit was either cursed or blessed by farmers as the pastures became threadbare, and fissures of erosion afflicted the soil. We girls liked to think our dad was seamlessly blessed and thanked by everyone in town and from the farms about. It might have been so. He did have some sense of social justice.

When Leo Waterhouse, our house guest, was not around, my cousin Mel told me that Leo's father had been a farmer somewhere up on the North Coast, but had lost his wife and taken a job in the administration of the Solomon Islands. Leo had grown up partly under the care of an aunt in Grafton, and in Malaita. He certainly looked to me as if he had spent his childhood in places which did not inhibit growth. He had already done some law at Sydney University.

From the kitchen window of the bank manager's residence, I saw my cousin Mel and the tall visitor creep up on each other in the backyard, practising falls, occasionally miming slitting each other's throats with a swipe of the hand. I saw Mel land, after one encounter like that, in an oleander bush. They were both playful and serious, those tussling young men. Some of my girlfriends who called in from around the town were hopelessly and frantically attracted to them, as women were to beautiful doomed boys then. He looks like Errol Flynn, all the girls said of Leo. I thought he was more of a young Ronald Colman, the moustache, the tropic-weight uniform, and the big secrets he carried lightly. His mother had died when he was ten. When seen as a motherless child, his appeal was more intense still.

I continued to watch the two young men too, as Leo Waterhouse became less and less apologetic, tripping my cousin up spectacularly, cutting his throat more ruthlessly. But they were so discreet for young heroes. Returning to the kitchen for lemonade and tea, they told me nothing about their expertise with explosives or knives or folboats, a term I would learn about only later. But I knew then they were involved in something more exotic than ordinary soldiering, even though this tumbling and tripping and ritualised throat-slashing was all I saw of what they did for a living.

And do you still want to go back to your law studies after the war? my tall father asked at the meal table. Certainly I do, said Leo, below his new brushy moustache.

It was a good summer. I was a wary, reticent girl, too tall and angular to be utterly happy about myself. My reticence was only partly induced by my upbringing as a model child of model parents in a small country town. It was temperamental as well. You will see from the story I tell that I am watchful by nature. Yet without an exchange of many words, within three days Leo and I became totally enchanted by each other. I remember that we conveyed to each other a certainty of the other's perfection. Yet we were so uncorrupted.

Our few, momentary, stealthy physical contacts would occur when my cousin Mel and Leo and I walked my friends, the daughters of the town solicitor, pharmacist, general practitioner, stock and station agent and headmaster, homewards through the dark, browned-out town of Braidwood. Leo and I would lag behind or go ahead on the broad roads, and if we timed it right would find ourselves in the ultra-darkness between houses under a massive sky on the back streets of the town. The occasional straying of hands was a mere stoking of the fires. How ridiculous given that the war which changed everything was under way. Yet I valued his gallantry. At one stage outside the Braidwood School of Arts, as Leo reached for a kiss, he held my outer thigh to his inner and then repented of it. It all filled me with months' worth of fantasy at the Kurrajong boarding house in Canberra, where I normally boarded between returns home. Nothing as potentially intimate had ever happened to me before. In its way it seemed vaster than the movements of Japanese hosts in the Pacific, of German arms on the steppes of Russia.

We certainly did not know enough to understand that even in the Independent Reconnaissance Department, that bureau of noblest and most glamorous human endeavours, and amidst the intelligence organisations on which it fed, there were ambitious men who were willing to deny all that brave backyard tumbling of Leo and my cousin if it suited them: older men, soldiers for life, who had administrative gifts and who weren't going back to the field of war, and who could write off Leo's and Mel's valour if it embarrassed them in some way. Who might find it politically inadvisable to defend them even from the enemy. I could not have believed it, and it was probably just as well, since I could not have convinced Leo. And anyhow, that's the burden of my tale.

Inevitably during that Christmas–New Year period in Braidwood, the question came up one lunchtime. I think it was my mother who asked. And your parents, Leo?

She too was considered rather unfashionably tall – nearly five feet ten inches – and had not married until she was twenty-five, then considered a fairly late, spinsterish age. But she had seen what had happened and that her daughter was under an enchantment. Leo gave my mother a more explicit rundown than he had given me.

My poor mother took a drink of milk one day from a diseased cow, he told us. The family had been walking in the Clarence Valley; the farmer had had no malice in offering his milk straight from the cow. But bovine TB had killed her in three short years. My father, said Leo, took up a post in the islands afterwards. He was Superintendent of Agriculture in Malaita in the Solomons, and now I'm afraid he's a civilian prisoner of war of the Japanese. He's been moved on somewhere north, because the Americans haven't found him yet.

That must be very trying, said my mother.

It gives me an interest in the region, said Leo.

In an older man this would have sounded like irony, but in him it was understated purpose. It's very sad, Leo told us. He had a hard time in the first war, and now he's a prisoner . . .

Leo's aunt in northern New South Wales had got a Red Cross card two months past which said that he was in good health.

I was not in Braidwood all the time then. My father had not permitted me to join the Land Army or any of the women's military units. The war represented a great chance to escape stringent fathers, but my father saw enlistment as a prelude to becoming fast, wearing trousers, smoking, drinking, and the unutterable. But having attended a secretarial course and learned to touch-type I was permitted to work in Canberra for the Department of the Navy. If I had not taken my holidays when I did I would not have met Leo, since I normally made the long bus journey home to Braidwood only once a fortnight. When I worked there, the capital of the Commonwealth of Australia boasted a population of barely ten thousand, and everyone seemed buffered from the war by the acreages of pasture and the great insulating force of the eternal bush. I'd started work a few years earlier at the age of twenty, and at the time I first saw Leo tumbling with my cousin in the yard at Braidwood, I had risen to the rank of Procurement Officer, Stationery and Office Equipment.

During the week in Canberra, I boarded at the Kurrajong Guest House, a respectable, temperance boarding house whose manageress, a former Braidwood woman, my parents knew. If my parents had understood how much sundry politicians drank at the supposedly temperance Kurrajong, and how dented its respectability was by their desire to smuggle secretaries into their rooms, they might have summoned me home permanently.

A week after New Year, I said goodbye to Leo and went back to work, and Leo and my cousin vanished – to Queensland, as it turned out.

But soon, attentive Lieutenant Leo Waterhouse descended upon the plainness of my life again. One day in early 1943, when for some reason he was on his way to Melbourne (the city, not my cousin), the bomber he was travelling in made an emergency landing at Canberra's long, grassy airfield.

Let me say that most of what I now know of Leo's activities in those days comes from his own occasional letters and intermittent diary notes, and from official documents pushed under my nose by Mark Lydon, a man who once wrote a book on the adventures of Charlie Doucette and Rufus Mortmain and Leo (*The Sea Otters*, Cassell, 1968) and who has never lost interest in these men. What other sources contributed to this tale you will learn as I go along.

But I know now that Leo was on his way to Melbourne to commune with the officers who were department heads of a group called the Independent Reconnaissance Department over a proposed raid on Japanese-held Rabaul in which he was to participate. Thanks to the faulty bomber he appeared in our outer office in Canberra, in his winter-weight uniform and his Sam Browne (a swagger-stick underarm), like a fulfilment of daydreams. According to the serpentine mores of the day, such an apparition at a girl's workplace was a very serious gesture of interest. He was aware of it, I was aware of it. He was hopeful, it turned out, that the engine problem would require him to stay overnight in Canberra. We'd have dinner, at least that. I did not want to sit at table with him at the Kurrajong, where some of the regular women guests would have interrupted us. I wanted him to appear, be admired, and then we would go elsewhere, into the centre of town, Civic. In that way my female fellow boarders would be astonished at how lucky I was, the male guests informed that I was not available. As house rules required, he had me back by ten thirty, when the doors of the Kurrajong were locked.

In Melbourne, as well as conferring, he did some course on explosives, how to attach them to ships and planes. When it was over, he organised a Sydney leave and got a train to Goulburn and a car to Braidwood to seek my father's permission to ask me to become his fiancée. I was summoned home from Canberra. On an afternoon walk through the quiet streets, amongst gargling magpies and fluting currawongs, with light slanting through the wayward colonnades of trees, he asked me the huge question. We kissed. As it got suddenly darker he touched my breast and then apologised, making it impossible for me to say, Go on please. And then we went back to my parents' place, announced the expected news, and slept feverishly in our separate rooms.

On our afternoon walk he had told me that he would be gone for a time, and that out of fairness to me, we should not marry until he was back. At this stage I knew nothing of bunches of initials like SOE or IRD, I had not heard of Boss Doucette. The lack of specifics made it seem all the more grand in scale. Of course he told me he was confident he would be coming back. We would marry then, he suggested. Was that all right?

Here was the lure of delayed fulfilment – men and women both like to play that game even now. An immense anticipatory excitement grew, calculated to fill banal days with consecrated light and profane heat. The idea that a man must go on a quest to earn the company and solace of his woman is ancient, is literally Homeric, and is a handy one for nations who are organising their young for war and bloodshed.

First Leo nominated June of 1943 as a possible wedding date. By then he believed he would have been into the Minotaur's cave and slain the beast and been rendered fully a man. But by April he wrote to me announcing that all timetables had been changed and he hoped to see me next by October. He said he knew that that was a long time, and though his affections and intentions were fixed, he felt he should offer me the chance of freedom. A beautiful girl like me must have many suitors, he acknowledged. Of course, I wrote back. I told him of my willingness to wait. Indeed, I'd had a nasty experience that Easter, when one of the senior men at the ministry, flushed and alcoholic, had asked me to sleep with him. He was nearly my father's age, and that made me feel sluttish and frightened and ugly and even took my mind in directions I did not want it to go. It was, that is, what my granddaughter would call *creepy.* It rendered the prospect of waiting for Leo and his unspecified heroic business to be attended to all the more attractive.

By letter from Leo, and other means postwar, I got a picture of the training he was engaged in during those months. Cairns in Queensland was one of the ports from which our troops and the Americans in New Guinea were supplied. It also had a hillside training camp for the officers and men of the Independent Reconnaissance Department, of which Leo was a member. There Leo met and worked with Free Frenchmen and British and Australian and Dutch, all pursuing plans to infiltrate various sectors of the new Japanese empire.

Their chief trainer was a tall English sailor named Rufus Mortmain, with whose wife, the writer Dotty Mortmain, I would become friends. The men trained in the thick rainforest of the Atherton Tableland west of town. Trucked down to the coast, Leo and the others, faces blackened, spent nights in the sort of collapsible canoes they called folboats, navigating from Palm Cove to False Cape or out to the coral reef and back. Leo's usual companion was a tidily built young Russian Jew who could speak Mandarin and Shanghai-nese and whose family had come to Australia via Harbin in Manchuria and Shanghai. His name was Jockey Rubinsky, and he was a leading seaman in the Australian navy. It was thought his languages might be useful in operations around the equator.

The task of the folboat crews at night was to flit across the sea without being spotted from shore, and indeed they never were. The searchlight battery at False Cape, placed to pick up an enemy entering through the heads of Cairns harbour, became a special training tool for Charlie Doucette's men – if caught by a light, Leo and Jockey would instantaneously paddle the folboat stern onto the glare, and then they would freeze. It always worked. In those warm waters between the coast and the Great Barrier Reef they built up their invisibility, and so their immunity.

On land, by day and night they hiked and stalked through the bush barefooted, sometimes naked to avoid giving themselves away by fabric noise, or perhaps wearing a soft cloth thong around their nether parts. Their faces were black with commando grease designed for infiltrators by Helena Rubinstein. They crept into a coastal artillery battery making no sound, and stood within inches of sentries whom, in their imaginations, they despatched with their knives. Then they withdrew without being seen.

If in exercises they had to land on the sandstone jumble below headlands, they wore no footwear except woollen socks to enable them to creep over barnacles and oyster shells. With only starlight to guide them, nineteen-year-old sailors from Australian country towns learned to assemble an Owen or Sten gun in ridiculously short times and without anyone twenty yards away hearing them. And Charlie Doucette himself the magnetic Irishman loved exercises of this kind, the way only an irregular regular soldier could.

Not to cast any doubt on their skill or athleticism, it was nonetheless true that this style of life suited some men. There are always men who are happiest with other men, dreaming of women as a remote mountaintop above the plain on which their Spartan camp lay. I didn't understand this, but Dotty Mortmain, wife of the trainer, the naval lieutenant Rufus Mortmain, believed this and would pass the certainty on to me. This hiking-running-tumbling-paddling-infiltrating caste might have been happier and more certain with yearning than fulfilment, since fulfilment was demanding in a complicated way. And as I said, yearning suited the times.

In any case, most of them were babies, and I too a bush infant.

And of course, the young Australians and occasional British, Dutch and French, training in the rainforest to turn darkness into a gift, learning how to breathe and move invisibly, were not aware of the great struggle of ideology and imperialism raging between American General Douglas MacArthur's headquarters, and the British and Australians.

We'll get to that. I became educated. Widowhood was my education.

One day, during his training, Leo found himself paired for a race in a folboat, not with Jockey Rubinsky, who had a tooth abscess, but with a magnetic Ulster Irishman, an exile from Singapore, Major Charles August Doucette. Doucette was a compact, muscular, gleaming man. He had been an intelligence officer in Singapore before its inglorious fall, and a rare valiant figure from that fiasco. Leo had been until now assigned to a different proposed raid than the one Charlie Doucette was slated to lead, but he knew something of the mythology and rumours surrounding Doucette. He was a Dubliner of French Huguenot descent. His people had been architects and soldiers who acquired land cheaply in the west of Ireland in the nineteenth century from the over-mortgaged Anglo-Irish nobility.

Doucette was a regular soldier of the kind who was attached to an ancestral regiment. The Doucettes' regiment was the Royal Ulster Fusiliers, which had been the Royal Dublin Fusiliers until the Irish Free State was established, at which time it moved north to garrison Northern Ireland. He was quite jolly about telling me this one evening at some eventual party in Melbourne, and letting me know that ancestors of his had helped the Crown put down a rebellion in Ireland in the late 1700s.

Mark Lydon, author of *The Sea Otters* and thus virtually Doucette's biographer, records that Doucette was a long distance sailor and, before the war began, had spent a lot of time sailing the South China Sea – mainly for his own delight, nominally for British Intelligence. He had identified the beaches up near the Thai border where he believed the Japanese would land in a future attack on Malaya, and he also informed British Intelligence that the Japanese would not slink through the jungles but would roll down the good north–south roads in trucks and on bicycles, flanking any line the British might set up. So he had been a prophet ignored, and General Percival and the others had lost Malaya and Singapore in precisely the way he claimed he had warned them they would.

During one of his delightful reconnaissances by small boat, he met the daughter of a Belgian businessman in Macau, and married her. In fact, as she told me after the war ended, he had heard that there was a beautiful Belgian girl in Macau, and ensured that on his long sweep across the South China Sea, he took his mess uniform with him in a duffel bag, to charm the family and to court the girl: Minette Casselaine. Not a maiden in a tower as it turned out but a young, sadder and wiser divorcee with a child named Michael. He courted Minette and married her at his regimental church in Singapore.

The month before the fall of Singapore, Doucette had shipped Minette, whom he called Netty, and her son Michael, out of Singapore and to Australia. By the time Singapore surrendered, Minette and her son were living in the suburbs of Perth in Western Australia.

After the fall, Charlie Doucette had got together some escapees, Singapore civil officials, police, members of the judiciary, and British officers and men, put them in a lumpy, 25-ton fishing vessel named *Johannes Babirusa*, and relayed them to Sumatra to the estuary of the Indragiri River, which he knew from his peacetime recreation of sailing. From the point where he landed them they could reach, by a last hectic road trip, the port of Padang on the west shore of Sumatra, where Dutch, British and Australian rescue ships waited to pick up the strays from the catastrophe. He went back to Singapore to a rendezvous on the west coast many times after the fall to rescue groups of officers and officials.

For these exploits alone, Doucette – by the time Leo met him – was already a legend. Men in the know shook their heads, laughed and felt better when his name came up. I record this fact plainly and in sadness. It remains to me in part to record only the thickening and ongoing strands of Charlie the Boss Doucette's Homeric status. The legendary state traps not only the hero himself but exercises a magnetic pull on other men. Stronger than breath, stronger than sex, as Dotty Mortmain would say.

Once Doucette could no longer rescue anyone from Singapore, the gaps in Japanese security having closed, he escaped from Sumatra on the *Johannes Babirusa* with sixteen Special Operations men, mainly British. He was navigator, and steered for India. On the way, he once told Leo and myself, the *Johannes* had been attacked by a Japanese aircraft, but although the sails were riddled and the decking splintered, neither he nor any of the other men were wounded. Just the same, this strafing seemed to have affected him in a curious way. He always mentioned it heatedly. He had been so badly hurt in other ways by the Japanese dominance of the region that for the sake of sanity, I think, he put all his grievance into that particular matter. It was as if it was the chief outrage of his military career and a final sign of Japanese malice.

The *Babirusa* reached Bombay, to considerable congratulations from the military in-crowd, and Doucette was sent to Delhi and attached to Special Operations Executive there. He wrote to Minette, announced his escape, and asked her to leave Australia and join him. In the meantime he went to his late father's friend General Wavell and proposed to him a raid upon Singapore harbour using a vessel rather like the *Babirusa*. The head of SOE Delhi decided now that the Australian Independent Reconnaissance Department in Melbourne had the best personnel for such a venture. In it, the raiders could approach Singapore from Darwin up the long Indonesian archipelago, hiding amongst islands, looking like a coaster doing normal Indonesian, Borneo or Singapore business.

Charlie now telegraphed his wife to tell her not to leave Australia after all – he was coming there. But the telegram arrived too late. Netty and three-year-old Michael had left Perth a week earlier on the *Tonkin*, with over a hundred other passengers. After five days at sea the ship seemed to have evaporated. Still in Delhi and about to leave for Australia, Doucette heard that the *Tonkin* had vanished with his wife and stepson. When I ultimately met Doucette, I somehow expected him to talk about this giant fact, directly or indirectly, most of the time. But it was the sort of thing he tried to keep to himself.

In Melbourne, the head of the Independent Reconnaissance Department, one Major Doxey, listened to the ideas of the dazzling newcomer. The chief idea was: get a Japanese coaster or fishing vessel to Australia, put on the right operatives, sail it through the Indonesian and Malay archipelagos and make an assault by canoe with limpet mines on Japanese shipping in the Singapore roads.

Ambitious Doxey loved this. He had felt cramped by the new relationship with the Americans, and dependent on them for submarines to land operational parties. But this plan didn't need permission or help from the Americans. And it would show the enemy that they had no safe harbour.

In any case, now, in 1943, preparing in Cairns for operations soon to take place, Doucette and Leo had made a unique folboat pairing. The most significant members of their families had vanished in the war. They might have thought it was a fanciful connection. But it was a connection nonetheless.

I imagine them sitting in pandanus shade on a beach waiting for the little canvas prows of inferior paddlers to show themselves on the dazzle of ocean.

In speaking with Leo, Major Doucette was reticent with the details of his life and let go of them shyly. Doucette remarked, as they sat on Holloway Beach, their race done, that the Australian other ranks were funny chaps.

Leo asked him in what way.

They always give you the impression they won't obey an order, yet they do.

Leo said they just wanted to assert their dignity.

Some of the things they say and do, reflected Major Doucette, would be the subject of a court martial in Britain.

Leo said it would be a waste of time charging them and would only make them sullen.

The major said he could do with an Australian officer to liaise between himself and his Australian operatives. Leo listened to this fanciful talk and didn't take it too seriously at first. His mind was given over to the proposed raiding party on Japanese-occupied Rabaul. I knew nothing of this constantly postponed plan, but it was the reason our engagement stretched out. The group of which he was a member were to be dropped and picked up by submarines, a prospect which Leo looked at as a pleasing extension of his experience and a fulfilment of filial duty to his father.

Much of the Australian autumn and winter he was in training for this Rabaul mission, which would never take place. His dreams of invading Rabaul Harbour by canoe with Jockey Rubinsky and others were ultimately quashed by General MacArthur's headquarters, which would not supply a submarine for the drop-off and pick-up. MacArthur's office had earlier said that it would all be okay, but then one of the American submarine fleet was destroyed in those same waters. And in any case, a new plan was in force to bypass the large Japanese garrison in Rabaul and to let it wither on the vine. Suddenly Rabaul was not worth risking any more submarines for. The Americans, I discovered later, also found it ideologically offensive, since it seemed to encourage the idea that British imperialism, even in its more modest Australian variety, would take up in New Britain after the war from where it had been in 1941.

The news came down to Leo that the operation had been cancelled. As delightful as that would have been for me, had I known, he was of course desolated. The war had been going for so long, and he had the capacity to infiltrate, to observe, to tumble, to extinguish life. But IRD was proving a melee of cancelled good intentions and projects which did not work – often because the Americans were singing from a different hymn sheet, and one which in time would be graced with God's evident blessing.

In any case, Rabaul being cancelled, Leo was ready now to join Doucette as a tamer of Australian personnel. He wrote me another letter. He expected still that we would be reunited about October, maybe November at the latest. Would I lose interest by then in a plain, uncultivated fellow like him? he asked.

# Two

It was easy to wait. Lots of girls in my office were waiting. A number had absent boyfriends, soldiering banally somewhere in northern Australia, or at greater peril in New Guinea or North Africa, flying in bombers in Europe. We compared notes, we drank tea together, and wandered in a mist of God-given and state-sanctioned longing. All this gave our plain jobs, the yellow folders of acquisitions I consulted and added to and filed all day, a holiness they would otherwise not have had. We went to the pictures on Thursday nights to have our heartache further teased by tales of heroic acts but heroic longing as well. *Action in the North Atlantic*, *So Proudly We Hail*, *Desperate Journey*, *Mrs Miniver* and *Sahara*. We emerged chattering like birds. I think only my shyness prevented me from a sort of crazed morbidity which afflicted some of the girls in the department.

In the meantime, without my being aware of it, Doucette was preparing to take Leo deeply into the oceans of the enemy. Doucette had already inspected a Japanese fishing boat confiscated by Australian authorities in Townsville at the start of the war. *Pengulling*, Doucette named it. The animal in whose honour it took that Malay title was the pangolin, a large anteater, many spiked. Cornflakes was the operational name decided on for what would be done via *Pengulling*. Why? Because on the morning after his proposed Singapore raid the Japanese would be too distressed to eat their breakfast!

The fishing boat was brought up to Cairns by coastal steamer and was moored by a naval workshop on the south end of Cairns, near the Yarrabah Aboriginal reservation. She was packed with the necessary limpet mines, on models of which the men had trained in the darkest nights around their camps. And so, on a May morning, Doucette and all his Argonauts – Leo amongst them – set off, brimming with clever training, skirted Cairns harbour and headed up Australia's long north-east coast.

After a day, his engineering officer contracted malaria and was put in a hammock on deck. Under the inexperienced care of a rating, the engine block melted down, and the *Pengulling* and its heroes drifted, called for help, and had to be towed back to Cairns. All Charlie Doucette's personnel, skilled in so many now irrelevant aspects of the craft of infiltration, were scattered back to their regular army and navy postings. Only Doucette and Rufus Mortmain and a highly frustrated Leo remained in Cairns.

Major Doxey of IRD put out a call to find *Pengulling* a new six-cylinder 105-horsepower Cascade diesel engine, with its spare parts, but the latter were apparently as rare as the Tasmanian tiger. Leo and the others were aware that Major Doxey, and the Allied generals to whom he reported, were now losing interest in Operation Cornflakes.

Conversations over evening drinks in the officers' mess in Cairns showed Leo that Doucette had absolutely no doubt that Cornflakes would go ahead. His wife and child being still lost and perhaps drowned, he clung to his Singapore dream. He kept writing for his new engine and the return of his crew, but Leo himself feared it might never happen. Leo had dreams, he told me later, in which his father, always a severe man, chided him for leaving him a prisoner.

So Charlie Doucette, the Boss, decided on an exploit to bring the efficacy of laying mines from folboats and onto shipping to the attention of their superiors. They would attach limpets to the Allied ships in the larger port of Townsville. Doucette, Mortmain and Leo prepared everything – the entire plan – but disguised it as a training exercise.

Doucette was able to gather a number of his original young men, Australians, and a Kipling-esque duo of Geordie and Welshman who had originally escaped from Singapore with Doucette, and took them south from Cairns on the train. Trucks loaded with their gear and with further members of the old group met them in the late afternoon by the railway lines north of Townsville, and there Doucette's people got down and then waved the coastal train and its passengers on towards Townsville. The trucks took them on a timber trail through the bush and to a stream named the Black River. Doucette's group spent the night and much of the day paddling and portaging down the river until it disgorged onto a wide-open and deserted beach. They paddled then for the high mass of Magnetic Island, where they rested in the bush behind a beach.

The next day they spent plotting through a telescope the positions of a dozen Allied ships at anchor in Townsville, and then at midnight set off in a series of folboats across the six miles of sea. Leo's partner was again the little Russian Jockey Rubinsky. One of the folboat teams attached dummy magnetic mines to two ships anchored in the roadstead, waiting for a mooring. The other four, including the team of Leo and Rubinsky, came on a current through the narrow entrance and past the navy's mine control point. It was so easy, a token of how easy Singapore might be.

The tale of this monkey business would tickle them for the rest of their mostly short lives; in fact, IRD people in general had some dreadful times ahead of them, and needed to have triumphs to sustain them, stories of impudent nights like this. Under, of course, their impudent cavalier, Charlie Doucette.

I know from Lydon's book rather than from anything I heard directly from Leo that attaching limpets to ships was done in this way: the man in the bows of the folboat attached a magnetic holdfast to the side of the ship. The man in the stern – Leo always took the stern position – used a foldable rod he carried in the bottom of the boat to pick up a limpet mine from the cargo space in front of him and set it against the boat's hull, as deep as he could get it below the water. Each folboat carried nine limpets, and each one was a hefty weight, so that to lift one from a sitting position required great strength in chest and arms, which Leo my beloved possessed. I had judged him strong, I had dreamed of being the client of that strength. Yet still I had probably underestimated it.

Needless to say, a sort of delicacy was also required to place a holdfast and three magnetic mines against the hull of a ship in which all sound resonated. But most of Doucette's men had by now been practising that technique for the better part of a year. Leo and Jockey placed theirs as ordered, three to each of three ships. There was a great deal of welding going on along the wharf, and up against one of the ships, a destroyer named *Warradgerry*, lay a lighter, a manned repair barge. But Leo set his magnetic training mines, incapable of doing damage to these friendly ships, without difficulty.

Upright in their slivers of canoes and without being detected from the wharves, Charlie Doucette's men put their strings of pretend fatality on the Dutch freighter *Akabar*, on the Australian freighter *Katoomba*, on two of Mr Roosevelt's American Liberty ships, and on a series of other vessels. One of the Boss's crews, made up of two sailors, were attaching their mines soundlessly to the

*Katoomba* when they saw a man on deck smoking, looking down at them. Just out for a row, mate, they told him, and he took it as a reasonable explanation and went to bed.

But what larks, as Dickens would say! On a night like that a young man – many young men – might mistake their stylishness for immunity from wounds.

Leo wrote an account of this which ended up in his office drawer in Melbourne. It was given to me after the war by Foxhill, one of Leo's best friends in the bureaucracy of IRD. Needless to say, it is written in the style of *Boys' Own Adventures*. But what else would you expect? To convince the authorities to unleash Cornflakes was for Leo the prelude to our marriage.

*Because of the barge anchored beside the destroyer, I wasn't able to work along the full length of the ship but placed a line of mines under the bows, deep as my arms would reach – we didn't want them to be exposed by the falling tide until just before noon the next day. There were actually men welding on the wharf, and the guards in their tin hats were discussing the previous year's Melbourne Cup which they'd attended baksheesh, for free. Jockey held us good and steady, as I leaned and reached, putting my own arms deep in the water. There was a metallic sort of gargle when the limpets attached. It is a wonderful thing to have an art, as my father used to say when he made my mother laugh. When I had done it, I put my hand on Jockey's shoulder so we could go.*

*We had an effortless row out of harbour on the tide. The moon had gone somewhere behind Mount Louisa, and our boats were pretty light now with all the mischief taken from them. Outside the boom, we turned south to the picnic ground near the mouth of the Ross River, pulled up our folboats there, and sat eating a breakfast of compo rations, and we would suddenly laugh, remembering something from the night's business.*

*The Boss organised accommodation for the men at the naval barracks. He's insisted that he take Mortmain and me to the officers' club. So a truck arrives for everyone – the same that dropped us off to the north the other day – how long ago I can barely tell. And so that's what happened – the officers' club. I got a very good room with clean sheets – wonderful. And I was so absolutely done in that I didn't hear all the alarms of the town nearby go off at ten o'clock, as the three highly placed fake mines we'd put along the length of a Dutch freighter rode up out of the water. The area near the wharves was immediately evacuated, I believe – various kids got a day off school. But I slept through all that, and I imagine Doucette was only mildly disturbed.*

*Sometime after three o'clock in the afternoon, a truck pulled up outside the same officers' club where we were resting up. There was a lot of loud yelling and officious orders given, and boots in the corridors and noise of the kind of soldierly drill provosts are good at. I got up and looked out my door and saw guards and a provost officer at the door of the room where the Boss was getting a rest. Mortmain emerged from his room wearing a singlet and khaki underpants and – I swear – his bloody monocle in his eye.*

*Boss, he called into Doucette's room.*

*I've just been arrested, cried the Boss from within. These gentlemen thought I'd slept long enough.*

*I told you the girl wasn't legal age, Boss, Mortmain yelled and winked at me, his eye without the glass in it. Could I be arrested with Major Doucette? he asked the provost.*

*The provost told Mortmain there wasn't any warrant for him, and Mortmain said he understood that, but they'd missed out on arresting him so many times in the past.*

*Lieutenant Mortmain is my second, I heard Doucette say. He'll accompany me. Mortmain looked over at me. And you can come too, Dig, he told me. (He always called me Dig or Digger in an exaggerated British way.) I got dressed. I have to say I didn't want to miss out on being arrested either.*

*I have transportation room only for two prisoners, said the provost.*

*We'll squeeze up, said the Boss.*

*They took us to the harbourmaster's office under Castle Rock. There were a collection of ship's captains in there, and an American colonel. One of the captains was a very angry Dutchman. We should not have dared to touch his ship. He had recently been attacked in New Guinea waters by Japanese aircraft, and he was very jumpy. When he stopped talking, Doucette apologised and said that he wanted to alert people to the vulnerability of Australian ports. (I think he'd earned the right to tell that slight untruth.)*

*And the thin-lipped old Scot who was harbourmaster asked him in a brogue that could have ground wheat if he was saying he wanted this outrage reported in the scandal sheets?*

*There were some naval officers in the harbourmaster's office and they all seemed calm, laughing now and then. But the Boss, Mortmain and myself were careful not to laugh. Mortmain merely shifted that ridiculous monocle around by the muscular force of his cheek and eyebrow as if he was laughing inside. The Australian captain of the* Warradgerry *spoke up and said he was sure this event was merely intended to be news amongst us.*

*And Doucette answered, It was a stunt unworthy of public attention, sir, but useful to those who have ears to listen.*

*The captain seemed quite jolly given that fake limpet mines had been put all over his ship. He assumed that Doucette had authorisation for this exercise? The Boss undid the top button of his khaki shirt and brought forth some documents which were wrapped in cellophane. He placed them on the table, not being too definite about who would pick them up first. The naval captain did. When the cellophane was unwrapped, two separate typed letters were visible. The captain read the first one and passed it to the harbourmaster. Then read the second and did the same. Then the letters made their way around the Dutch, the three French and the Australian merchant captains and were absorbed one at a time. At the end of the line they were passed to the American colonel. They did not seem to make a huge impression on him, but his face remained neutral throughout the whole thing. He excused himself, stepped through the line of merchant captains and returned the letters to the Australian navy man in charge of the port without comment or thanks. Then he resumed his place in the far corner of the room.*

*The Australian port commander declared it seemed both General Wavell and General Blamey had given Doucette open slather or* carte blanche, *and some of the captains might be angry and embarrassed, but a greater good had probably been achieved. He himself didn't seem angry and embarrassed.*

*As we all emerged, the merchant captains walking down the docks to their sundry ships, the captain of the* Warradgerry *stopped to talk to us. He invited us to attend drinks in the wardroom that evening. Doucette said we would be honoured to. The captain explained why he and the local naval commander were so friendly to us. He'd been telling the Scot for a long time that a complete boom needed to be laid inside the harbour. But the old harbourmaster, who'd held the job since the 1920s, argued some of the native captains coming in from the islands would get themselves caught up in it. The captain said the harbourmaster thought it was still 1935. He saluted and so we saluted back like real gents.*

For the sun was shining on their faces, and rewarding them, or making promises they could imagine were cast-iron. Leo's account continues exultant, and shows that even a mock-martial triumph can endow the heroes with the better lines, and a sense of divine assurance; exactly what I would have wanted him to have.

*There was no time to go back to the officers' club before drinks hour aboard the* Warradgerry. *We decided we would fill in the time by going to the Townsville Hotel and having tea on their verandah, and begging a piece of their stationery so that the Boss could write a list of the ships we had marked. He was doing this while Mortmain and I drank our black tea, exactly right for a warm place like Townsville, bringing out a sort of cleansing sweat. Then we saw the high-ranked American who had been in the harbourmaster's office was standing over us, very thin and tall. His shadow fell over the Boss's page, and he looked up. The American asked us if it would be an intrusion if he joined us.*

*Certainly not, said the Boss, but in that icy British way which actually means I'd prefer you went away. Doucette did not rise to salute this more senior soldier, and so neither did we. Strange, since the Brits were so crazy on rituals, but then we'd all got out of the habit of it during our training.*

*So the American took a seat. I looked at his uniform – it was great tailoring. The Boss introduced us. This was Lieutenant-Colonel Jesse Creed, he told us. Creed wore the insignia of the American intelligence corps.*

*The tall man smiled.*

*I was wondering if I could have a confidential word, Creed asked Doucette. The Boss said certainly, and then Creed looked significantly at Mortmain and myself, suggesting we should leave. I was already standing up to go. But the Boss said, These gentlemen can stay.*

*Creed agreed, making the best of it he could. He asked the Boss about the spare engine for the Japanese fishing boat,* Pengulling. *I hear it's turned up, he said.*

*Being installed as we speak, said the Boss.*

*That was the first I'd heard of it, but I really hoped it was true. It was time.*

*Creed shook his head and grinned. You English, you do things all your own way, he said.*

*I'm actually an Irishman, said the Boss. But he only said it for the sake of argument since he was one of those Irishmen who considered himself British.*

*You'd have a hard time proving that in New York, Creed told him.*

*I am, begorrah, said the Boss, without a smile. I'm Irish as Shackleton. Irish as that ponce Oscar Wilde, Irish as Dean Swift or Sheridan or Oliver Goldsmith.*

*Creed said, All right then. Since your cranky old boat's getting its temporary repair . . . the question arises. Was this morning to improve the safety of dear old Townsville, the delightful place destiny has placed us? Or was it a dress rehearsal?*

*It was an expression of brio, sir, said Doucette, but still without any emphasis in his voice.*

*Loosen up a bit, for God's sake, Creed said. Last time I read about it, we were allies.*

*So I could tell you everything, and you would say, That's absolutely splendid and we Yanks can help. But when the time came, you wouldn't be available. As happened with young Waterhouse here. Suddenly, no sub for his jaunt. That's what happens with you chaps all the time.*

*Creed was angry and his face flushed for a moment. He said, We did lose a sub off New Britain. That's eighty men who drowned, whose lungs choked with water. But a person would think we did it just to thwart IRD and cause you offence, Major Doucette.*

*The Boss murmured, If that's the impression I gave, then I apologise. But I think there's a policy on your side to keep us permanently training for ops which get cancelled. And it's just not good enough.*

*And he didn't give an inch.*

*Creed lowered his voice. There's a rumour around that you're going up to Java, to Surabaya, say, in that cranky old bathtub of yours.*

*That was indeed the rumour. The Boss might have spread it deliberately, though he told me it would be better if there were no rumour at all.*

*The American said, God forbid you got into trouble, but I could make sure your distress calls were acted on. I must be crazy talking to you like this, on a hotel balcony. I'll approach you more formally and, Major, I'll expect a private meeting and a polite answer.*

*Perhaps you should talk to Major Doxey at IRD, the Boss said, suddenly stricken with a fake air of helpfulness. And he smiled now, like a boy. He did have a boy's wiry build and lolly-legs, and seemed maybe fifteen years younger than he was when he did that grin.*

*Creed was pretty exasperated, standing and addressing us from that position while making a patting-down gesture that said we should remain where we were. It's like this, Doucette. I used to paddle boats when I was a kid. Life seems pretty simple when you're surrounded by water and it's kind of level with you. But then I'd come in at the end of the pier and moor the canoe and come ashore, and I'd be amongst complicated stuff then – my parents, my sister, and whether she was dumping this boy or encouraging the other, and all the financial secrets and even other secrets of my parents. That's your situation, Doucette. You're just paddling away, but there's a complicated big house somewhere, where your IRD and the whole Mountbatten SOE group and Central Intelligence Bureau all live. And you despise and don't understand the big house at all, Major Doucette. You don't know our secrets and you don't want to give any ground.*

*I should say not, said Doucette. All the more reason to stick to what I do best.*

*It's all the more reason to have a well-wisher in there, in that big house, to look after you.*

*I thought to myself that an argument like that might win the day for the American colonel, but Doucette stayed neutral to the point of contempt. Thank you, sir, he said.*

*You guys are more mysterious than the Japanese.*

*I felt a bit embarrassed for Creed as he walked away amongst the good afternoon-tea-ing women of Townsville who wiped their necks, and the chest regions above where their dresses started, with sweaty handkerchiefs. The truth was that to me Creed seemed a pretty generous ally. But the Boss must have had his reasons for rebuffing him.*

*We were saluted aboard the* Warradgerry *in the late afternoon and escorted to the wardroom by a midshipman. As we entered, applause broke out amongst the naval officers present – it was as if the captain had told his crew that that was the appropriate response.*

*When the congratulations were over, we were taken to a bar where a white-coated steward poured us drinks. I had the national diet – a glass of Dinner Ale. And the worldly Boss and Rufus ordered gin. I found myself drinking a beer with a young officer, and well forgotten in a corner of the room. Then the captain clapped his hands and gave a jovial introduction to Doucette.*

*We had some visitors last night, he said, and everyone laughed.*

*Major Doucette has kindly agreed to read out a list of fifteen ships to which dummy mines were attached last night.*

*Doucette came forward in that slightly distracted way which I think was a bit of an act.*

*The fifteen ships were the SS* Akabar, *the SS* Warrnambool, *the SS* Katoomba, Port Lincoln, Grafton *and* Eskimo, *the frigate* Geelong, *the frigates* Mildura *and* Portland, *the minesweepers* Echidna *and* Waratah, *the Liberty ships* Carolton *and* Duchesse, *the coastal steamers* Murray *and* Downley *and, said Doucette, HMAS* Warradgerry. *Until that second of seeing the captain's stunned face, I thought he already knew his ship had been marked. But it was obvious that he didn't.*

*Doucette said, I'm afraid it's my young friend over there in the corner, Lieutenant Waterhouse, who placed your mines very deeply. As you see, he's got awfully long arms.*

*The captain laughed, but there was a barking sound to it. He called for two officers to go on deck and look for magnetic appendages which might not have been visible in the first panic that morning, and had passed scrutiny since. The young man I was talking with gave me a small punch on the arm and asked, You did us? Bugger me! You really did us!*

*The captain told me that it looked like he must be indebted to me for blowing his ship up, and soon the two officers were back having launched the ship's boat and located the limpets and left seamen working at detaching them from the destroyer's side.*

*When it was announced we were leaving, we were cheered out of the wardroom. And I suppose, as Rufus said, we had a story which could make us warm on cold nights and cool on hot nights. We had a tale which we could use to revive ourselves and other men.*

*On the pier, which was conspicuously darker than it had been the night before, the Boss said that* Pengulling, *the fishing boat, was nearly ready. Are you still willing to sail? he asked me.*

*Mortmain was smoking. He closed the eye behind the monocle. Can paddle, he said of me. Strong lad. Good humour. Rough manners. Why not?*

*But I was always coming, I insisted.*

*And they laughed. I thought to myself, Creed's right. You can never exactly tell what the Poms are getting at.*

# Three

How was the sex? asked my granddaughter Rachel, one time when she was a student in the late eighties.

She meant in my life with Leo. She was always talking about and marvelling at my tales of Braidwood at the turn of the 1940s, the codes, the social restrictions, but she was also a clever girl and aware that she too was subject to codes, and that restrictions on people are a moveable feast. She was amused by the fact that in my day women had a duty to appear indifferent to sex and to treat it as a necessary evil, and that in hers women have a duty to be sexually fulfilled and satisfied.

So, how was the sex? she asked me.

It was very satisfactory, I told her, delighted to be prim.

Oh, she said, amused. Satisfactory. Very well.

In many ways I have never in my life been able to talk to anyone as freely as I have talked to this girl. This was a conversation I could not have had with Laurie Burden, my second husband. It's still the way.

Rachel's a museum curator in Brisbane now (*now* being the early days of the twenty-first century), with three children and a husband, but when we meet even after a year's separation, often at my son's place at Christmas time, we simply begin again with the same level of mutual confidence.

*Very* satisfactory. That's what I said. One weekend in that winter of 1943, when the wedding awaited some ordeal of arms I could only vaguely imagine, my mother came to my room and gave me a book in a brown paper cover. Her face was red, but obviously she felt she must perform this duty.

She said, Men think they are worldly, but often they're not. They think they understand women, but no! Sometimes the wife has to educate them. Treated in the right spirit, that book will help you a lot.

It was a surprisingly weighty book. I found it as abashing to accept as she did to pass it to me. I started nonetheless to open the front cover.

No, my mother said. Wait till I'm gone.

I waited till ten seconds after she closed the door. The opened titlepage read *Sex Without Fear* by one Samuel Aaron Lewin. It possessed the heaviness of a medical tome and was published in America, where – I presumed – life was racier. This book was revolutionary, I would later discover, in that it placed an onus of pleasure, and of educating husbands, on wives. It proposed that men were sexually primitive and that the wife must teach her spouse to seduce her, and that the husband be led to have in the forefront of his mind his wife's delight. And it illustrated widely and clinically and without pornographic relish how that delight could be achieved, and counselled women to discuss these matters with their husbands, and not to be constrained by any artificial fear that their husbands would think them 'pre-violated'.

Where had my mother acquired this exceptional book? Did all the women of Braidwood possess a copy? I was thrilled and repelled by that idea. Obviously she must have got it on a visit to Sydney. She probably needed to have a medical prescription to buy it. Had my parents resorted to such hearty stimulations as the book recommended? I decided not to contemplate that.

I read the book on icy nights in Canberra with the acuity of an athlete absorbing the rules of a new, higher sport and getting ready for the contest. In the spirit of preparing the way for my lover, I engaged in solitary explorations, though they seemed a dim pre-echo of what might happen to me, once Leo's test of war had earned the nuptials.

This was, I know now, the beginning of the golden time for Doucette and Mortmain and for Leo. Dour government records are nonetheless full of hints of their mutual creativity and confidence in each other's company. Now that the new engine was aboard the *Pengulling*, Operation Cornflakes was a go-er, a starter in the great planetary power stakes. The attack on Townsville had been a mere mock play. Now they were to be in the great theatre, and would become legendary even to themselves, blessed men. Alfred Tennyson provided the text for Doucette's life with lines he could recite at parties.

> . . . but somewhere ere the end
> Some work of noble note, may yet be done.

That might have been the trouble. The men were living according to Tennyson, whereas Dotty, and soon I, were determined to live in the age of Auden and TS Eliot.

*Pengulling* would bring Doucette and Leo through seas of all colours, of abrasive tropic blue, through blinding golden sunsets and the bruisings of storm, to their *work of noble note.*

Despite all the planning, Doucette had to grab for a few extra people at the end – the only cook he could find was a malaria-prone veteran of the fighting in New Guinea earlier in the year. It was appropriate to every odyssey that there be such flawed men. The navigator was flawed too – a wanderer and barely repentant alcoholic, already in his early forties, though gifted at his job. After an unhappy spate in the navy during World War I, he had spent the Depression in Queensland and New South Wales digging for opals along the New South Wales–Queensland border, or descending upon nineteenth century gold rush sites to rework the tailings and mullock with arsenic. For his brief World War I experience as a sailor in the Australian navy, upon re-enlisting for this new war he had been commissioned. The Independent Reconnaissance Department had chosen him, yet he had been through none of the training rigours of his young fellow crewmen. His name was Lieutenant Yewell, his nickname was Nav. I have seen his photograph and his face is a complex one, leathered by remote suns and in which the struggle with his demons was plainly written. Doucette tended to take a very positive attitude towards such men, an attitude that was good for them, and made them behave better than perhaps they were. He made heroes out of quality men like Mortmain and Leo, and a passable fellow out of the unredeemed Yewell, who'd been assigned to the *Pengulling* purely because he knew tropic waters.

*Pengulling* cast off. Everything went cheerfully as it easily penetrated the dangerous coral reefs of the Torres Strait, and reached westwards through the Arafura and the Timor Seas, sighting peaceful Melville Island north of Darwin. Down the shoal coast of Western Australia they came to the American base at Exmouth Gulf, Potshot. All the way they practised on their silenced weaponry and by day kept their large Caucasian jaws and shoulders and hands under the awning. As for the routine, some men could sleep on the deck, unless there was bad weather and they could then sleep in the wheelhouse. The hold contained three officers' bunks and a sophisticated radio run by batteries. The head, the lavatory, used by all ranks without distinction, was on deck in the stern. The galley and various cupboards were also there, and there were water tanks and a gravity tank to the engine which was used as a mess table. A tarpaulin covered much of the deck, and I know it was decided that only those who could pass as Asians would be in the open – Doucette, the boy terrier of an Irishman; Rubinsky, the olive-skinned Jewish rating from the Australian navy; and Nav himself.

At sea by night they had taken off and dumped some of the *Pengulling*'s bullet-resistant cladding, and were thankful for the good weather to that point, for they saw that the armour's two tons had reduced the freeboard to a mere ten inches, and that would not have been enough in stormy seas. Now they rode higher but would splinter to matchwood under any attack.

The American rear admiral at Potshot was very kind to them, and was convinced that their destination was the Japanese naval base at Surabaya in Java, though he told Doucette solemnly that everyone believed the hopeless little vessel was bound for Fremantle. In any case, *Pengulling* was repainted here with camouflage grey.

There was a load of gear awaiting them, flown from Melbourne by IRD. New British-built folboats, spare parts for the engine, anti-glare glasses, binoculars, etc. Leo would later tell me that he was a bit amazed when Doucette declared he was going to drop inland a little way and see some of his relatives who had a cattle station east of Exmouth – some first cousin from Ireland had settled there – and a transport plane flying to Perth agreed to take him.

Mortmain looked over the new British folboats with Leo and said that the stitching of the canvas was appalling, a real wartime economy job. We used to laugh at Japanese manufacture, Mortmain told Leo. But he and Leo and their partners went for a warm-up paddle of twenty miles or so, and suddenly the stitching meant nothing. For Leo, excitement and daring would prevail over any deficiencies of thread.

How often did these men mention their women, I wonder. Mortmain his – as I would discover – wily wife, or Leo his fiancée? I never thought about it at the time, I presumed we were talked about, boasted of, envisaged constantly. The older I get the more I doubt it. It was simply that they were engaged in an all-absorbing task.

Doucette returned from his cousin's cattle station, and he and his men took to their little fishing boat again and sailed north out of Exmouth Gulf. The forward hold was full of armaments and other gear, and there were flaps in the superstructure to enable men to take up battle stations in an emergency. The horns of a submarine supply and maintenance ship, USS *Wagram*, sent this little grey sliver of a vessel on its way. It made half a mile before the engine instantly overheated and choked. Some mysterious components named the centrifugal pump and the coupling key of the intermediate propeller shaft had broken. The Americans had *Pengulling* towed to *Wagram*'s side, and the engine and most of the drive shaft were hauled aboard and worked on. The Americans replaced the centrifugal pump.

When they left Potshot, it was thought by the Americans that they were going to Fremantle, and that the repairs were meant for a journey down the Western Australian coast. The mechanics earnestly told Doucette to nurse the engine along.

And now our voyagers were away on an afternoon tide again, the opinion being that the new pump would last them a long time. Interestingly, once the course and rudder were set and they were heading north-east along the desert coast, Doucette read snatches from a little brown book, *Homer's Odyssey*, translated by Chapman. The men listened as if for a code. He had won the book as a prize at Eton, and the kid leather cover was a scuffed brown. Tea and beer had both been spilt on it. Did he see himself as Ulysses 'detained by the goddess Calypso'?

A great storm hit them that September night. The decks were awash with fluorescent foam, and the *Pengulling* was a mere tub before waves which Leo said were big as blocks of flats, and came up behind, and lifted the little boat high above a nauseating trench of water, dropped it in, awaited its emergence, and began the process again. All night, the water across the deck was waist-deep. Mortmain chopped a hole in the hull to allow the volume of deck water to escape. Above or below, sleep was not possible. Most of the muscular ratings and soldiers were sick, and lay on their sides helpless, humiliated so soon. Leo too was sick, but in a practical way, stepping outside the wheelhouse, retching, coming in again with a clear mind for the next little while.

It was when the storm abated and the sky grew brilliant again the next afternoon, and the men returned to being hungry, that Doucette told *them* what he and Leo and Rufus and a few others already knew: where they were going. Leo's partner Rubinsky, for example, had not known until now. He and the others were astonished and enlarged by the news.

Singapore. Three boat crews and one in reserve. Nine limpets per folboat, as at Townsville, but live ones this time. After the exhilaration, for the meat of the long journey, there were only three books on board – the novel *The Sheik*, an erotic story tame by the standards of today, that little leather copy of the Chapman edition of *Odyssey*, and a black-covered devotional book, *The Imitation of Christ*, by Thomas á Kempis, which belonged to Sergeant Pat Bantry, and which only Bantry had any interest in. Most social life took place on the after-deck behind the wheelhouse, which was adequately covered by the tarpaulin to enable gatherings including those men whose big hands and feet and large features deprived them of any chance of resembling an Indonesian or a Malay. Mortmain told stories of life on teak plantations in Burma and Malaya. The malice and whimsy of elephants figured a lot in them. Able Seaman Jockey Rubinsky told stories about his Russian father and uncles in Bondi Junction, a location where Hitler was unlikely to disrupt their energies. Meanwhile, the man keeping watch stood on the gravity tank within the canopied area and stuck his head through a hole in the awning roof.

For a time off the north coast of Australia, *Pengulling* had aircraft cover. But even this early the navigation officer was surly and wanted a drink. He snapped at Jockey's tales. He did not get the point, or didn't have the mental space to, and expressed a hatred of Jews which Leo said wouldn't have been out of place in a Nazi. A distance grew between him and the other travellers, not because he badmouthed Jews but because he was not far behind in badmouthing everyone and wanting whisky.

At this stage, going to the fair, Doucette did not permit too much conversation. He had already told them he hated regular soldiering and been expansive on his unregimental sailing adventures in the South China Sea. But now he used all the regular military tricks, filling the hours with the business of dismantling and reassembling weapons, and of watches and drills. If that wasn't enough, his occasional lectures on the Punic Wars were very successful. Having heard that fantastic word *Singapore*, they did not worry anymore about propeller shafts or seas. It was as if the augustness of the target itself, and the supreme dangers it stood for, would keep them safe from lesser issues like drive shafts and rogue waves.

Approaching Bali they saw Japanese planes flying high, with intentions to inspect and destroy bigger shipping than them. From now on they would wear sarongs – all uniforms were put away, and they covered their bodies with a brown stain. Leo says the stuff was utterly lacking in fragrance and grew smelly on the body. The Japanese flag was raised at the stern – it had been sewn up by someone's wife in Melbourne. When other small ships were met in the fringes of the Indonesian archipelagos, most of the crew concealed themselves in the wheelhouse or below, or under the awning, while Doucette, himself slight of body with delicately designed hands, and fluent in Malay, together with the navigator and swarthy, small-limbed Mandarin-speaking Seaman Rubinsky were to remain visible.

There is a photograph of Mortmain, his monocle still in his eye socket, his body streaky brown, his lantern jaw a frank tribute to his ancestry, and of Leo, similarly bare-chested, standing together before the wheelhouse wearing their sarongs, demonstrating the hopeless innocence and valour of the idea that all that sea could be covered without the subterfuge being easily seen through. But they did take wise precautions. All smoking was forbidden, lest cigarette butts cast overboard might serve the Japanese navy as a clue to their infiltration. Toilet paper could not be used – it was too dangerous a clue as well. At night there was total blackout. Garbage and the leavings of their mess table were put in sealed tins which the men cast overboard and then filled with holes using Sten guns with silencers.

I see them cheering in particular in their sarongs as with mock ceremony the home-made Japanese flag was let fly from the stern. They did this without much thought for the situation international law placed them in now. Deceptive men ripe for punishment? They did not feel that way.

They lined up with the two volcanoes of Lombok Strait, and found themselves a little way off course at the western end of Bali, and then crept along to the strait, where the waters surged through so strongly against them that they were held there all night, watching the lights of Japanese trucks on Bali. Then while vapour still clouded Lombok, they crept through by daylight. They did not want to hug any coastline, in case they met Indonesian *prahu* or junks or patrols, so they made course north towards Borneo and then turned to port, lined up on nearly an exact north-west course for Singapore.

They had the cheek now, in these enemy waters, to begin to feel bored. 'Bored' was their reaction to a sea too broad and bright, and a sky too enormous, a brazen sun and their tiny refuge beneath the tarpaulin inadequate. I don't pretend to understand how this might be called 'boring', since normal people would have brought an active anxiety to every second.

In fact the navigator, Lieutenant Yewell, was not bored at all, and so was out of step with these fellows. One day a Japanese seaplane appeared above them. The aircraft circled the *Pengulling* as the navigator stood in his cabin swearing and preparing badly for death. When the craft flew off on a tangent, the others had to reassure him that it was not going off to summon forth patrol boats and other ships of war. But he was sick over the side, while having enough whimsy to tell the others he wished he was an alcoholic again, stuck in some mining camp, safe from everything but the arsenic and dynamite he managed, and his own hand.

Now they eased up the Riau Strait and in amongst that bouillabaisse of islands on the approaches to Singapore. They found there were too many Malay fishermen around big Pompong Island, which Doucette had thought of using as a base, but about which he now changed his mind. On a mid September day in the tropics, with the Boss planning to turn west to another of his hides from the time he was rescuing people from Singapore, they found themselves under the scrutiny of a Japanese observation post on Galang Island. The navigator was again tormented, but Doucette decided it was best to keep north beneath the broad gaze of the marines of Galang. They calmed him in the end by letting him look through the telescope at the indolently chatting and smoking Japanese at the post, who were obviously unimpressed by their passage.

At night, in case, they puttered back to a little pyramid of jungle named Pandjang Island, and it was here that the three boat parties were dropped. Leo would tell me of the disappointment of the reserve canoe group, two Australian kids, one nineteen, one twenty, ordinary seamen by rank, rather extraordinary in their way, however. These two were to wait on the *Pengulling* with the crew. It was the first day of October. The raiding parties would have the help of the last month of the south-east trades. On a dark beach, all but the navigator were ashore at the one time, helping the three folboat crews to creep their gear and a little depot of rations amidst the palms behind the beach.

Here Doucette brought Leo to one side.

I want you to do me a favour. I want you to take aside the reserve boat chaps, and I want you to tell them to *make* the navigator come back. By that I mean by shaming him, bullying him . . . by whatever means. Do you understand? All right?

Leo was secretly comforted by this order, and since he didn't want to ever become a permanent soldier, saw no problems with telling young men to coerce an officer. And so he spoke to the two youngsters, and passed on his message. Can we shoot the bastard? one of them asked him.

I don't think you'll need to, said Leo. Not unless you can navigate as well as he can.

On these infants of the Australian navy the reunion between *Pengulling* and the folboat men depended.

In the dark a question struck Leo that he couldn't let himself ask. What if, combined with Yewell's reluctance to come back, the engine simply blew up? It was the dark hour at which Leo felt he was in great danger, a feeling from which he would recover, he said, as soon as the *Pengulling* vanished to sea again before dawn to stooge around Borneo until it was time to meet them again here, at Pandjang.

I look back to 1943 now and ask who deserved such an outlay of gifts as these innocent young men intended to bring to Singapore. While Nav and the others hid and flitted and felt bored off Borneo.

It was cold in Canberra, and snow fell on the Brindabellas. The new girls in the typing pool by my small office called me Miss, which made me feel ancient. On Thursday night a group of us, office veterans, went to dance at the Allied Forces canteen with air force men, Australians and Americans, and landlocked sailors. There were chaperones and most of us got away, flustered and talkative, by ten pm without what we called *damage*. The cold stars above the

Kurrajong Guest House attracted my gaze but were merely an enigmatic clue to the stars Leo might have been under at that moment.

Doucette knew all the islands between Pandjang and Singapore, though they seemed more numerous than the stars of the Milky Way, denser than the Clouds of Magellan, their off-shore waters studded with *pagar*, fish traps of bamboo, sometimes with a rickety little hut on top. Indeed, hardly anyone else on the *Pengulling* knew the names of the islands, for they all had code numbers – Pandjang was NW14, but the final island before the run into the Singapore roads and Keppel Harbour was NC11, a tiny hill of an island from which they would be able to observe Singapore before and after the raid. The boys knew how to paddle around the NWs, NCs and NEs like angels on pinheads.

They had two days of rest on Pandjang before they set out for NC11, for they needed to wait for the right moon. They spent the time moving their food dump further inland to a pile of rocks under the island's hill in case it would all be needed later by them or by downed airmen. And so they hid, and talked very little, and sketched in their diaries and made observations of shipping.

While their first day there was still not at its hottest, a Japanese patrol boat hove around the point of Pandjang, anchored in the blue bay and sent two boats ashore. Japanese marines landed from them. Mortmain and Doucette grinned at each other. The joke was: what would Nav do if he were here? Shit himself, sir, suggested Jockey.

The Japanese marines cooked up some fish and rice for a brunch ashore and drank from coconuts.

Then they lay down without sentries and slept, while all the time their patrol boat swung on its anchor, and Doucette and Mortmain and Leo and Rubinsky and the others sat by their depot and the day's heat began to strike. After an hour and a half, a Japanese NCO woke on the beach, rose, urinated and kicked his companions' legs. They dragged their dinghies down the beach and rowed back out to their boat, and so departed.

A more complicated test came the next morning. A fishing *kolek* appeared, and the Tamil fisherman who owned it began to head it in for the beach. Here was the dark side of the Doucette proposition. He sent little Jockey Rubinsky and a young rating named Skeeter Moss down into the fringes of the palms, figures who could be mistaken as fellow natives, to kill him with knives once he was ashore. They had to, went the reasoning. Their presence could not be announced by anyone – they intended to announce it themselves. And yet to think of these two: a dairy farmer's son, a jeweller's son born in Russia, come all the way to Pandjang to slaughter the head of a Malay family! What did Leo think of that? The first damage they would do was to an innocent! Well, we're used to that reality from modern wars, but it was an unaccustomed thing for Leo. His training in tripping, garrotting and knife-work had always had an imagined enemy as its object.

The Tamil man saved his own life by detouring to another island. No one ever said whether they were relieved or disappointed. I think they were in a way chosen for their unlikelihood to ask themselves that question. At dusk, their hands bloodless, our boys went swimming off one end of the beach, with Mortmain acting as lookout in the shadows of palms and rocks, while the others played and dived with a sportive sea otter family with whom they found they shared the water. A day in the life of an infiltrator. Ashore again, they each put back around their necks a bakelite container with its cyanide tablet inside. Have I mentioned that? They had apparently each been issued one in Cairns in case pain or torture or fear of revealing too much overtook them.

Tides ran hard through the channels between these crowds of islands, and going north that night they had a difficult time against the current and were ten miles short of the island NC11, when the dawn came up. They put into a small island between two bigger ones, Bulan (NW7) and Batan (NW8), both Japanese garrisoned, and dragged their folboats – no small weight, some 700 pounds with their mines aboard – in amongst the mangrove roots and lay still all day, within earshot of a village, eaten by carnivorous insects, with mud itchy on their bodies under that dreadful sun, unable to say anything. A person couldn't put up with that sort of wait, I don't think, unless he was able somehow to be remarkably at ease with himself inside the very kernel of the moment, or unless he lacked too much imagination. They stewed there anyhow.

It's the sort of thing I think of whenever I've been to Singapore. The sun is a ruthless threat – it comes down amongst the great steel towers, slapping your face aside. In the lout-less streets of that ersatz modern city, it is the lout. Anyhow, one way and another, they all proved themselves up to that sort of endurance and that stillness. Mortmain with his optic in his eye, a sort of lantern-jawed giant, the colour of mahogany but impossible not to identify as a European. Big jolly Chesty Blinkhorn, who claimed to have been thrown out of the Goulburn Convent School for being unruly yet who had the discipline for this particular classroom in the mangroves. Sergeant Bantry, veteran of the North African desert and of New Guinea, and aficionado of *The Imitation of Christ*. Doucette with his Chapman's *Odyssey* jammed as a talisman in the breast pocket of his shirt. And Leo, of course, used from his childhood in the Solomons to this intensity of heat. A thunderstorm gave them brief comfort during the afternoon. I think that if Leo could reduce his mind down to muteness as a means of lasting out the sandflies and the heat at the apex of the day, then the rain must have come like a huge act of grace, must have carried with it elements of motherhood and rescue sufficient to endow him with confidence.

That night the currents were running their way, and they could see off to their right as they paddled past the oil refinery at Samboe, no distance at all from Singapore, and were suddenly at NC11 three days before they were to make their foray. Here there was a lot of what they called heather, but not of the Scottish variety; just enough cover for them to hide, though they would not be able to move about by day. At dusk they saw Singapore begin to glitter, a secure, wide-awake, electrically lit city. Using Doucette's telescope, Leo was able to read the time on the clock of the Imperial Insurance Company tower, and to see fabled Raffles Hotel where, as Doucette said, the Japanese were drinking Singapore Slings tonight. From NC11 too they could see and covet the docks of Keppel Harbour, and due ahead the core of Singapore, the Empire Dock, with the superstructures of ships rising above its mole. They could see the great containers and superstructures of the Samboe Oil Refinery, and dead ahead the wireless masts on top of the Cathay Building. Doucette drew their attention to the many native craft coming and going in those seas without molestation, wearing their Japanese registration numbers and not having to worry about mines.

There and in the roads were many freighters and tankers, all lit up. They began in the last of the day to select their targets, always allowing that what they chose now might have moved on in three nights' time. We need the Australian Waterside Workers, said Chesty Blinkhorn proudly, to bung on a strike. Then the bastards'd still all be there in a month.

For three days they lay in undergrowth in the enervating tropic sun which failed to enervate them. As with any tribe, stories were always part of the day. Leo's stories of growing up in the Solomons, barefoot, shirtless, a South Pacific motherless urchin, with a casual Melanesian nanny who allowed him the same latitude given native children. Based on tales he told me his stories dealt too with natives who trod on stingrays in the shallows and suffered an immediate, agonising cone-like excision of flesh. There were excruciating native remedies involving lime juice in the wound, and mysterious herbal remedies to prevent paralysis, and sometimes death.

Mortmain as ever never moved far from his old repertoire of casually scatological tales of monkeys in tea plantations in Malaya who fell for plantation women, and the standbys of elephants with diarrhoea in the teak plantations of Burma. Rubinsky spoke of the Jewish quarter in Shanghai – everyone called it Little Vienna for its cafes. There were synagogues and rabbis too, and an occasional scandal when a Jewish trader's daughter fell for a Chinese man, and a little half-Chinese Jew was born and accepted into the family of Judah. So far from home, so endangered, all the men of Cornflakes recited their favourites.

At four o'clock in the afternoon of the appointed day, Doucette told each team what they were to do, and the bearing they were to take, and the targets they were to approach, and Mortmain and Leo recited it all back. I have no doubt at all that the mere recital of these details filled the men with certainty. They let the dark settle and slipped their folboats into the open at last. Mortmain and Chesty headed due north, right through the unguarded boom gate and into Keppel Harbour, into the very mouth of the port. The Empire Dock was so heavily lit that they were forced to stay in the outer harbour, choosing first a 6000-ton heavily laden cargo vessel, *Moji Maru*, which they surmised was carrying rubber. After placing three mines along its length, they sidled up to the 6000-ton vessel *Tatsula Maru* – it still had its English pre-war lettering under its Japanese title. A 5000-to-6000-ton vessel, unladen, was their next. Fixing the limpets, the contact, the fuses, three by three per ship, they were able to time themselves by the chimes at St Andrew's Cathedral clearly heard across the water every quarter of an hour. They were done in less than an hour and a half and slipped away south for Pandjang, as ordered by Doucette, and were greatly favoured by the tide.

In the Singapore roads, the three boats had diverged. In the darkness, Doucette and Bantry could find none of the ships they had been watching and selecting over past days. All shipping at Examination Anchorage was gone or impossible to see out here in the fast-flowing Phillip Channel. But Doucette found a fine big tanker, the *Tiensin Maru*, 11 000 tons, and placed all nine mines by the engine room and along the stern and the propeller shaft. He wanted it to explode in all compartments, to create a Singapore sensation by being dramatically and visibly blown apart.

Leo and Rubinsky went right into the Bukum Island docks, a few miles south-west of Singapore, and as in Townsville months before, heard sentries and welders yelling jocularly to each other. It was ten o'clock, so Leo and Jockey had the time to examine the entire length of the wharf. They mined the dark side of the bows of a 6000-ton freighter, *Subuk Maru*, and then, exhausted by stress and effort, Leo wrapped an arm around the ship's anchor chain for a while and he and Jockey rested, within earshot of the sentries' banter and the sizzle of oxy torches. They ate chocolate in the dark, surveying the wharf area, of which Leo made sketches and notes as they tarried, invisible in the shadow of the enemy's bows.

The tide changed at eleven o'clock, and they let it take them to their next ship, a modern freighter, the *Hoshi*. A curious thing happened to Leo and Rubinsky while they were working on their second ship. A light went on in a porthole above them and a face appeared, a Japanese face, seeking the cooler night air in his sweltering sleeping quarters. He looked right at Leo and Rubinsky but did not see their stained faces or notice their breath. Mortmain had taught them a technique for breathing so shallowly that an animal three yards away would not hear them.

He was a very ordinary merchant seaman, a little bald, certainly no warrior. But he had chosen his ship, and so he had to be there for its destruction.

They could see their next target anchored in the stream, and it was well laden and of a good size, but when they slid under the dark side of its stern, and Jockey held fast and Leo tried to affix the first magnetic mine under the water, the ship's hull proved too rusty to take it. Leo did something extraordinary then, either out of determination or the obduracy of stress and excitement and frozen intent. He drew his commando knife, reached below the water and began scratching away patches of rust. The next time he tried the mine held, and so he had to repeat the scratching twice more, as Jockey played out the connecting detonation wire. Did any merchant seaman taking his rest in the targeted ship hear the sound? Was he too tired or accustomed to the noises of a crowded port to report it?

The third limpet having stuck, a whistle on Bukum signalled a change of shift. It was one o'clock in the morning. They could get away now before the tide turned against them. Through helpful currents Leo and Rubinsky were in fact the first back to NC11. Next were Mortmain and Chesty Blinkhorn, who had suffered a harder time with currents. Then Doucette and Bantry came in, happy but complaining only half jokingly of the impact of a collision they had had with Mortmain in the dark the night before, and the fact that it had affected their steering and timing. Doucette was inspecting the problem by feel in the last dark hour of night when they heard the first mines go up, and then as they stood and stared during a short two and a half hours, they heard periodic explosions all over the Singapore roads, and sirens of patrol vessels and sub-hunters.

In a sharp-edged early light they saw Doucette's tanker explode beyond all possible ambition in flame and smoke as deep-dyed and effusive as that of a volcano. Doucette wept and smiled and wept, and no one blamed him. The rusty third ship marked out by Leo and Rubinsky off Bukum, already a scene of frantic alarm, seemed by full day to erupt spontaneously and as if by its own will, not theirs. Leo could see its bows and stern both standing clear of the water, but only for seconds it seemed, before it accepted the force of Leo's and Jockey's daring and disappeared. It was a matter of awe now. Chesty Blinkhorn, muscular but very young, and his world until recently restricted to a country town, said, Poor bastards, as if he had not expected till now the scope of his commando ambition, and how much mayhem it could cause. And as repetitive explosions and repetitive alarms enlivened and stunned their morning, they drank their water and ate their rations and felt like the gods and demons they had become. They hadn't only stolen fire, they had planted it on others.

For them, exhilaration overrode all other impulses. Each detonation enlarged their legend. Doucette was keeping count by means of his telescope. With their rods and fuses and magnetic make-fasts they had sunk at least 40 000 tons of shipping and God knew what in the enemy's cargo. Leo felt that he had nudged open his father's prison gate, that the walls were closer to falling. And he intended to give the walls a further nudge if asked to do so. They laughed and wept on the cloud-feathery peak of NC11 as explosions tore the sky. Nothing would ever be as wonderful a riposte as this, nothing would ever be as stylish. They had intended to steal the enemy's sense of safety, but were astonished now they had done so.

They did not fall asleep until late afternoon, and behind their closed eyes the wonderful explosions recurred. With his head down, Doucette had murmured, Did you fellows notice how easy it is for native junks and *prahu* to come and go? They slept on groundsheets on their inured backs, and when they woke the awe at what they had done recurred to them and authorised all their future plans.

That night they took three separate courses back to the meeting place at Pandjang Island. They were next to invisible on a normal sea. They knew and believed that. With daylight, Leo and Jockey simply turned to a convenient island shore, hid their folboat, and found the boon of a Chinese graveyard, where they were able to hide and rest, having been assured by IRD that the Malays kept away from Chinese graveyards. They needed a deeper sleep than they were able to get amongst the dead that day, but they were still stimulated. The tale of what they had done fuelled them overnight, and the repetitiveness of their single blade stroke induced in them a sort of euphoric meditation. In the darkness they skirted *pagar* lit by kerosene lanterns and heard fishermen within or from the shore, and they were as unseen as their deeds entitled them to be.

A Sumatra came rushing out of the west and blinded them with rain and jolted them about on waves, but did not much delay them in the end. Before the next dawn, at two in the morning, they got to Pandjang and the bay where they had swum with the otters. The others all turned up within the hour, the Boss still complaining of the damage Rufus Mortmain had done to his steering.

They took turns to watch for *Pengulling*. In last light they spotted it far out to sea, heading south as if towards home. Nav had come back, and they had somehow missed him, and he them. *Pengulling* looked like a vessel on which there was no dissent now, as it moved definitely Australia-wards.

That was the night the monsoon started. They sat up under groundsheets and discussed their situation. Maybe they should paddle south to Pompong Island and live there off the cache of supplies till the monsoon ended, and then when the native *prahu* set off westwards on the trade wind, they would capture one and sail it to India, like Doucette had earlier. A little disappointing they wouldn't be home for Christmas, but they'd be home in the end. And they were not depressed, said Leo, except that he knew the marriage would be postponed further. He confessed later that he nonetheless had a sense I would tolerate such a thing.

They began to build a hut. An old man and his grandson rowed in in a native *kolek* and this time Doucette went down and negotiated with the old Malay for food – a risk, but it had to be taken now. They completed their rough thatch shelter, and then finished some of their tinned rations with the fish the old man gave them for dinner, and lay down very tired and ready for a sleep, with Rufus Mortmain on watch.

And then at eight o'clock there was a sudden frail density of blackness on the water. *Pengulling* was back. The young men had made the nerve-wrecked Nav return yet again. Doucette and his five abandoned their hut and paddled out. The reunion – well, it can be imagined. Nav the outsider, a bucket of worms, said Leo, talking endlessly. When Leo and the others briefed them, a form of intoxication possessed the men of *Pengulling*. They had all voted to come back, they told Doucette, except for Nav, who had been incapable of electoral activity. Yet he still got the navigation and steering right, and so there was a kind of admirable quality to him also.

Everyone agreed, around dinner tables afterwards, that the trip back had been – yes, *boring*. The warrior Doucette claimed that these were the necessary longueurs a professional soldier had to face, and that they should be grasped for the sake of contemplation. (As if he were not himself the soul of impatience.) The blazing blue nothing at the centre of each second, he asserted, had to be seized.

Meanwhile, as his sailors spoke of boredom, Doucette knew that Ulysses did not get home without passing through Scylla and Charybdis, Scylla being the six-headed monster which guarded its cave by lashing forth and devouring mariners by the half-dozen; and Charybdis being the maelstrom. Doucette knew that in surviving Charybdis, Ulysses lost a swathe of shipmates. Doucette's Scylla and Charybdis were that narrow hole in the gate, Lombok Strait. Nav was anxious about it for days before, in a continuous frenetic state, barking at the men but fussy about the duties of navigation which would get him safely back between the two monstrous shores, Bali to the one side, Lombok to the other.

During the afternoon of the approach to the strait, Nav was in a flighty condition, repeatedly talking to himself, said Leo, mumbling co-ordinates. In darkness he was calmer and worked better, and he hoped to be through by dawn. Chesty Blinkhorn, who was on lookout with his head through the awning atop the wheelhouse, reported the phosphorescence of the bows of another ship coming up on them from astern and overtaking them with ease at a distance of a mile. It looked like a Japanese minesweeper or a patrol boat, but seventy-five yards long, he reported. Blacked out, it had the muteness of a blind monster, but its flag could be seen. In the wheelhouse Nav recited to himself a continuous stream of prayers and curses. Mortmain, naked but for a monocle, packed explosives around the radio, enough to break the back of the *Pengulling* if they were set off. Bantry put his rosary beads around his neck, Leo noticed, and lifted a silenced Sten gun to one of the flaps in the after-awning. Every one of them resigned himself to bloody, explosive death. Mortmain and Leo, observing through glasses, could see the lookouts on the Japanese vessel. On somebody's order, the Japanese ship kept pace with *Pengulling*, slowing down to a crawl to do so.

What were Leo's true thoughts at this moment, if he knew them in the first place? He would have told me in the end, of course, if we had been married long enough, or it would have emerged in some illness or night scream. Five minutes passed of the most intense anguish. The minesweeper or whatever it was kept level pace with the creeping two-knot *Pengulling*. The Japanese vessel possessed two cannons, one on its foredeck and the other on the apron in front of the bridge. Leo did not know their calibre, but it was obvious to him that either could have obliterated them. So they lived for five minutes with the bitter certainty of what was to befall them, a certainty which only the young and irrationally hopeful could sustain.

But for no reason then, the big vessel peeled away westwards, in the direction of Surabaya. It was surmised, as the men hugged and clapped each other's backs, that the Japanese watch officer, who must have had authority over the helm, had decided that so late at night, and so close to the end of his watch, he did not wish to initiate the rigmarole of searching a fishing vessel for little result. He had been sloppy, he had wanted his bunk, and his discretion and sloppiness had saved them.

I wish I could have heard that laughter. I wish I could plug into it at will. Rosary beads and suicide pills hanging not yet required from their necks. The rest of us are cut out of its echoes, however. It was one of those moments you had to be present at to understand how succulent it was. Another item for the legend, and another chain. The lucky Boss Doucette. Even Japanese naval officers-of-the-watch succumbed to the spell inherent in his blessed plans.

On a permissive riptide, *Pengulling* swept through the Lombok Strait. And after what had happened to them, they did not mind the tides which then, beyond the strait, ran up contrary to delay them. For after a further day they pulled down their Japanese flag and the flag of the Singapore port administration. They were in range of Australian coastal bombers. Nav suffered a burst of manic delight, and ordered the wireless operator to send a message to a friend of his, an American at Potshot, with the news that Lombok Strait was lightly patrolled.

The others could hear Doucette chastising Nav in the wheelhouse and later in the day Doucette made a speech over the evening meal, eaten under awnings on the tank amidships, which Leo recorded in his occasionally kept diary. It would seem, said Doucette, from a rash radio message recently sent, that some of the party expected to be welcomed back with parades, and to have our expedition written up in the weekend newspapers and made a newsreel of. I'll tell you now, said Doucette, that will not happen. *Pengulling* will be used again, and then there may be further raids on Singapore and other places using the methods we used. If you think your exploits are going to be spoken of in pubs, and that decorations will come plentiful and fast, then I suggest you should avoid any further association with this type of operation. In the meantime, you have the satisfaction of the secret knowledge of what you did.

Nav sulked, but so did some of the younger men who thought their motivations had been questioned. Five days later, they made it into Exmouth Gulf and its desolate but well-supplied shore station USS *Potshot*. This was a desert shore richly endowed with the plenty of American logistics, but lacking in any extensive population and any atmosphere of triumphant return. Ulysses might have said, I resisted Circe and fought the Cyclops, and all the rest – Scylla and Charybdis, and the rudeness of the sirens – for this banal docking? Mooring there with sealed lips was not an exhilarating experience. Mortmain was left in charge, and Doucette and Leo were flown by bomber over the huge vacant earth to Melbourne for a debriefing. However secretly, they would be permitted to speak to select officers.

# Four

Leo and the Boss travelled to Melbourne in the belly of a bomber, the noise atrocious, the vibration worse than the *Pengulling*'s at the point of engine strain, and the cold far too intense for tropic-weight clothing. When they landed at Essendon, Leo, waiting for a car to take him and Doucette into Melbourne, made a trunk call to my office.

Dear, dear Grace, he said plainly. My sweetheart.

I said, You're back! And I began bawling, as was normal. I did not know where he had been and would not for years yet, but I knew he had gone into a forest dense with perils and come back with a voice still fresh, if not refreshed. I believed till that second I'd been confident he'd come back, but now my previous naivety on that point seemed ridiculous and I could see I had been oppressed by the waiting.

Are you still un-booked? he asked. Has some Yank claimed you?

What a question! But how are you?

You wouldn't believe how well I am. Would early December be okay?

He had a calendar in front of him.

What about Saturday, December eighth? I know I can get leave. The Boss has assured me.

Yes, I said. That will be it then. My darling.

I had never before called anyone *darling* in my life. Endearments sounded rusty yet compulsive in my mouth. I would just the same need to be accustomed to using them. I also knew well enough what would accustom me. Sex without fear.

From Essendon, Doucette and Leo were driven to a big old house in South Yarra, Radcliffe House, the sort of place built by someone who made a fortune in the gold rushes, more lately having been a temperance boarding house and now the headquarters of IRD. The sentries on the door saluted them – they wore blanco-ed webbing and gaiters on the rare occasions I went there myself. Piss-elegant, Leo said. Leo and the Boss, who had worn sarongs or gone naked on the deck of *Pengulling*, were rewarded now with military ritual. And there was more to come.

They entered an office, where the saluting mania continued. The three officers who had stood up to meet them were, as I imagine it, like publishers greeting their best-selling authors. One was Major Doxey, the chief of IRD, and another Major Enright, Director of Plans/Army, and the third a strange, merry-looking fellow wearing a sort of Highland cap with ribbons and tartan pants. This was

Captain Foxhill, an officer at IRD who had escaped with Doucette from Sumatra, and who would prove a good friend. After meeting the genial Foxhill later at a party, I wondered how he managed to walk around the streets of Melbourne in those pants without attracting catcalls from Australia's common soldiery. The answer was that he did, and that he didn't care.

The other two were professional soldiers of administrative talent and stultified instincts – my opinion, of course, based not only on Leo's but on ultimate social contact.

These three officers made a huge fuss of the two visitors and the whole Cornflakes operation. Major Doxey said what they had done was top hole, it was the ploy IRD had been waiting for, not that it had been totally lacking in earlier success, but this had been on a scale which none could ignore. SOE in India and Britain were beside themselves with delight.

Foxhill told them he was probably the humblest officer who would congratulate them, because there would be a party at Government House that afternoon – the Governor-General Lord Gowrie was visiting Melbourne, had come down from Canberra by plane and was installed there, the regular governor of the state being away on some civic duties in the bush. General Blamey would be there, and although no public announcement or fuss would be made, both gentlemen wanted to meet Doucette and Leo.

Foxhill asked about the mention in Doucette's report that native junks seemed to come and go in the Singapore roads without much molestation.

Doucette confirmed it, saying that next time a party should simply take a ride by sub, pirate a junk and use it to launch folboats. After the operation, the folboats could return to the junk which, having finally met with the submarine one night, could be sunk with explosives. Everyone already took it for granted there would be a next time, and Doxey said it was the right moment to bring in Colonel Creed. He picked up a chunky black phone in front of him and spoke into it.

Doucette's success, Leo noticed, had not made him kinder to Creed. When Creed entered there was hand-shaking all around, and Creed congratulated them, but Doucette seemed a little upset that Creed even knew what had happened. The American laid on the praise, which, as Leo told me, was not a bad experience.

Creed took a seat at the table. Why am I here? he asked. Well, for one thing I'm here to tell you we have unimpeachable and independent information that the enemy was genuinely shaken by your activities.

He said that his boss General Willoughby was very impressed, and not just General Willoughby, head of intelligence, but *the* boss, MacArthur himself. He said that it might at last be possible for the Americans to help out in some way in some future, larger scale operation. The idea of cooperation pleased him. Everyone loves a winner, said Creed, and this will convince my people you are winners.

I can see in my mind's eye the way Doucette lifted his head then, the little half-inch toss of the head, a sparse gesture full of infinite contempt which I would sometimes see at parties, particularly if Doxey were about.

We know from the record of this meeting, as conveyed to me by the indefatigable Mark Lydon, who tracked down the minutes in the archives, that Doucette said the offer was most kind but that anyone could see from the success of Cornflakes that there was a strong source of brave, competent and adaptive young men amongst the Australians.

Doxey, Enright and Foxhill seemed alarmed at this rebuff. The lean Colonel Creed remarked that Major Doucette saw him as a crass opportunist, but he hoped to prove otherwise.

And in that spirit, said Creed, in that spirit . . . And he exposed a great and dazzling plan to Doucette and Leo. Sounding all lazy and languid and like a cowboy. What if a permanent raiding party were put ashore at Great Natuna Island, east of Malaya, south of Indochina, north of Borneo? With junks built in Melbourne but convincingly Oriental. From Great Natuna a raiding force could operate throughout the South China Sea. If Free French commandoes were involved, there could be attacks even on Saigon.

Doucette nodded and frowned. He looked towards Doxey and Foxhill. They both gave confirmatory nods. Doxey said General Durban from SOE London had been out to see General MacArthur, and had got a pledge of cooperation. Creed looked gratified. He seemed to be convinced that Doucette would soon be looking at him with new eyes. Basically, old sport, he said, you'll be raider-in-chief in the South China Sea. We'll have you raiding airfields and shipping. Everything you tell me you like!

Even Doucette was impressed and excited, though warily so. He was still distracted, trying to reconcile his mistrust of Creed with the golden idea that had been held out to him. The idea that he could be a pirate chieftain!

When Doxey told Doucette then that first the British wanted to see him in London at SOE headquarters, they had a few things they wanted him to look at, Doucette said, That's good. I can go and visit Mother.

They put Doucette and Leo up at the Windsor, the flashest of old gold rush hotels. A pressed uniform with captain's pips on the shoulder sat on Leo's bed, so he went to Doucette's room to report a mistake had been made. It appears not, said Doucette. Doucette had just discovered he was a lieutenant-colonel as well, and Rufus Mortmain was lieutenant-commander. Doxey said Mountbatten's headquarters in India were so impressed that they intended to recommend decorations. Doucette said, Makes my rant to the men look pretty silly.

At the time, Leo wrote to me a letter which was an account of that heady afternoon. *I have to say*, Leo would write, *I feel a bit of the vanity of it all. There's something intoxicating about getting an extra pip on your shoulder. Stupid, I know. Gives you ideas of military self-importance. I wish you were here, to see how seriously we're being taken.*

In the dusk that afternoon, they were driven by a staff car up the long botanic garden-like grounds of Government House to the front door, where a fellow in a frockcoat opened the car door for them, and another with an umbrella led them into the portico and told them he hoped they had not got too wet, sir. They were taken into a great hall lined with portraits of former governors, whose names adorned rivers and mountain ranges in the great State of Victoria and the immensity of the Commonwealth of Australia.

Inside a ballroom, a waiter asked Leo would he like sherry. He didn't like it, but equally, he didn't fancy his chances of getting a beer. He saw Foxhill across the room in his tartan pants and started to cross to him, but was all at once taken by the elbow by a young English captain in dress uniform who steered him directly to the centre of the room, into the open veldt of the place, away from paintings and ferns and other items of protection. Here in the middle of the floor, where the more important dancing couples would have danced had this been a wedding or a state ball, Doucette was speaking like an equal with three men, two of whom Leo knew from newspaper pictures. One, dressed in a morning suit, was the Governor-General Lord Gowrie, a lean man, popular for having toured the troops in northern Australia and New Guinea. The other was a very portly fellow, famous General Blamey, former Commissioner of Victoria Police, pudgy and yet somehow commanding, and swaying a little, toe to heel, with a glass of Scotch in his hand.

*Some of our boys like the fact he's a bit boozy*, Leo would write, *and that he looks such a man's man. I think he could have been a bit less so. He had interesting, crinkled-up eyes full of roguery, and all up reminded me of a cross between Santa Claus and a pub-owner.*

Tall Lord Gowrie extended his hand to Leo and spoke, thus condemning him to further danger. Easy for Lord Gowrie, in his vice-regal serge. And what he said would draw hoots of laughter now, if it didn't cause widespread incomprehension. He said to Leo, Captain, may I express the admiration of the British Empire.

*The admiration of the British Empire!*

All the grandiloquence of one age becomes one-liners for a later generation, before becoming utterly incomprehensible to the next.

And General Blamey was muttering his version of the same thing. Bloody fine, said Blamey. Bloody fine.

Lord Gowrie said that his friend, the governor of Victoria, who had so kindly loaned him these digs, possessed some excellent maps in his library. He turned to Doucette and asked him whether he and his young friend Waterhouse could perhaps show him, after the party, their operational movements on an atlas.

General Blamey was pleased with the idea and passed his glass to a waiter for a refill. Leo decided not to judge him for that. He was, after all, one of the fellows who beat Rommel. But then Doucette adopted a solemn air which confused Leo. Doucette said, I was so distressed to hear about Patrick, Leonard.

That's most kind of you, said Lord Gowrie, and I wish I was a rarity amongst parents who've lost sons in the Desert campaigns, but I fear I am not. He knew General Blamey here, by the way.

Yes, said Blamey solemnly. He was a very fine young man, Lord Gowrie's boy.

Lord Gowrie found even this much reflection on Blamey's part painful and changed the subject, asking after Doucette's wife and son. Any word?

No news, Leonard, said Doucette. Thank you for asking.

Lord Gowrie said he didn't want to offer false comfort. But it takes ages for the Red Cross to get news . . .

Doucette declared that a kindly thought. In a half-embarrassed voice, Lord Gowrie explained to the other generals that Mrs Doucette and the little boy were missing. They'd been on the *Tonkin*.

Doucette, perhaps to distract attention, nodded in Leo's direction. Captain Waterhouse . . . his father is a POW of the Japanese.

General Blamey looked solemn and said something Leo quoted to me occasionally, sometimes half joking in boastfulness after sexual athleticism, for like many he thought Blamey ludicrous. Well, he said, they've felt the sting of the family, son. They've felt the sting.

The British general who had till now been silent, whose red tabs looked so much more vivid than Blamey's desert-bleached ones, now joined the conversation. He seemed to address Doucette and Leo. He hoped that his own journey from London, specifically to visit General MacArthur, had broken down the American resistance to cooperation and the use of MacArthur's submarines. MacArthur was very worried that the British and Australians would use their occasional special operations as the basis to claim back the whole region when the war ended. Now according to the Americans, that couldn't be permitted, because it was imperialism. But, complained this general, it's not imperialism when *he* declares he will return to the Philippines.

Lord Gowrie murmured, Well, of course, we'd expect Malaya back. I mean, after all, it was taken from us without benefit of international law.

The tall English general turned out to be General Durban, the head of the Special Operations Executive in London. He said that with a bit of American cooperation, he could see the whole of the Southeast Asian zone busy as a church fete with airfields and ports blown to pieces by Australians and Free French and wandering Britons like Charlie Doucette.

Later, after everyone had left, Lord Gowrie got one of the Asian atlases from the Government House library, and Lord Gowrie and Charlie Doucette and Leo ended up with it spread on the floor, recounting their dartings back and forth, Subar to Bukum, Pandjang to Pompong.

By the time we were finished, Leo told me, we'd pretty well managed to amaze even ourselves.

How I loved him for choosing a sherry at Melbourne's Government House instead of asking for beer. He really was just a boy from the bush, a Grafton boy, despite the fact that he also lived in the Solomons amongst the colonial administrators and their children. They were the bush gentry in places like that, their civic dignity paper-thin and under threat from marital or alcoholic scandal. Leo was therefore fascinated by real gentry, the members of English or Anglo-Irish ennobled clans who produced a governor-general in the family like the king of spades out of the magician's hat, yet who had never mentioned it before.

I'm sure if I showed Rachel some of Leo's occasional scribblings on events like the first wonderful day back in Melbourne, she would point out that I get one mention from Leo and Doucette gets so many. I notice it myself. But this was a statement of the preoccupations of that day of glory, that hour, that martial – not marital – moment. Doucette was *there*, and so was triumph, and triumph is a two-dimensional condition. That's why Leo wanted me there, to add an element. A man, a woman and a hotel room, the simplest joy. The young Leo would not have wanted to hear me talking like that, of course. But it's longing and misery that are three-dimensional.

Even as he remembered the evening, and relayed it to me (without any of the geographic details of the mission) during our honeymoon, Leo runs the risk of looking from the perspective of the present like a stooge of Empire. But it was not about Empire. It was about Doucette and Rufus. And apart from that, it was *his* region the Japanese had taken, *his* island childhood in the Solomons they'd tried to annul. Yet it has to be admitted that the concept of Empire was not offensive to him, or to any of us. He – like me – had made our school procession to country showgrounds to celebrate Empire Day. The Empire was a system as eternal and fixed in structure and God-ordained as the solar system. Besides, nine-tenths of all we made went to feed, clothe and steel the Empire. But that aside, it was something more ancient and eternal still that drove Leo. Something mythic or chemical or cellular or all three in Leo and his friends. The summit of their lives had so obviously been that liquid darkness in which they had affixed their limpets!

That was so clear that I did not question or feel particularly threatened by it. It would be Mortmain's wife Dotty who would try to make me more discontented at that reality than I had so far thought to be.

# *Five*

Dotty Mortmain, black-haired, pretty, watchful and lithe, came up with her monocled husband Rufus Mortmain to the wedding, all the way from Melbourne. She was tall for a woman, coming to Rufus's shoulder. Other visitors included Major Doxey and Foxhill in his tartan pants, and above all Doucette. Thus I clapped eyes on the man, not as egregiously handsome as Leo, far more compact and neat-featured but endowed with an extraordinary presence, a teasing mixture of reticence and command that even I noticed. They were all in dress uniform and had brought their swords to make an archway for us from the door of the Anglican Church in Braidwood when we emerged married. There was a reception at the Braidwood School of Arts, with a keg of beer laid on by the owner of the Commercial Hotel to honour my father's local importance.

I was in a daze but remember pretty Dotty Mortmain, smelling of cloves, lavender and gin, asking me softly what I thought of Doucette. Dotty Mortmain seemed an exceptional woman to me, from a wider and more diverse world, and such a couple as she and monocled Mortmain did not exist in Braidwood or in any other place I had ever been. You'll have no trouble from other women, Dotty told me, with that connubial knowingness I had seen in some wives. Leo is utterly under an enchantment. Just remember bloody Doucette is your rival. Look at him smile. He's quite a smiler. I've known the bugger since we met in Singapore.

Leo and I travelled to Sydney and stayed at the Commonwealth Hotel, where I put into action without fear the tenets of my mother's manual. I thought I'd be the master, Leo told me with a lusty smile. I find I'm the pupil.

We visited all the sights, catching the Manly ferry, and then going by train to the Carrington in the Blue Mountains, the traditional hotel of the newly married then. It was all marvellous. I can say that without quaver even to my knowing, slightly mocking granddaughter, although the sex was not utterly without fear. As in all great arenas, courage had to be acquired through repetition. But we were set on an excellent, happy marriage. I suppose that part of the test is I barely remember the conversations we had. All was a golden, unified sphere of delight and very ordinary reassurances to each other that we had never been happier.

One day when we could contemplate being on less than intimate physical terms for some hours and went walking in the luxuriant dampness of the Jamison Valley, Leo told me that he might be sent on operations again, and suggested therefore that we should try stratagems to avoid the conception of a child. He felt that was only fair to me, he said. There were moments when, swept away, we risked conception anyhow. Within nine days of the wedding, however, he went to Melbourne, and I prepared to follow him.

It was Dotty Mortmain who told me after I arrived in Melbourne as a young bride that the wondrous Doucette had gone to look at new gear and wonder-weapons in London. She said that we could enjoy our husbands' company as long as he stayed there, so she did not wish him a speedy return.

But more of her in a while, because what happened to me on my train journey down would have something to do with Dotty. For a country girl like me the journey from Sydney to Melbourne was considered significant travelling. It was, after all, nearly six hundred miles, a distance which in Europe would have placed the traveller in another country. The trains were crowded with troops, American and Australian. But I, being an officer's wife, had a sleeping compartment, which I shared with another wife, seemingly unhappy and older, who had obviously, like Dotty, passed through the veil I had not yet breached between girl- and womanhood. She was probably in her mid-to-late thirties, and I noticed she was very pretty in a slightly hawkish way.

I knew her husband was a major from the fact that the nameplate on her bunk said *Mrs Major Enright,* in the same way that mine said *Mrs Captain Waterhouse.*

As the train rollicked south-west through endless pastures, I could hear her weeping during the night in the bunk above me. I was very grateful that I was married to Leo, because I knew he would never give me any need to weep the sort of tears Major Enright's wife was shedding loudly and without any embarrassment.

For lack of a standard rail gauge between Victoria and New South Wales, we all had to be dragged from our bunks in the small hours, and given a cup of tea, and then told to get down on Albury station and sit in the first-class lounge. This was a primitive room – hard benches around a coal fire even in summer. Or else we could go to the refreshment room, while the standard gauge (4 foot 8½ inch) train from New South Wales was emptied and shunted out, and the broad gauge (5 foot 3 inch) train from Victoria took its place.

My cabin companion chose neither of the proffered options, and I found the waiting room very uncomfortable, and the refreshment room full of soldiers calling for beer at four thirty in the morning. She sat on one of the station's benches and began smoking with a vengeance. Innocently, I asked her was she well. Once I did, the tears dried, as if she had been waiting all night for me to say something like this. She set her face as if she had at last decided on some solution to her grief.

I was just making up my mind to start a plain conversation with her, something about, It's an endless journey, isn't it? when she offered me a cigarette from her silver case. I said no thanks.

She told me to take a seat beside her if I wished to. She said, I'm sorry I was such a grump at the start of the trip. You would have guessed. It's always men. Those absolute buggers. Enjoy being young, anyhow. Once you show the slightest flaw, you can expect to weep a great deal.

It's just as well I have flaws to start with, I told her. I was probably annoyingly blithe, like most people in love. I was amazed myself about the perfection of things with Leo, what a bright companion he was, what a dazzling man.

Oh, we're all amazed, dear. At first, they mimic our needs, but they don't really feel them, or meet them or give a damn.

These were, I realise, not particularly original ideas about men, but you have to remember the time. I had never heard them uttered before except by racy, world-weary women in films. They weren't the sorts of things my mother had ever said – somehow I felt naively certain of that. She pulled out a silver flask and unscrewed the cork with the hand which held the cigarette. Gin, she told me. Do have some.

I smiled so that she wouldn't think me rude. Look, thanks. I've had gin once before, and I don't think Albury station's the right place for a second try.

Fair enough, she said. She took a long swig herself. But the time might come, she said, gasping with pleasure, when you'll find it's good at any hour, and absolutely anywhere. You see, I have to brace myself for a fight. My husband wrote me a letter a week ago, telling me that there was no place for me in his flat in Melbourne, that another woman has taken occupation. He was so sorry. He intends to marry this other tart. I sent him a telegram, telling him to cut out the nonsense and that I was coming anyhow. He sent me a reply that addressed nothing. *If you have to come, I'll meet you at the station.* That's the other thing I didn't mention. They're bloody cowards. Oh, they'll charge a machine-gun for you. But the idea of a scene, especially a scene witnessed by other men . . . that's what terrifies them.

She adopted a gruff male voice. *I can stand anything except screaming women*, she mimicked.

She snorted. Well, all that rough soldiery hanging round the refreshment room are going to see a major subjected to quite a scene at Spencer Street Station.

I thought, Leo and I will have to be subjected to that as well.

The woman looked up at me with her stricken eyes. I apologise in advance, she told me. But I'm a woman fighting for her life.

I've got very little experience at any of this, I said, but it might shame him if you appealed to him. To his better nature.

No, she told me. None of us must ever do that. That puts you at their mercy. Look, I'm sorry to load you up with this utter shit!

I told her not to worry. A new train came into the station to take us on to Melbourne, and Victorian Government

Railways conductors began yelling at the soldiers in the refreshment rooms to leave their beer and get aboard. Mrs Enright and I had to sit up, in an admittedly comfortable carriage, all the way to Melbourne, as the summer sun came up over the mountains to the east of the rail line. We were not alone. There were three officers in our compartment. Everyone tried to sleep, but only Mrs Enright, helped out by her gin, managed it. It was not a graceful nap, however, for her mouth opened and she began snoring. I gave her a nudge to save her from unconscious embarrassment. You might well say I was a bit priggish to do that. I had an innocent assumption that decent women were too angelic to snore. Again, that's the way we were. We were closer to Jane Austen than to Madonna or Julia Roberts.

When Mrs Enright woke up properly, and everyone definitely abandoned their attempts at sleep, the youngest of the officers, a freckled young man of about twenty-one years, spoke to her across the compartment.

Mrs Enright. I'm Lieutenant So-and-so. I attended a party at your place in Sydney. How is your husband?

Mrs Enright gave him a washed-out, How are you?

That was one of the best parties I've ever been to, the young officer said like a schoolboy.

She nodded. He could tell she didn't want to talk.

I hope I didn't interrupt your sleep.

It's quite all right, she said. But she closed her eyes again.

Later, when our train came seething into Melbourne, and I got down onto the long platform, I saw Leo running towards me, and from the corner of my eye snatched a glimpse of Mrs Enright met by an older-looking officer. She allowed him to scrape his lips across her cheek, and she went off unhappy-looking, but without creating the scene she had promised. I think it was the meeting with the young officer, who'd been to her party, which made her think how momentous and final it would be to stage a brawl in front of officers. Yet I did ask myself why she had made my journey miserable and had not then punished the cause as promised.

I walked that platform with Leo, the blue and red ribbon of the Distinguished Service Order on the chest of his light-weight uniform, like the most blessed woman at the centre of the warring world. Now that he had grown a moustache, he looked like the film actor Errol Flynn, everyone said so, except younger, and somehow more serious. He was also heavily tanned, in exactly the way that made it seem he'd faced danger in places none of the other soldiers on the platform could imagine. For women have our part in relishing the warrior myth, the place in the legend that, although I did not know the details, I knew Leo had achieved.

Indeed, women could feed the immolatory furnaces too. In Braidwood in 1916, my mother confessed to me once that one night on a dare she had handed a white feather to a farmer's son who had not yet volunteered. He had gone to France in 1917 and not survived the year. It was her greatest sin, she said, and she told me lest I repeat it. My adoration on Spencer Street Station might itself have contributed an ounce more to Leo's willingness to extend the range of his heroism and the scope of the Doucette legend.

Ahead I could see sallow-looking Major Enright, talking hard to his wife and trying to hurry her off the platform and away to a sullen breakfast somewhere. Mrs Enright hung back like a four-year-old being dragged. It was true what Susan Enright had said. An army major was frightened of a scene, and the bodies of both Enrights were full of tension. Whereas Leo and I were side-by-side, walking in casual lockstep, my shoulder against his upper arm, hip to hip, at prodigious, godlike leisure. I was amazed and delighted at how bodies could send a promise to each other through fabric. Also, I felt beautiful at his side. Effortless Gene Tierney and the inwardly radiant Merle Oberon had nothing on me. And I had no sense at all that I would ever be punished for the glory of that instant. That's why ecstasy is ecstasy – it carries with it the idea that it will easily outlast all the rest.

On our way to the car and driver Major Doxey had loaned him, Leo told me again – as if it might be a problem – that we were billeted to share a big apartment with the Mortmains. It would prove to be a pleasant, white, art deco block of flats just by the river in South Yarra. Our place had plenty of space, considering the way people were living then. As Leo had promised by letter before my move, there were two smaller flats between which the wall had been knocked down, so that you could move from living room of one to living room of the other, and each half-flat had its bedroom.

The Mortmains were easy to live with, he reported. Dotty Mortmain had published a novel. Neither of us had ever before met anyone who had published a novel. The only trouble was, Leo reported, that sometimes she gave Rufus the rounds of the kitchen, and Lieutenant-Commander Mortmain might come creeping into our side of the flat begging for sanctuary and a drink. Leo hoped I wouldn't find that a problem.

Nothing was a problem that morning. It was a late summer's day, the humidity was low, and even that contributed to the perfection of things.

On arrival, I saw that the table in our living–dining room had nothing on it, but I could see through the archway the Mortmain table on which lay two dumbbells, newspapers, a number of stacked books, and a big typewriter. Leo saw my glance and said, Dotty works for the Yanks three days a week. The rest of the time, she does her own work. Something literary. They'll be in later today. Look at the knife.

On their dresser lay a large Malay-style knife beside an empty teacup. Rufus has knives of all kinds spilling out of drawers, Leo explained. He grinned and his eyes glittered. Australian eccentricity was not like the worldly eccentricity of the Mortmains. And again, the idea of someone doing *something literary* on an extended basis was new to us as well.

Our bedroom looked out across a tree-lined street to the grassy embankment parkland and the narrow water of the Yarra itself. For people from New South Wales, and particularly from the great harbour of Sydney, the little Yarra is considered a joke, a river which runs with its bottom mud on top of the current. But its water was a pleasant blue that day, and when we arrived, eights and fours and scullers were practising on its surface, cutting even wakes as sharp as joy itself.

By the time the first of the Mortmains got home hours later, Leo and I were sitting, decorously reading books. It was Dotty, the wiry Englishwoman, with her remarkable slightly doleful green eyes and her lustrous black hair. In ordinary weekday gear, she looked even more like an outdoors woman who had been rendered sinewy, as I would find, by a life of trekking and sailing far from Britain. Oh, she cried, setting down the string bag with groceries in it by her typewriter. This is your young wife, Leo? I couldn't get enough time with her at the wedding.

Leo and I both stood up and advanced to the archway. She embraced me like a sister and asked us to sit down with her and have tea. We were drinking it when the front door opened, apparently of its own accord. We could see nobody there from where we sat, but Leo started chuckling. Come off it, Rufus! groaned Dotty Mortmain. But still no one appeared. Then there was a blur of white, which I worked out later was Lieutenant-Commander Mortmain, in white shirt, shorts, socks and black shoes, somersaulting into the room and ending on his knees at his wife's chair. Instantaneously, he leapt from the floor to his feet, grabbed her black hair and lifted her bodily from her sitting position into the air, her feet off the ground, as he and she laughed wildly. It amazed me by being more like a circus act than something done by people one shared a flat with but Leo seemed used to this kind of behaviour, and laughed heartily at it. I suppose, by contrast, my own hilarity was a bit shocked.

Rufus Mortmain lowered his wife to the ground again. He bowed. And for the next trick, he announced, I shall throw a series of native knives at Captain Waterhouse and pin him to the wall by the hems of his shirt and pants. But maybe, first, let's have a real drink to welcome Errol Flynn's handsome bride!

I was naively delighted Leo's colleagues saw the resemblance to the movie star too, and I found that strangely reassuring, a sign that the Mortmains and Doucette were not as different in perception from me as I had feared.

Rufus Mortmain – the name still amazes me with its wrong-headed exuberance – extracted a bottle of gin and one of whisky from the cupboard. Glasses were fetched, Leo going back to our kitchen to collect a couple. That was merely fair in terms of our semi-communal living. Dotty began clearing up some papers by her typewriter to make room for our drinking session.

Mortmain asked me what I would like. A little gin, I said.

Bravo! Mortmain cried, as if he knew that I wasn't a drinker. He turned to Dotty. He said, And you, light of my life, temple of my desire, companion of my mortal days?

Dotty said, Gin-and-it, thank you, sailor. You bloody reptile!

The two men drank whisky, and added a little water

from the tap. Then Leo sat and took my hand and raised his glass. Darling Grace, he said, you know I can't go on with all that palaver Rufus does, but I drink to you.

I sipped my gin and tried to look normal, but as it shuddered through my body, Dotty noticed and offered me some tonic water. That was better. I've liked gin and tonic since that day. But it wasn't to be the only mystery to which Dotty would introduce me.

By the time we got to a second drink, Mortmain announced, To absent friends!

I hope you don't mean that Irish chancer Doucette, snarled Dotty, her face narrowing and her eyes full of passion. I hope a Number 18 bus runs over that bugger.

Nor did she smile as she said it.

Ahem, murmured Rufus. Charlie Doucette is a sore point in our family.

Dotty shrugged. He is a madman born out of his time, she told me. I hope they're not filling his mind with rubbish in London. They can dream up all sorts of things behind their desks. They find some eccentric like Doucette to try it out, and expect my husband to go along. It's just not acceptable. I don't know where in God's name you've been last time you went.

Rufus interrupted her, and winked, and said to me, Dotty is just saying that out of piety. She knows where we were from her friend the Yank Colonel Creed, who's quite keen on her.

Dotty took some more gin, shook her head and would speak no further.

Leo turned to me. Dotty . . . Mrs Mortmain . . . works for a Yank we know. Colonel Creed. Very smooth sort of bloke.

Rufus said, The Boss gives him a hard time. The Boss has a bit of a thing about Yanks. I have always found Creed one of the better ones myself.

Leo declared, He certainly seems to be trying to work with us now. But better not say any more.

Leo then smiled at me. He told me he had to go into the barracks the next day, and then to meetings, but would be back in the evening with Rufus. Dotty tossed her head. Altogether, she had made a fairly sombre drinking companion, and the more melancholy she became, the more wary Rufus Mortmain looked. It was clear Doucette and the present employment of Rufus himself was an issue of argument between them.

On my way to the toilet, I glanced out of our living room window across the river and the shunting yards to the browned-out city, and on a bench in the parkland across the road, I saw Susan Enright sitting wearing a hat and with her suitcase beside her. I called to Leo to come and see, and the Mortmains came as well. I said, That's the woman I came down with from Sydney on the train. Mrs Enright.

Not Peter Enright's wife? asked Mortmain. The poor lady has my sympathy.

What's she doing down there? Dotty worried.

Rufus said, Obviously she caught Peter with his woman. He lives on the top floor. The almighty Director of Plans.

Leo murmured to me, Perhaps you and I should go down, Grace, and see if there's anything she needs.

Dotty said, Shouldn't you leave it to Enright himself? He might be out and she is waiting for him to come back with the key.

She could probably do with a drink while she's waiting, said Rufus.

In the end, Leo and I insisted on going down together. We crossed the road to the bench she was sitting on by the river, and she turned to see who was coming. Hello, she called with a sort of manic gaiety. It's Grace. And her gallant husband.

Leo asked could he help her.

No thanks. It's very kind of you. I'm waiting here till I'm arrested for vagrancy. My husband won't let me into my apartment, so it's become a matter of shaming him.

Her voice was high-pitched.

Please let us give you a cup of tea or a drink, Leo offered.

You can't sleep here, Susan, I told her.

Maybe I could do an Ophelia in the waters of the Yarra, she suggested. Don't worry, Grace. I have a room at the Windsor reserved very kindly for me by my treacherous spouse.

Could I get you a taxi then, Mrs Enright? asked Leo.

Please, no! I am not your responsibility, young fellow.

We have a settee, I said, as a girl did if she came from the country, where accommodation was freely offered. Ours is the double apartment, number five and six.

Look, said Mrs Enright, you're both very kind. But you must please leave me free to humiliate the mongrel.

Perhaps because of the gin, the tension of my own happiness, and certainly because of lack of experience, I was suddenly moved to tears.

Please don't put yourself through this, I begged.

But in the end, we had to leave her there, and were both very uncomfortable about it as we re-entered the lobby. Leo kissed me on the forehead. Let's go to bed, he whispered.

Upstairs, abashed at the brush-off Mrs Enright had given us, we said goodnight to the Mortmains, who intended to stay up a little longer. We were half undressed when our doorbell went. Leo put on a dressing gown and answered it. It was Mrs Enright. I saw her over Leo's shoulder. She was crying. I'm a weak woman. I will take that settee your dear wife mentioned.

I found some sheets and blankets, as she stood in the kitchen being introduced to the Mortmains. I quickly made the settee for her. When I re-emerged, I found that she had been induced to comfort herself with some gin.

Rufus told me, We'll point Mrs Enright in the right direction. You must be tired after travelling last night.

I was awakened in the morning by the sound of angry voices at our opened front door. Putting on a dressing gown and going to check, I saw both Leo and Rufus in shirt sleeves arguing with a man similarly half-dressed in uniform but very angry. It was of course Major Enright.

Mortmain was saying, You surely couldn't expect us to leave the poor woman in the open.

That's exactly what I expected you to do. She would have got sick of it. As it is, you played right into the hands of that mad woman. But you knew what you were doing, too. I know you understood exactly what you were doing.

Leo said he resented the accusation.

The woman had a perfectly fine room at the Windsor, paid for by me. But you look out your window and you think, Let's make a fool of old D/Plans. In civilian life, you fellows would be little better than criminals, and I know the way you think. God knows what your purpose was in introducing that woman into your flat.

Mortmain declared with the calmest authority, and with a certainty Dotty must have relished, that he and Leo were both married men. I'd knock you down for what you have said, he told the major, except you're beyond yourself. I ask you to show a little restraint and dignity. We all have to sit at the same planning tables for weeks and months yet, and Colonel Doucette isn't even back.

Leo, of course, despite his role as an official hero, had a temperament which would go a long way to make peace. He said, My wife has just arrived from Sydney – by the same train as your wife, in fact. I have to ask you not to make a scene, sir.

I felt silk brush by me in a hurry. It was Susan Enright, coming from the bathroom to join the conflict. She took up a position in the middle of our living room, from where she could lob her own high-calibre commentary over Leo's and Rufus's heads onto her mad-eyed husband.

How dare you find fault with these decent men! she raged. You're just embarrassed to be shown up as a skirt-chaser in front of your brother officers. Yes, both their wives are here, and you're offensive to them too. As for your room at the Windsor, take your tart there and leave me the flat. By the way, any chance of your being sent on a suicide mission? I don't suppose so. Far too flabby compared to these two.

You're making a fool of yourself, Susan.

Good. And you're playing me for one.

Suddenly, Enright began appealing to Leo and Mortmain. You see, she doesn't mind using your flat as an arena of battle. Well, I'm not biting today, Susan. Excuse me. I shall see you at the office, gentlemen.

He turned on his heel, in a way which implied not a retreat but a dignified withdrawal.

Coward, Susan yelled. Craven bastard! Back to your whore.

His retreating steps could be heard on the stairs, and Leo closed the door, shaking his head.

Mortmain said, The bugger needs a broken nose. I don't think we should take that from anyone, Leo.

Leo looked at me. I'm sorry, love, he told me, as if the madman at the door had soured everything.

Susan turned, taken out of herself by Leo's concern, and came and hugged me. At that second, I began to resent her.

She said, I'm not going to risk that you'll be bothered any further. I'll go to his bloody room at the hotel.

We told her to stay for breakfast first. But Dotty was not as warm towards her as the men. And later Dotty would tell me she believed that from that day, Major Enright, despite all conscious professionalism, at some level wished them ill, and even wished them dead.

# *Six*

*At morning tea time during that day's meeting, I approached Major Enright to make the normal speech, which would have consisted of: Sir, I don't care who you are. I don't intend to stay in the army after the war, and so I don't have to kowtow to anyone. I'm surprised a regular officer would come to other officers' doors making the accusations you did. And I won't have my wife upset by outbursts.*

*I had to queue – I saw Rufus giving him a bit of a shellacking too. But Enright's face remained set though he was very pale. He was probably copping mullock from his girlfriend as well, and so he should.*

*Later, he came to Rufus and me voluntarily. He said, Unfortunate scene this morning. That bloody woman has the power to put everyone in the wrong. Sorry for anything untoward I said. The woman knows I'm seeking a divorce, and that's that. Divorce is a big enough disadvantage for a professional officer, though many colleagues have remarked to me how inappropriate a soldier's wife Susan makes. And of course, I overlook anything extreme you might have said. Can we all be men about this? And gentlemen as well?*

*That was as good as we could hope for. Rufus nodded with a half-smile on his face. Later at lunch, he said to me, The bugger only learned to talk like that from a West End play, on secondment to British regiments in India. He gets it all out of sequence, anyhow, and he gave himself away at the end by pleading.*

*I wondered where he thought I learned to talk. But I think he was saying the major's utterances were only skin deep. In any case, we agreed, it was as good an apology as we would get from Enright.*

After Leo and Rufus had gone to work on the morning of the confrontation between Major Enright and Leo and Rufus, I decided to go into town by tram to look at Myers and other department stores of Melbourne renown. You cannot imagine the attraction of such an idea to someone raised in the Braidwood and Canberra of the time. Captain Foxhill had lined up a part-time job for me doing filing for the Transport Corps at Victoria Barracks, where Leo frequently did his afternoon gymnastics. But I did not have to start for a few days.

I was thus able to leave Dotty to work on her mysterious book, and would be able to return in the afternoon and ask her, as if I routinely asked people this, How is your book coming along?

Susan Enright, still on the premises, complicated all this in a peculiar way. She asked if she could come to town with me. She seemed quite cheery, ready for a day's window-shopping after the scene with her husband that morning. I couldn't say no, but from her typewriter, Dotty asked, Didn't you say you intended to book into the Windsor?

Susan said she would collect her luggage after lunch.

I had expected to catch the tram, but as, wearing our finest, we left the block of flats, a taxi appeared bearing its great bladder of coal gas in a bracket on its roof. She insisted we catch it, and when we reached Collins Street and I offered, like the bumpkin I was, to pay the driver, she cheerily permitted me to. In Myers, Buckley and Nunn, Foy and Gibson, she entered into crazily jolly conversations with girls in the jewellery and cosmetic departments about what her habitual choices were in these matters. It was as if she hadn't been rebuffed by her husband at all. Or else she was confident her husband would take her back. Again, girls from Braidwood didn't behave like that in shops. You've got no idea what a constrained bunch of people we country girls were, terrified that someone would think us flash, or skites, or having tickets on ourselves, all of which were the greatest crimes a person could commit in the bush. But Mrs Enright was free of such fears.

At lunchtime, she tried to talk me into a hotel dining room instead of the cafeteria at Myers. She was rather depressed that you couldn't get a drink at Myers. At least the Windsor has a bar, she said.

We got home by tram at midafternoon and could hear from the stairs Dotty still working, like a real writer in Hollywood pictures, with a quite feverish clatter of keys. I wondered whether we should go back and sit in the parkland a while, lest we interrupt her. We'll just creep in, Susan insisted. I must pack and get going.

That prospect of her going was so pleasant that I let myself be talked into opening the door to our half of the flat. Dotty, of course, looked up from her work. I'm just creeping in to pack, Susan explained, moving in a stagy creeping gait.

I said, Please don't let us disturb you, Dotty.

While Susan packed, I sat in a chair reading *Smith's Weekly* and its rollicking attacks on Generals MacArthur and Blamey. To them MacArthur was a poseur playing to the American press in hope of the Republican Party nomination for the presidency. The Australian General Blamey was a well-connected tippler. Satire is its own reward, and often it is outdone by reality itself – I realise all that now. But *Smith's Weekly* was considered rather seditious in the household I had grown up in, so I enjoyed it all the more now. I was a little disturbed that with Susan and me in the house, the pace of Dotty's typing had fallen off. I began to doze and woke to see Dotty standing over me.

How're the shops this dreary season?

They're flourishing, I told her. At least that's the impression of a woman who's visited only two cities in her entire life.

She smiled and yawned, and sat in the neighbouring lounge chair.

Have you ever written any poetry? I don't mean about flowers, or some ballad about rounding up cattle. I mean, *poetry*. I mean about loss and fucking and the misery of children, and why chaps love war and are such deadbeats in bed? Have you read *The Waste Land*?

Trying to appear at ease with her earthiness, I said no. She tramped into her half of the apartment and came back with a Penguin book.

Read that, Grace, she advised me. Image is everything, so I'm afraid I'm not much of a poet myself. I'm good at outrage, of course. I feel a lot of that. But when I was young in London, and hanging round writers, I always thought my style was pretty thin. A reviewer described my novel as understated, as if it were a virtue.

What was your novel called?

*Sweat*. It was about the lives of women in Malaya, or a colony like it anyhow. They weep sweat from every pore, I said. They shrivel and pretend it's a life. A film company showed some interest in it, but then the war came.

I was fascinated by this.

Writing poetry is wonderful, she assured me. If the beloved is away for a time, it's a sort of vengeance.

Against who? I asked.

Against the loss of time and beauty, Dotty told me. Or if you want to look on it positively, you could say it was a prayer for a golden world in which men loved women as much as they say they do, and the other way round, in which all wars are merry, and all children loved with equal ardour. You are a sweet and beautiful child, Grace, full of rejoicing. Poetry's about that too. But you haven't been betrayed yet.

She sounded remarkably like Susan.

Surely you haven't been? I asked. Betrayed, I mean.

By Rufus? Oh yes. He does that, poor fellow, but men are like dogs. When an arse is proffered, they can't turn away. Pardon my putting it so simply. It is simple for them, I'm afraid.

She lowered her voice. The sooner that tart gets out of here, the better. Look, I don't mind showing you something I dashed off today – it's not perfect, but it helps me stay sane. Like some gin?

Surprisingly I found I would like some. But something in me didn't want Susan to have any with me.

Maybe after our guest's gone.

Quite! Dotty whispered emphatically.

She went to her table and brought a page back. Officially, she told me, I'm supposed to be writing a novel. Really, I want to write about what a shambles the whole fall of Singapore thing was, but the publisher says it would not be looked on very kindly. So I'm trying to write simply about Englishwomen on one of our overcrowded steamers to Australia. Chaucer should have been there. He could have done justice to it. In between, when the thing is seeking its way out of me, I write about Rufus and myself. Despite what I say about men and dogs, he does love me, you know. As far as his sort of fellow possibly could.

She gave me the sheet. Don't feel you have to tell me anything – whether it's good or bad. I know exactly how good and how very bad it is.

What she gave me was entitled *Mercator's Projection.* It read:

And in love's bed, caresses seemed
a holy vacuum.
Since lovers seek to force the air
from every cavity and intervening space.
Love's pressure is enormous,
the normal terms of gravity becoming trite.
But then, I catch his eye
and see the shoals and surfs
and archipelagos
which fill the other mind,
the tides that go on running
when his tide is spent.
The Projection of Mercator cannot save me
from concluding:
Love is the longest distance between two bodies.

I don't know why I was impressed. I thought until then that poetry had died with Tennyson. And the remarkable thing is, I remember understanding the meaning. I must have felt the same thing she did, without knowing it. I knew at once I wanted to write something like this myself.

At last, Susan emerged with her suitcase, and we saw her into a cab, which Dotty was forced to ring for, using the shared phone. We were delighted when she left, and then, as if we'd known each other for years, we broke out the sisterly gin.

I did not have an exact idea of the work Leo did at the requisitioned boarding house and temperance hotel, and at Victoria Barracks. Women were of course counselled even by the *Women's Weekly* that they should not ask too much. The women's papers, the motion pictures, novels, and even the traditions inherited from mothers all underlined the idea that we lacked a right to be too inquistive.

I knew, though, that Leo and Rufus worked together literally, having desks in the same room at Radcliffe House. While in that office, they were supposed to read the latest files on new equipment, from groundsheets to spirit stoves to weaponry. Leo told me this made pretty dry study, worse – he said – than contract law. So Rufus and he developed office games. Samples of commando daggers lay about the office, some of them in filing cabinets. Leo or Rufus would close and lock their office door and compete at hitting the doorframe with knives. Only embeddings counted. Bounce-offs were a crime. If a thrower hit either the surrounding plaster wall or door itself, he lost all his points acquired to that stage.

That was part of their éclat as well. Officers in D/Navy's office or Major Enright's D/Plans were not permitted to waste time on such knife play. They had to keep writing reports and coming up with the correct admixture between destination and plan and technology. But then they had not personally invaded Singapore. They would tolerate the heroes' games at great length, whatever spririt stoves or groundsheets waited to be assessed and initialled.

When not employed on their files or their knife practice, Leo and Rufus attended roundtable meetings at which questions of equipment, transportation, tactics and strategy to do with the coming huge operation in the Natunas were discussed. These meetings were attended by Colonel Creed, who remained an advocate for the idea of many well-equipped operatives, landed from many US submarines, undermining Japanese structures and lines of communication, ships and airfields, transit of supplies, etc etc, in Southeast Asia – which to us, of course, was Northwest Asia.

The idea that the Independent Reconnaissance Department should build its own Indonesian, Malayan or Borneo junks was still being discussed, and Mortmain in particular made suggestions about the way that should be done, on everything from the contour to fitting-out and the supply of drinking water. I know now that the building of a number of junks was begun in a Melbourne shipyard, which was then afflicted with strikes, so that they would never be finished.

In the afternoons, a succession of hefty NCOs kept up the fitness of Leo Waterhouse and Rufus Mortmain and others, introducing them to new methods of tripping, knifing and incapacitating mortal flesh; and causing them to climb ropes, run through mud and surmount improbable barriers. They came back home to Dotty and me full of muscular vigour, though, as Leo said, absolutely buggered.

*They were about to truck us to a private abattoir in Fitzroy, so that we could practise slitting throats on pigs, when a corporal came running to us from a nearby office. There was a call for Commander Mortmain. Rufus jogged double-time across the parade ground to take it. By the time he got back the truck was ready to leave for the abattoir. I was sitting in the rear with a group of soldiers and sailors who were going through the same training for perhaps the same purpose. His monocle was glistening when he crawled aboard and sat beside me. Aussie soldiers and ratings who hadn't seen him earlier nudged each other and whispered, Cop the bloody monocle on the Pom.*

*That was Mrs Enright, he whispered to me. Wants to shout you and me a drink. To repay us for our kindness. Windsor bar, five thirty.*

*He inhaled and the eye which did not have the duty of bearing the monocle, arched.*

*She wants us to bring our wives? I asked.*

*I don't think that's the purpose, said Rufus, looking ahead. I also think she knows you won't come, Dig. I feel I should go out of politeness, don't you think?*

*Up to you, I said, a bit surprised. I can't go. I don't want to.*

*No need to bother Dotty with the details, he told me. I don't think Dotty likes her.*

*I thought I knew him. I didn't think he was an altar boy. But I didn't know he'd compromise me like that. For a drink and God knows what else with a good-looking mad woman. On our operations, life is so simple, and we all know everything we need to know about each other. Now, on the way to knife pigs, he was making the world complicated again. I wanted to go home and hug Grace. But I had to cover myself with pigs' blood before they'd let me.*

# Seven

During our joint tenancy, Dotty and I liked to get ready for the return of our men by cooking a communal dinner – a pleasant exercise of sisterhood. Talking, talking, we cleaned and mashed the spuds, debated how much butter we could spare to make them appetising, and shelled heroes' quantities of green peas. Occasionally, as we chatted, she might go and find a book from the bedroom, stand with a frown thumbing through it and, finding the page, hand it to me to read while she went back to stirring the vegetable pot or reducing the flame beneath it.

I have said this before, in one or two literary magazine interviews, that Dotty was my chief educator. I thought Spender's poetry, which I read at Dotty's urging, astounding. That's putting it mildly. Spender, with his talk of the treachery of banks and cathedrals and the insanity of rulers, had nothing in common with me, and my innocent father, a good servant of society and a survivor of the world Depression, would have found his socialism offensive.

Spender also had little time for punctuation. He was too busy educating the reader in the space of one poem.

Before the war, before her travels, Dotty had met Louis MacNeice at a party in Bloomsbury. Evelyn Waugh, of whom until then I had never heard, had told her offhandedly that he disliked stringy women like her, that they generally had narrow opinions and tendencies to 'improve' men. That was after she had published her novel, and was ripe to be put in her place by other writers. Breaking away from such posturers, she had begun her rough travels in Turkey and the Middle East, and met Mortmain on the beach in Penang.

Let's have a gin before the men get home, she always suggested, and I agreed to the idea as if it was something daring and revolutionary, which indeed it still was in my terms.

On my second afternoon in Melbourne, we hadn't finished it when Leo let himself in. Seeing me evoked such a frank joy in his face that I felt myself instantly exempt from the wistfulness of Dotty's earlier poem. Cooking's afoot! he yelled, and lifted me and carried me around the living room and back to the kitchen. Dotty was smiling too at this demonstration of exuberant love. He put me down.

You're stacking on the weight, old girl, he said, imitating a husband of greater age, a Braidwood pastoralist, say.

Then he frowned. Rufus won't be back for a while, he told Dotty, and her face clouded.

Where is he?

Leo said uncomfortably, I'm not sure. I think he might have gone down to Port Melbourne to inspect something, a vessel, you know. He can't always tell what they might expect of him.

How long is this inspection to take? asked Dotty.

Leo made a pained face.

Dotty asked again, Will he be home for dinner?

Leo told her, Well, he didn't actually tell me he wouldn't be.

We turned down the stove and waited, and Leo kept on apologising to Dotty as if it were his fault.

He said, Grace and I might go to the pictures. If Rufus is back in time, perhaps you and he would like to come too. It's Errol Flynn.

Then you'll be looking at yourself on the screen, I joked.

Wasn't he arrested this year for rape? asked Dotty, as if our happiness bothered her.

I'm not sure, said Leo. I hope not. He's a Tasmanian, you know.

Leo and I were pleased to eat dinner hurriedly while listening to the ABC news and then get away to the pictures. Errol Flynn was a Norwegian villager who stood up against the Nazis. He was starting to look older than Leo, like an elder brother. But his eyes still glittered on the screen and I was sure he couldn't possibly be guilty of rape.

When we got home at eleven, the flat felt cold and we heard a shrill question from Dotty in the Mortmain bedroom and the appeasing rumble from Rufus.

Let's go to bed, said Leo, looking very grim but then smiling broadly.

The next morning, Leo and I encountered all the worst aspects of sharing the flat. Dotty was thunderously silent, and Rufus behaved like someone in a play, the breezy fellow who enters towards the end of act one, tennis racket in hand, sweater over shoulders, oblivious to the crisis that's overtaken all the other characters. In as far as he could dance, he danced around Dotty, his comedic glass in his eye, trying too hard. Could I pass you the milk, dear? Try this marmalade a Yank gave me. And so on.

I now know what was happening with Charlie Doucette in England at that time. He had fallen in love with an appliance of war, a sort of sub-submarine, a little boat piloted by one man. This vessel could proceed on the surface by battery power, it required no paddles. It could also submerge, so that only the driver's head was visible, or it could go underwater entirely, the driver wearing goggles, and with an oxygen supply device clamped between his lips. The record shows it was an Englishman, Major Frampton, who introduced him to it and to a young instructor named Sub-Lieutenant Lower who could do the loop-the-loop with it underwater. Doucette wanted a go at it. If he could handle it, it would be very suitable for his buccaneering plans.

I believe that, when he practised aboard the submersible in the deep, dark water of a reservoir outside London, Doucette dealt easily with the normal human problems of fear of drowning, of underwater claustrophobia in water greyer and dimmer than the greyest, dimmest English sky. Doucette was first of all a creature of water, and I doubt he had too many of the normal phobias. Doucette had to be lived up to by other men who knew normal, pedestrian fears. A man who would know fear, the Englishman Frampton, the inventor of the little submersibles, reacted to Doucette's enthusiasm for the machine and pleaded to be allowed to come with Doucette and have a role in Doucette's new enterprise. Doucette said, I'll fix it! From some of his men he required months of punishing training. With others, a burst of enthusiasm was enough.

On his English journey, Doucette also visited a British mine-laying submarine, and found out that if you built special containers for the submersibles, a number of them could be transported in the compartments generally devoted to mines.

His mother, Lady Doucette, was living with her English relatives in Wiltshire. She had left Dublin for the time being as a protest against de Valera's insistence that Ireland remain neutral. She was the descendant of those hard-up English gentry who had married into the Doucettes' ready cash, giving the Doucettes social cachet while the Doucettes paid the bills. For whatever reason, Doucette had given SOE her address as his care-of address in Britain. Lady Doucette was a robust woman, but she later told Mark

Lydon she sought the normal reassurances from Charles that a mother should. In his book, Lydon sets down, accurately or not, a standard mother–son conversation:

How are your quarters?

Quite comfortable, thanks, Ma.

And you wouldn't do anything ill-advised?

Of course not, Ma. I intend to come back and take you dancing.

The conversation sounds credible. Though it's dying out, that understated language is still used by the sort of British gents my second husband, Laurie Burden, had business with. But in Doucette's day, it was a sort of safety net thrown over the cruelties that young men could inflict, and have inflicted on them.

The evening of his visit to his mother and aunt, Doucette caught the village taxi to the local railway station. He was about to be returned to Australia by a succession of military aircraft. A quarter of an hour after he left, an urgent telegram arrived for him. After some discussion, Lady Doucette and her stepsister called the police to come and collect the telegram and rush it to the station. The train had already left for London by the time they got it there, so they brought it back to Lady Doucette. They must open the telegram, the two women decided, so that its contents could be relayed to a number at SOE in Baker Street, London.

The telegram, from the International Committee of the Red Cross, begged to inform that Doucette's wife and son, Minette and Michael, were alive, and prisoners of the

Japanese. They were presently held in Satsuoka internment camp in Japan, and were in moderately good health. The SS *Tonkin*, on which they had been travelling to join Doucette in India, had been intercepted in the Indian Ocean by the German raider *Jaguar*. Its commander gave *Tonkin*'s captain a choice between capture and being blown to pieces. For the sake of his passengers, the captain chose capture. The Germans put a crew aboard *Tonkin* and sailed it to the Japanese port of Yokohama. From there, the one hundred and thirty passengers were taken by train to the upland town of Satsuoka and internment in a convent building.

The personnel at SOE failed to get the news to Doucette before his plane took off from Croydon airfield, but it was waiting for him when his plane touched down in Malta. Immediately, he sent a message to IRD, and Captain Foxhill passed the welcome news to Mortmain and Leo, who brought it home to Dotty and me.

By now, Dotty had forgiven Rufus for whatever had happened earlier. She and I had become firmer friends still, and on the days we didn't work, she showed me things to read – Auden, and TS Eliot's *Prufrock* verses and *Mrs Dalloway*, *Sons and Lovers*, and Stella Gibbon's *Cold Comfort Farm*. I began to write a few tentative verses myself, a sign that Dotty was having a potent influence on me. The other thing about her was that she spoke with great frankness, to the point that would actually be considered impoliteness in my own painfully polite family. In a bush town, a bank manager like my father was considered one of the gentry, and although the children of undistinguished English and Scottish immigrants, my parents did their best to behave in the manner in which they thought the British privileged classes did. With only an occasional etiquette guide, and tips on good behaviour in the weekend papers and the *Women's Weekly* for directions, they avoided uttering bruising truths. Dotty didn't. Thus the morning after Leo and Rufus brought Doucette's good news home, I found Dotty very depressed and, over tea, she was quick to tell me why.

This will make Doucette even more unstoppable, she told me. I'm glad the woman and her bairn have been saved, of course. But Jesse Creed showed me a report about how short the Japanese are of steamships. Doucette will want to blow up the entire Japanese merchant fleet now, and end the war. And he'll want Rufus and Leo with him. And Rufus will go of course.

I felt a pulse of fear too, and for the first time. Leo was so much part of my world that I had never doubted his survival. To an extent this was a symptom of my innocence. Young captains bearing the DSO and resembling Errol Flynn weren't in any real danger, were they? Leo had told me he and Rufus were chiefly advising IRD on equipment, and they kept fit because at any stage they might be needed as instructors. Leo had also mentioned that he and Rufus might be sent by sub on a non-attack run to lay a depot here or there in the islands, but would I keep that to myself. I asked him was he comfortable in a submarine, and he said, No reason why not. I mean, they've got air down there.

It was partly Dotty's unconscious demeanour of knowing so much more than I did. If she, a novelist and a poet, had grounds for alarm, then alarm must be the proper mode. I wanted Leo to be like Major Enright, stuck to a desk in Melbourne, going out to Essendon now and then to practise putting wing charges on military aircraft, so that he could in turn instruct commandoes on how it was done.

The simple truth was that I found it easier to believe in my own death than in Leo's. Earlier in the war he had come through the bombing of Darwin, and through whatever he and Rufus and Doucette had done. And in fact, the main lesson he took from the good news about Doucette was that *he* might now learn something about his father. From his contacts in intelligence, he told me, he suspected his father had also been shipped to Japan. But at least I had not got from him any sense that he intended to blow up Japanese fleets as a way of personally liberating his father. His father's capture was a phenomenon locked up in the giant nature of the war, beyond any individual input.

But Dotty's concern about Doucette and his plans put the first shock of panic into me.

As Doucette himself approached Australia, aircraft by aircraft, outpost by outpost, it seemed that the entirety of IRD devoted itself to interpreting Mrs Doucette's and her son's imprisonment. And Captain Foxhill had acquired through Colonel Jesse Creed a remarkable American aerial reconnaissance photograph, taken from a few hundred feet, of the building and its grounds, a photograph which

Leo would show me one lunchtime when I came to his office. It was of a convent like any Catholic convent anywhere, but surrounded by rich farmland. The letters PW were hugely visible in the front garden of the place. The weather on that plateau, Foxhill had ascertained, ranged between 0° F and 75° F.

It struck me as very strange for the returning Doucette that he should know exactly where and at what temperature his wife and child were held captive. It doesn't seem so bad, said Leo of the place in the photograph. You could see in him the hope that his own father was held somewhere equally unthreatening.

One evening, Leo and Rufus came home with a gleam in their eyes. Doucette had returned. There would be a party at the Foxhills'.

# *Eight*

*In the office we congratulated the Boss on the news about his wife and son. Rufus and I noticed how hollowed-out he looked though, but he was excited too. When he smoked he left his cigarette unlit for a time and jabbed the air with it, telling us about the Silver Bullets, the new submersibles he had ridden in England. He showed us photographs and plans of them. He had a feverish light in his eyes which picked us up too.*

*We realised, I think, that we'd got a bit flabby in his absence. Our dagger-throwing skills improved marginally, so that maybe we could have got a job in a sideshow. But we had been drifting. Now we could feel the current was back, and the current was Charlie Doucette, the Boss.*

*He told us the submersibles would be testing for some chaps. Some of them wouldn't like this new device, there'd be cases of claustrophobia and panic, since you could lose all sense of up and down when riding them. I knew I was going to find it hard, just from the description of the tight mask, but I can't imagine that Rufus or Rubinsky or Blinkhorn or Doucette's old bowman Pat Bantry will have any problems. And we were exhilarated to think of as many as twenty of these near invisible craft creeping into anchorages with loads of limpets.*

*At calmer times, the Boss said that he had been rather comforted to see that reconnaissance photograph of his wife's prison.*

*Good old Jesse Creed provided that, Rufus reminded him.*

*Kind of him, the Boss admitted. The place, he said, certainly didn't look like a hellhole, and the good thing was in that climate Minette and the boy were a long way from the risk of malaria and dengue fever and beri-beri. He didn't make much of it in military terms, he didn't make the news the basis for any 'once more unto the breach, dear friends' speech. So we were a bit surprised by his intensity in the next overall planning meeting.*

*We were all in the conference room with its empty fireplace and a late afternoon hot wind from the Western District was blowing in at the door to the balcony. Everyone seemed awed by Doucette for a number of reasons – the submersibles as well as everything else. That stale old bugger Doxey had the chair of course, and there was Foxhill, Enright, D/Plans, the head of Navy Plans as well, then the head of IRD intelligence, and Colonel Jesse Creed. Rufus reported on the junks a shipyard in Melbourne was making for us, and the fact that the shipwrights thought the war was as good as over, and had no inhibitions about going on strike. It couldn't be predicted, said*

*Rufus, whether the junks would be ready in time for use before that year's monsoon. Jesse Creed reported that the proposed base on Great Natuna would be equipped with Bolton long-range radios, but that operatives would be fitted out and trained in the use of the new hand radios called walkie-talkies. The Boltons would enable contact with IRD and the Melbourne Ultra signal centre, of which Jesse Creed was supervisor.*

*All at once, the Boss said, That's all very well, nice equipment I'm sure, Colonel Creed.*

*He was punching at the air with an unsharpened pencil. There was blueness round his eyes and I don't think he'd been sleeping well since coming back.*

*But, he said, I'm a little disappointed to find that no US submarine reconnaissance reports on the Natunas grace our agenda.*

*Creed said, I too am disappointed by that fact. I hear from General MacArthur's office that the combat demands on our submarines are delaying all that. I can assure you that I have labelled all my requests URGENT.*

*The Boss looked away towards a far corner of the room. He asked, But will we be waiting this time next year, and fobbed off indefinitely with the same excuses?*

*Creed told him he would certainly not expect that and would be personally disappointed if that were the case.*

*Well, said the Boss, I can only judge from results. I proceeded to SOE in London on the basis that something pressing had to be done, and that I must find some device to achieve that end. I have returned, the equipment has been loaded on a freighter and is on the way to us, and both the engineer-cum-inventor and the instructor from SOE are also on their way to take their role in the enterprise. I can't do any more, but you have not done what has to be done.*

*Creed said he was not the final authority on sub deployment. He said it was a matter of negotiation between himself and General Willoughby, his boss.*

*Our Boss said, Oh, General Willoughby! That very good friend of all British enterprises!*

*Creed got angry at that. He hoped the Boss wasn't accusing him of insincerity. That would be a serious hindrance to our new relationship, he declared.*

*But the Boss really put it to him, and not for the first time I began to feel sorry for the American, who didn't seem such a bad fellow. That's the whole point, the Boss told him. There's been no cooperation. You sit in on our deliberations, while yours remain undisclosed and mysterious and inconclusive.*

*We could all see that Creed was very angry now. But the Boss did not let up. For all I know, you might go off to General Willoughby and say, This and this are what that curious Doucette and his Australian chums are up to. So let's keep them busy with great dreams and promises.*

*Major Doxey ineffectually called for peace, gentlemen.*

*Doucette declared, I have an entire regiment of friends, and my own flesh and blood, not to mention eighteen thousand Australian prisoners, held by the enemy. I resent the Americans depicting my motives as empire-reclaiming.*

*Order! cried Doxey, and reminded the Boss that in his absence we had all managed these meetings without any rancour.*

*Then I have to tell you, said Doucette, that I'm appalled by the lack of progress you've made. We might as well have rented out the work to the British submarine flotilla on the other side of the country.*

*Major Enright shook himself like a dog who has just woken up to find there's a bone of interest to him in the room, and he put in his tuppence worth to cover his posterior. He said, You'll see in the minutes I've put a request in to the air force chaps to see if they can do a reconnaissance of the Natunas for us. I've also been onto D/Plans at MacArthur's HQ in Brisbane, and they report there has certainly been an unavoidable delay with submarine reconnaissance.*

*This did nothing to soothe either of the combatants. Creed said he didn't need to prove to Doucette that he was trying as hard as he could to get the joint endeavour off the ground. You treat everything I do, Doucette, like an arrogant Limey eccentric.*

*I happen to be an arrogant Irish eccentric, the Boss reminded him again, just for the sake of contradiction.*

*Doxey ended up clapping his hands, demanding that both gentlemen desist from further insult and innuendo. The Boss managed merely an icy imitation of being polite. He said that submarine reconnaissance will be essential to the Natunas plan. But he hadn't seen any indication that our friend Colonel Creed was as anxious as we were to get things in place.*

*Creed did a more diplomatic job, speaking about how he could understand that after the stress of a journey to Britain, and a long airborne return to Australia, anyone might be a bit edgy. And he himself wished he had made more progress.*

*I think Rufus and I felt a bit guilty. We knew as well as anyone that there'd be no running of a junk into Singapore once the monsoon turned against us. Yet although Rufus had visited the shipyard, to see the craft being built, we had personally placed no urgency on American reconnaissance. The Boss, coming back, had clarified everything, had got us all out of our file-skimming stupor, all our lazy initialling of memos and reports. It was like Peter Pan coming back to Neverland and straightening out the boys.*

*Back in our office after the meeting, the door with our knife scars in it firmly closed, Doucette sat behind his desk and made a gesture that Rufus and I should grab a chair each and pull up to it. The Boss's calm had returned. It was as if he had never lost it in the first place.*

*You're the pair whose opinion means something, he said. What do you think of Creed?*

*Rufus told us Dotty thought he was a decent fellow. She said he really liked that last jaunt of ours, Boss.*

*The Boss thought about this and remarked that Dotty's loyalty to all of us was exemplary.*

*Oh yes, Rufus agreed, but he reminded the Boss she saw through people pretty easily too, and she'd see through Creed if he meant us any malice.*

*The Boss thought and then declared, Doxey and the others will never understand my position. In some ways I don't blame Creed because he's been put in place in this committee to spy for General Willoughby. A fellow has to do what his superiors tell him. But I blame him for the hypocrisy of pretending to be a friend and supporter while he's doing us in.*

*Rufus said, I wouldn't have thought it was all pretence, Boss.*

*But again the Boss said Rufus was a kind man. Creed might amaze everyone by coming up with a reconnaissance of Great Natuna in the next few weeks. But the Boss didn't think that likely. So he wanted us to start planning a mission of our own. Back to where the Japs and MacArthur both don't want us to go, he said. We'd have to build up some records and files but we'd keep them amongst ourselves till it became clear Creed was useless. We wouldn't be left high and dry without a plan when Creed fails us.*

*Rufus asked him, Back to Singapore?*

*The Boss said, That's the neighbourhood we know. We'll call it Memerang. Remember those Malayan otters that we swam with that afternoon at Pandjang? Charming little blighters, but you can't see them coming in the water, and with these submersibles . . .*

*We talked away with each other, spinning theories. One idea was that Rufus could captain one of those junks they were building in Melbourne, and take it up off Sumatra to Pompong Island, say, while the rest of the party travelled by sub with the submersibles aboard it in the mine tubes, meeting up with him within reach of Singapore. There was that group of British subs operating from Western Australia, and the Boss knew the flotilla commander, Shadwell. So after junk and sub met, everything could go over to the junk which could take us right up into the Singapore roads. We'd use twenty of the little submersibles, the Silver Bullets, said the Boss. Imagine the mayhem. Whereas I'm sure that this big pirate show they're talking about now has as much reality as the Wizard of Oz.*

*So you don't want to involve D/Plans? asked Rufus.*

*For God's sake not yet, Rufus, said the Boss. He's hopeless.*

*Rufus murmured, Yes. I can't say I'm sorry I tupped his wife.*

*This confession Rufus made wasn't up for discussion by anyone. The Boss asked for no further information on this, and as for me, I knew enough to confuse me already. I didn't like it, the fact Rufus took his chances with other women. To tell the truth, I'm a bit scandalised about the whole thing. For poor Dotty's sake as much as anything. And even though I know he's the bravest man there is, I have this permanent suspicion that it might affect the way he behaved, way out in some archipelago somewhere.*

# Nine

I learned a great deal through the Mortmains about life in Malaya before the war, and of how Rufus first met Doucette.

Doucette, and a friend of his from his garrison life in Belfast, Billy Lewis, owned a 19-foot yacht. They used to sail up the east coast of Malaya on the south-west monsoon. The east coast was not much used for recreational sailing, because it took some doing to get out there on the south-west monsoon, and during the north-east monsoon it was impossible.

Billy Lewis and Doucette shared a similar hatred of peacetime garrison work in Selarang Barracks. Rufus seemed to think that Billy and Doucette also had problems keeping up with the mess expenses, and living cheaply on the boat was a great saving as well as a great relief. In a 'good' British regiment, an officer might need hundreds of pounds a year to keep up with mess and sporting activities, and the Doucettes sent their son only a modest yearly allowance.

It was difficult to get boats in over the sandbars of those eastern rivers, but Doucette and Billy managed to do so, and one day Mortmain had met them drinking tea and practising dialect Malay at a village near the mouth of the Terengganu River. Mortmain, as yet unmarried, had descended from his timber plantation to buy regional daggers, his chief passion. That was how they had met, in an outdoor teahouse in a Malay village. Some military gentlemen were stand-offish even with other Englishmen, in particular with someone like Mortmain, a mere timber estates manager. But that had not been the way of these two. Doucette was always too curious to be aloof.

Mortmain himself would have been a military man, as was his older brother, if his parents could have afforded two regimental sons, but they couldn't. Rufus too liked to sail, and they sat over tea talking about the testing sandbars of all those north-eastern Malayan rivers. It was up here, Doucette already believed, that the Japanese would one day land, now they had China by the throat. Why not? There was a good highway all the way south to Johore. Mortmain agreed and advised Doucette to tell the blighters in Singapore. They think they're protected by the Malay jungles. In reality, the roads they built themselves lead right to their front door.

Doucette liked Mortmain and invited him down to Singapore for weekends. On a typical weekend, they might sail from Changi to the Singapore Yacht Club, and begin their drinking and discussions there, chatting with other boat enthusiasts. It became apparent to Mortmain that Doucette *had* made an intelligence report on his journey up the east coast.

As their Saturdays waned, they would sail round to the west coast, to the Coconut Grove nightclub. Both the soldiers had their pipe dress uniforms and shoes with them in duffel bags, and Mortmain similarly had his dinner suit from up-country. They changed and rowed ashore in their dinghy, overcrowded as it was with a beanpole civilian and the two more compact but sturdy officers. Their shoes hung around their necks, they climbed the sea wall, brushed the sand off their feet, tied their laces, and selected girls to dance with. Infiltration was already their style.

It was clear to me early in my Melbourne days, Dotty did not have the same gleaming view of Doucette as Rufus and Leo did. During the afternoons in the flat, when we were both trying to write, an activity which if communally attempted always leads to conversation, she would tell me about her contacts with Charlie Doucette in pre-war Singapore.

There had been a six-month period, before Minette consented to marry him and join him in Singapore, during which he used to confide in Dotty a great deal. He knew Minette was torn two ways. She was used to living in style in Macau. But there she was a Belgian Catholic divorcee – though she had some sort of Papal document of separation, she could not talk in any real way to the men of the colony.

Dotty said she didn't know whether in those months of waiting Doucette saw her as a sister or as a potential lover, a solace for his bewilderment. Dotty spoke to me about all this with a characteristic frankness I did my best to pretend was normal to me too. She said, I found him very attractive in all sorts of wrong-headed ways women are fools for. Of course, he respected Rufus too much, and so did I, but I'd be lying if I said there wasn't some sort of magnetism there.

Minette was always worried about Doucette, you know, Dotty further confided. He'd taken her by storm. I mean, to sail the South China Sea from Singapore to Macau in a 19-footer just to see her face . . . that would have an impact on any woman. And when she asked him why he did it, he didn't tell her one of the reasons was intelligence gathering. He told her, I had to see you because I was deteriorating into nothing in the East.

And so he was, Dotty told me. Doucette once showed me a letter he'd written to Minette – this was before they got married, and he wanted to ask me should he send it off because he was worried by its frankness. On one hand, he compared himself favourably to his hidebound senior officers and felt sorry for them, poor old men who would never know the sort of love he and Minette had. In the next sentence, though, he was warning her he was unreliable and a bad man, but that she was a superior enough soul to ignore that. Minette didn't find out that in everyday life he was a hopeless boozer until she moved into married quarters at Selarang Barracks. I heard her express her anxiety about all this while the boys were out sailing, and

Minette and I would be stuck in the clubhouse waiting and trying to space out our gin slings. Minette hated his drinking. She thought it was because he was so torn between sailing and garrison life. And the big boys in Singapore laughed off all his intelligence, you know. The only person who read his reports on how easy it would be to take Malaya was a chap we knew in the civilian administration. But he couldn't influence the stupid soldiers. That also drove Doucette to drink, the fact that some officers were actually looking forward to taking on the Japanese and, since they were missing the European war, could hardly wait. Minette told me that one day when they were sailing he looked at her and said, I'd go to the depths of hell to escape ordinary soldiering in barracks.

Doucette's now-widowed mother, Lady Doucette, was a renowned dragon, said Dotty, and Charlie was the favourite son. He sometimes said he had become a soldier for her sake – she wanted him to follow in the tracks of his father, the late Major-General Sir Walter Doucette. At a party in Singapore, he said something like, I dread the time I go home and she has to realise I don't resemble the small, model boy she thinks she's been writing to. He was, as he said, a frightened six-year-old scared of his mother.

He also confessed to Dotty that he felt like a fraud with Minette, because she was so generous and rated him at a higher moral level than he deserved.

To Rufus, said Dotty, Doucette has always been the King of Ulster, but I think he's always been a mess. Sometimes he'd go to pieces and smoke opium in Chinatown, and Billy

Lewis or Rufus would have to nurse him back. He hated himself for that, and his drinking. And then Chinese boys, one in particular, in his bachelor years. Not that he was alone in that. But he really hated himself for that as well. It was as if he really believed his terrible mother would find out.

I was not shocked so much as scared for Leo. Does Leo know these things?

Don't worry too much, said Dotty. He's an extraordinary commando. That's how he punishes himself for his sins.

I'd rather he didn't have any sins, I admitted.

In Rufus's eyes he doesn't, said Dotty.

*After the Boss's argument with Creed, we all started on the new plan, Memerang, but for a while the Boss seemed down. As the Americans delayed and Memerang became more official, at least as an idea Doxey tolerated, we had to work with Major Enright. He was good at many things – working out the number of Compo and Rompo rations that should be dropped off, and where, and when. I have to say I got a tinge of respect for him. He was earning his keep now by writing into the plan such easily forgotten items as waterproof containers for wireless equipment. He had himself designed new packing methods. Every given load we took on our adventures was to be limited to 35 pounds, what an operative could easily carry. Enright himself designed the sealed kerosene tin-like containers, which had special lever lids and rope carrying handles, so that they could easily be moved in the confines of a submarine.*

*Boot A. B. Australian No.2, Tropic Studded, was decided on as most suitable for us, and it had been designed by a committee on which Enright had served. He had also designed the marspikes with which explosives could be stuck to wooden hulls – the device silently released a spike into wood through a bracket on the charge. And so on. He had talents. If I didn't already know it, I began to realise you had to have people like him.*

*It looked likely that the training for Memerang, on Doucette's wonderful machines which were still on their way to us, would happen on the other side of the country, where the British submarine flotilla was, at Garden Island, just off the coast at Fremantle. I was disappointed, for no wives were permitted, but I suppose it had to come to that.*

*The Boss remained silent and edgy and suspicious of Creed. He definitely has the blues, Rufus told me. He was like this sometimes in Singapore, he'd work himself into a black hole, the deep dumps. After he came back from a long sail he was always mopey. Can't say I ever blamed him.*

*I hadn't seen much of that before. I was a bit surprised. As for Rufus himself, he never seemed to feel entitled to be down.*

*There was a party at Foxhill's that Grace and I had gone to, but we'd come home a little early. We wanted our own company above all. And when we left Foxhill's, the Boss seemed much better, and the life of the party. He was playing a ukelele he'd picked up on his long trip back from Britain. He'd learned to play it in the bellies of bombers and DC-3s, where he couldn't be heard over the noise of engines. And that night he'd played for us 'The Umbrella Man', 'Paper Moon', 'The*

*Teddy Bears' Picnic'. He'd stretched his mouth comically and done George Formby, then a tinkly Arthur Askey, and a Cockney Stanley Holloway, followed by some Noel Coward. He'd been full of the joy of life when Grace and I got our coats and left, and through the blacked-out streets on the way to the tram we laughed about his performance.*

*For the next day Major Doxey had called the first big minuted meeting for the Memerang plan. Even he believed Creed was no longer of use to us. D/Sigs, D/Navy, D/Plans were all there at Radcliffe House for the meeting, and Rufus and I, but the Boss didn't turn up. It was strange. The Boss was winning his argument with Creed and Doxey, so I thought only something severe or unexpected had delayed him.*

*Nonetheless Rufus waited until the afternoon before he called Doucette's flat. No answer. He called Foxhill, who was at home, about it, and Foxhill told us Doucette had drunk quite a bit later in the night, and got a little bit weepy very late, after Mrs Foxhill had gone to bed. The Boss had said something about he should have felt greater excitement about Minette being safe. And that he would hate anything he did to hurt her – if he caused the Japanese to get revenge on him by punishing her or his stepson.*

*It was later still, apparently, when the Boss began to plummet a bit. He got on to the whole thing of it being his fault Minette and young Michael were on that ship, on their way to India. They could have stayed in Perth all the time, as it turned out. And he began to say again how he thought he wasn't pleased enough to find they were alive.*

*Before Foxhill went to bed, he set the Boss up in the spare room because it was too late for him to be driven home. Foxhill was woken towards dawn by a racket from the Boss's room. He found the Boss tangled in the sheets and fighting them. It turned out he had a sort of waking nightmare, something about guards taking blankets away from Minette.*

*I know what that is like, the nightmares. I have this nightmare where my father and I are in the same camp and he's asking me for food, and I keep on saying, of course, I know a barracks where there is some, and I wander off to get it, but I keep on being delayed, and I always find myself at the opposite end of the camp to the hut where the nourishment is. I have conversations with other men who try to put me off the search too, and I'm bullied by guards with indistinct faces who tell me that I have to do certain duties, including latrines and unloading trucks, and I'm fretful to get to the supply hut and then back to my father. I explain to everyone, The thing is that my father doesn't know I'll be so long, and there's the risk he'll start to believe I'm not coming back. So I know why the Boss might have a nightmare, particularly when he'd drunk a lot.*

*Foxhill himself came to the office later, looking white and shattered. He had totally forgotten the meeting, and apologised and said he had felt bound to stick around the house until the Boss woke. Doxey was censorious about it. You could have called us, Captain, he told the Scot. Foxhill told us the Boss had said when he woke up that all he needed was a few days by himself, somewhere in the Dandenongs or a beach house where he could fish and go on long walks. He obviously needed a few days off, said Foxhill – he'd come straight off the plane from England and got to work, and he'd had a shock he hadn't absorbed yet. Foxhill's wife's family – as it turned out – had a nice beach house on the Mornington Peninsula, and Mrs Foxhill would get the keys from her brother that day and drive him down to the place with his ukelele, his fishing line and some books.*

*At the meeting, Foxhill turned to Rufus. Actually, I don't want to barge in at the beach house and check all the time on how he is. But I'm sure he'd accept a visit from Leo and you over the weekend, since you're his golden boys. You could take the girls down there and have a picnic. Just let me know by telegram or phone how he is.*

*We were even able to get a car from the office to pursue that task. On Friday night, though, Dotty said she would not go. I've dragged the bugger up by his miserable puppet-strings too often, she told us. We knew her well enough by now to understand she wasn't likely to change her mind. Grace said in that case she wouldn't go either, because she didn't want to cramp Rufus and me. But I wanted her to come. I wanted to sit in the sand dunes with her and drink beer. As for the surf, it was getting a bit cold for that, but I imagined that we would dare each other into it.*

*Dotty stayed abrasive overnight about everything, spiky about Rufus and the Boss. Tell him to have a nervous breakdown once and for all, she advised us while we packed a picnic basket the next morning. I said, I don't think the Boss is crack-up material.*

*And she replied in her tigress way, Oh, he's fine when he's sneaking around and exploding things. It's just daily life he can't handle.*

*And yet, while Rufus picked up the car, she came to Grace and me and said, All right, I'm going, but only for Grace's sake. And to show you what a lunatic Doucette is.*

*He's not a lunatic, I said. He's been through a lot.*

*Haven't we all? Dotty sniffed.*

*Grace saved me from further arguments by winking at me. The ride south with Rufus – driving through Brighton and Frankston – was very pleasant. Through those suburbs with low-roofed houses behind the dunes and flashes of bright sea seen across vacant plots. At last we got amongst the bush of the peninsula and followed the directions Foxhill had written out for us, from Rosebud on the inner side of peninsula across red hills to the ocean side. We found the family name on a board hammered to a tree by a stock gate. Beyond the gate a tall timber house with a verandah all around it looked out at the Southern Ocean. Nothing stood between it and the South Pole, and it felt like that. Pleasantly though, not cold but certainly the end of the earth.*

*We walked up the timber stairs to the house and around the verandah to the front – the sea-facing side. Here there was a slung hammock, and on the verandah boards, an open novel and a bottle of whisky two-thirds gone. Rufus stood by the back door, crying, Boss, are you there? There was no answer, and Grace suggested he might have gone down to the beach. It was a hopeful sort of idea, but I think we could all tell that things were not right.*

*Rufus said, I'll just creep in and see if he's asleep.*

*We nodded, and Rufus disappeared into the dim house. Grace and I looked out to sea. It was so immense it seemed to promise us settled times. A roar from inside the house took us by shock. A stooped Rufus was retreating to the verandah, his arms spread wide. No, it's me, it's Rufus, he was saying. The crazy-eyed Boss, in nothing but shorts and greatly needing a shave, was yelling at him in what must have been Malay and swiping at him with a machete.*

*Boss, it's us, I called out, because he didn't seem to know Rufus.*

*Have you got malaria? Rufus asked him, but the Boss sliced the air with the machete.*

*At the end of the Boss's backswing, Rufus hit him in the face and his legs gave out and he fell sideways onto the verandah boards with his mouth crushed open. I'd never seen him look like this before, and I was shocked by the belt Rufus had given him, and knew I'd have to explain its force to Grace without understanding everything myself about what it meant. Perhaps I could say, Rufus isn't trained to hit people softly.*

*In fact Rufus himself seemed appalled to see the Boss flattened like this, looking like a dipso in a gutter.*

*He said, Let's put him to bed, Leo. No, better bath him, I think. He doesn't smell so good.*

*Does he have malaria? asked Grace. It was obvious she wished we could say yes.*

*No, muttered Rufus as I helped him lift the Boss. He's just beyond himself, poor laddy.*

*There was a sour, acrid smell about the Boss as we carried him inside, where thank heavens the girls didn't follow us. He was not heavy, slight as a kid, really. Such a big personality you forgot he was a squirt. Very sinewy, but very thin legs and arms. If they weren't so brown, we would have called them Pommy legs.*

*We ended up in the primitive bathroom of the beach house. Two tarantula-like spiders watched us from the ceiling. It was the sort of place the fauna would always invade – possums and insects.*

*Hold him tight, Rufus ordered me as we lowered the Boss to the floor. He's been on the opium pipe and it always does weird things to him. You'd think it'd make him docile, but he goes haywire.*

*Well, I thought, opium! Of course. Singapore. These two fellows had a shared history and knew each other well in places where you pick up exotic habits.*

*While I held on to the Boss, he had a fair bit to say. He said, Come to the wedding, Colonel. Come to the wedding, you fucking fat bigot! He adopted a pompous voice. Doucette's done it now. Wants to marry some Belgian tart from Macau!*

*That fit passed and he yelled over my shoulder at Rufus, Malaria, you say? Good for you, doctor! Malaria! And blood poisoning. Went crazy, took four damned orderlies to hold me down. Remember that one. Four fucking orderlies!*

*Rufus began to fill the bath with the cold tank water which was all that was available here. He cried out above the noise of the water splashing into the zinc bathtub, Yeah. I remember that time, Boss. The tropical ulcer went septic. Lucky you lived, you mad bugger!*

*The Boss writhed and began crying, and that and the sweaty and shitty stink of him made me feel embarrassed as I held him fast. I was discovering he was more human than I wanted him to be. I hoped I could forget the raving, stinking imbecile he was at the moment. I took comfort from the fact that all this didn't seem to shock or come as a surprise to Rufus.*

*The Boss began to work his jaw where Rufus had hit him. Well done, old chap! he screamed. But watch out for Round Four. I'll eat your guts hot.*

*Okay, Boss, said Rufus, turning the tap off. Are you going to be good for me?*

*Can you imagine, the Boss asked, weeping, they take her blankets away?*

*No, I think you're dreaming that, Boss, said Rufus, removing his uniform jacket and rolling up his sleeves. Grace knocked on the door to tell us she and Dotty had started on a lunch and the clean-up in the kitchen. Are salmon sandwiches okay?*

*I called out, Yes, and we'll be out to eat them soon.*

*Ah, cold blankets, said the Boss as we stripped him off and smelt the full staleness of his opium and whisky sweats and his urine and shit, and lowered him into the water. The cold water did not seem to worry him, but he argued with himself and the Japanese and God and Rufus and me as we washed him down with soft cloths. As he began to cool off and shiver he started abusing Belfast weather, blaming another country for what he was feeling in Australia's cold tank water.*

*When the bath was over, we towelled him and dressed him in a fresh singlet and shorts I got from his kit in the melee and fug of the Boss's bedroom. As he briskly dried the Boss's under-groin Rufus dared to make a joke about the Boss's penis, saying, You don't exactly own a love truncheon, do you, Boss? For such a charmer?*

*Get fucked yourself, Mortmain. Women don't want a bloody elephant.*

*Ah, said Mortmain. It speaks!*

*In the kitchen, Rufus sat him down and hand-fed him salmon off a spoon, as Grace and Dotty and I looked on, awed and frowning. After getting a little food into him, Rufus and I put him into bed, and then we ate our own sandwiches and drank our tea. Hearing an occasional yell from his bedroom, we knew we couldn't leave him alone, and Rufus asked if Grace and I would like to drive into the seaside village of Flinders and call Foxhill at the office – he was waiting there all day for a report – and tell him the Boss was still a little indisposed and Rufus would stay with him here overnight, but he should send a car and driver for the rest of us. Rufus would bring the Boss home to Melbourne the following afternoon.*

*You're not staying alone with that maniac, said Dotty.*

*My dear, no need for you to spend a night here.*

*I bloody will. If he comes at me with a bloody machete, I'll shoot the fucker dead.*

*Grace and I were pleased to get away from the house and drive amongst the melaleucas and she-oaks on the sandy road to Flinders. I was not an accomplished driver, but Grace wanted me to drive. This was a little adventure we both could cherish. She was silent for a while. It was almost superstitious.*

*We both wanted to get well away from the house before we started talking full voice, as if we were afraid of waking the Boss, though I knew that wasn't it. I was edgy about what impression everything we'd seen had had on Grace.*

*The sandy back road met some bitumen and took us into the village of Flinders. I got out and made the call to Foxhill, who said, Oh dear! and promised to send another car the next day.*

*I got back in the car and started the engine. But Grace put a hand on top of mine as I reached for the gear-stick.*

*Will you be going on any more operations with that man? she asked.*

*I said, He's just a bit ill at the moment. He's not like that when we've got something to do. They're just messing him about, that's all. The Yanks and the desk boys.*

*It seems as if he ought to be in hospital.*

*No, I said, look, he's found out about his wife and the little boy, and he feels pretty powerless about that too. I know how he feels. I have the occasional bad dream about my old bloke. And as well as that everyone's been frustrating him, trying to scale things down . . .*

*Grace grabbed my hand harder. But it wasn't in her nature to be sharp like Dotty. She said, I hope they scale him down all the way, to be honest. I don't like sending you off far with a man like that.*

*I begged her to suspend judgement. I told her he was a different man when we had something on. His face shone. He never touched liquor then, even if it was available. It was the first time, though, that I thought I'd need to go along next time, whether it was Memerang or the Great Natuna plan, to keep an eye on the Boss, instead of doing things under his gaze.*

# Ten

As Rufus and Leo had promised, Doucette came back to his best. Charming at parties, he was again forthcoming with the ukelele, and sang 'When I'm Cleaning Windows' in a range of regional accents. Uncertainty was over for him now, and a course had been set. Leo devoted a lot of energy to persuading me that what came next would be the climacteric of clever endeavours, beyond which we would have earned the right to breed children and live tranquilly.

One Saturday that winter, Leo was given two tickets to the stand at the Melbourne Cricket Ground for an Australian Rules game between Carlton and Collingwood, which the newspapers said would be the game of the season. Under a severe Melbourne sky we went off on the tram, carrying all that had happened and what was to come on our shoulders with apparent ease. I was unversed in Victorian football, and so to an extent was Leo, but he reacted to the contest between leaping and kicking men with an excitement that flowed into me when he grabbed my shoulder as if to protect it against the cold at moments of high sporting tension.

A chill wind was dimpling the surface of the river when we got home. Coming inside, we found a very sombre Foxhill drinking with the Mortmains. We could see the traces of tears on Dotty's cheeks, so that at first we thought there might have been an almighty row between her and Rufus.

Foxhill rose. Leo, he said.

Dotty and Rufus had also risen. Dotty said, Please, Foxy, let us get out of your way. And she and Rufus disappeared to the interior of their side of the flat. I felt a distinct pulse of fear at that moment. What could be so bad that Rufus and Dotty needed to make a space for it?

Foxhill said, Jesse Creed has access to a lot of information, you understand, Dig.

But we knew that already. How do you mean? asked Leo.

Well, you'll be getting notification from the Red Cross. But I'm afraid your father . . . he's been killed, Leo. After he was taken prisoner in Honiara they shipped him to a camp in the Philippines, and a month ago he was put with two hundred others on a ship for Japan, the *Terasao Maru*. It was torpedoed by an American sub. The only survivors were a handful of crew members. Both Japanese and Red Cross sources concur.

I felt that primal convulsion of grief and the surge of

tears, and began clumsily hugging Leo, trying to make hard contact with his flesh despite the fact that he was sheathed in an army overcoat still.

We have independent confirmation of it, Foxhill told us, to ward off any argument of hope. Of course, the American sub commander had no idea the ship was full of POWs.

Leo had not shed a tear but his mouth was open as if he was pathetically rolling probabilities around in his jaw.

Let's sit down, he said. I insisted I take his coat off, as if that would ease the hour. Then we both sat down. I held him. Foxhill fetched him some whisky.

They were all below, of course, Leo reasoned with himself. The prisoners. The sub commander couldn't have known.

Foxhill said, That's right.

So he's with my mother now, said Leo in a burst of primitive faith. Foxhill nodded earnestly, encouraging this sudden theology in Leo. That's right, Dig. That's exactly right.

Well, said Leo, blinking. He was a very skilled man. Never got over my mum dying like that. It changed the whole direction of his life.

The thing would have been sudden, I guess, Dig, Foxhill insisted. The commander said the thing just exploded amidships. One great explosion, no, two actually. The ship went up and then settled in an instant.

The sub commander said that? asked Leo.

Pretty much, said Foxhill. Just one thing – we can't say anything yet, or have any public memorial service. I mean, for the moment can you just keep it in your own circle, Dig? It shouldn't be in the paper or anything.

Leo looked at him, but dully.

What I mean is, said Foxhill, we're not supposed to know about this yet. The Japanese don't know we know. You understand, Dig? After the Red Cross tells you officially, by all means go ahead. But I suppose you'll be off . . . on your adventure by then. If you're up to it.

Leo shook his head. No, of course I'm up to it. No. This alters nothing.

But my fear was that it might alter a great deal, not least in Leo himself.

Eventually Dotty and Rufus reappeared. Foxhill informed Leo, I did tell the Mortmains why I was here. I hope you don't mind that, Dig.

Leo stood up to receive Dotty's embraces. This bloody, bloody war, she said.

Yes, said Leo. But it will end, you know, Dotty.

Rufus muttered, a sort of melodious condolence, and poured more drinks. We all sat down. Leo began speaking spontaneously about his father. He had a hard life, you know. We have a good farm, but dairy farming's tough. We were better off than most. Landed gentry.

He laughed at the idea.

Bush aristocrats. Seven hundred good acres. Flood plain. An educated man, too, my father. An agronomist. So when my mother died, he turned the farm over to his sister, my Aunty Cass, and her husband. And he took this job with the British administration in the Solomons.

But what was he like? I wanted to ask. This man I had never known. I did not even know if he was gregarious or reserved, loud or quiet. Leo had lapsed into deep thought in our midst. We were not going to find out much more.

That night as I held him, he said, He wasn't without his faults, you know. I wouldn't want to say that. He started drinking too much in the Solomons. But everyone did. And he let me run wild, and he had a woman. My nanny. Delia. A great, full-bodied Melanesian woman. A really jolly sort of person. I loved her. I didn't quite understand that he did too. I can see now why the colonial wives were sniffy about him. Anyhow, most of them probably died on the ship, and Delia is probably still on Guadalcanal, getting by.

After a silence, I thought Leo had gone to sleep but suddenly he said, He was a bloody good fisherman too, you know. And then, It would have been an awful death. Locked in the hold. It would have been hot, about 120 degrees, and it would have been foul and cramped. And then all at once the concussion, and water flooding in.

I could hear a little stutter of tears from him, merely a stutter, the habit of easy tears had been suppressed since his wild Solomon Islands childhood.

I said, You don't have to think about that. Most death is hard. He wouldn't want you to dwell on that.

Leo said, But I have to.

The flat was unheated, and for the first time I felt the malice of the cold of that southern city in winter.

Only two weeks later, Leo and Rufus left by train for Western Australia. It was another dismal night – we had

had a last supper at the flat and went across to Spencer Street in a taxi. Rufus had a lot of business to attend to, supervising the loading of gear into the goods vans at the back of the passenger train. I met little Jockey Rubinsky, the young man of many languages who was too awed by the occasion to say anything meaningful to me. I was astonished to meet my cousin Mel Duckworth, the one who had brought Leo home to Braidwood in the first place, amongst the men boarding. Leo had not mentioned his possible membership of the Memerang group, and I thought until then he had a comfortable training job in Queensland. I'm just in support, said Mel. I'm like the lighting man on a student production. He had none of his New South Wales family and no girlfriend to see him off, and he gave the impression of being a little more lost than some of the others.

Leo took me aside. I'll be back for Christmas. It's going to be wonderful. I agreed with him. I'm not making empty promises, he said. The weather conditions mean we've got to be back well before Christmas anyhow. That's between you and me.

I'm pleased to hear that piece of information, I told him.

Look, he said, you're allowed to worry a bit. Just a bit.

I remember saying – wittily, I thought, for a woman doing her best – All right. I'll indulge that luxury.

And listen, he said further, you don't have to worry about other things. I believe there's a searchlight battery of women at our training ground. You don't have to worry about any of that. You're the woman. There isn't any other.

He put his lips to my ear. As for Rufus, he said through crushed lips, I can't give any guarantees.

I'm not worried about women. I'm worried about your father.

I meant the influence his father's death might have on him.

He kissed me. I'm not Hamlet Prince of Denmark, he told me. Don't fret about that.

For some reason, on the cold station, the assurance was a comfort.

Doucette turned up, with bright eyes utterly lacking in doubt or the madness I'd seen at the beach house. He was compact, full of a burning energy. Kissing my hand, he assured me he would look after his young friend Dig, and that I was to live blithely until Leo's return. In the coming months I would remember and cling to Doucette's air of certainty, and I would not tell Dotty about it for fear she would diffuse it with another story of the Boss's Singapore berserkness.

The train was delayed and delayed, and it got to the point where everyone wanted it to be gone, and to have done. We had said every possible version of goodbye and exchanged every consoling promise, and invested ourselves into too many farewells, so that by the time the whistle went there was a sense of staleness in the air. At that second, a revived, mad Rufus did a lanky somersault on the station platform and delivered himself upright into the doorway of the train. A small group of soldiers and sailors further along the carriage whistled and cheered him, and his smile went crooked and toothy beneath his eye-glass.

Goodbye, goodbye. Dotty and I and other girlfriends and wives ran along the platform as the train gathered speed, until the barrier at the end stopped us.

I know from Mark Lydon's book *The Sea Otters* most of what happened in the training of the group for Memerang on Australia's west coast. Rufus and the Boss instituted a severe regime at the base near Fremantle, on an island connected to the mainland by a spit of sand, Garden Island. The camp was primitive and tented, but the British submarine flotilla was nearby. Here was stationed a mine-laying submarine named *Orca*. It had been assigned the job of taking Doucette's party to a well-wooded island off Singapore where a pick-up base could be established. Then it was meant to convey them further throughout the region till they found a junk that suited them for their attack on the port of Singapore.

The winter nights were severe, and Leo and the others spent many of them in folboats at sea, between Fremantle and Rottnest Island, named by Dutchmen making for Indonesia. Those men who came down with exhaustion were thereby eliminated by Rufus. Dig – Leo – passed every test of course. Jockey similarly. Old hands. The news came that the submersibles, the Silver Bullets, had arrived in Melbourne by ship and were being flown across. For many of the young soldiers and sailors, they would be the ultimate test for membership of the raiding party. They arrived in specially built canisters designed by their inventor, Major Frampton. By this time their English instructor, Lieutenant Lower, had also arrived, with Major Frampton.

After the first Silver Bullet was un-canistered and displayed to the men, there was enthusiasm and some secret anxiety. Lower warned them that the vehicle proceeded well on the surface, travelling on its batteries at more than four knots, but it was harder to handle in the mode in which the operator's head was just above the surface and the Bullet below, and it also took some skill if the operator drove it down below the surface altogether. The mask had to be breathed into in a particular way. Otherwise carbon dioxide would build up and kill the breather. If any of them got disoriented or otherwise panicked and abandoned the Silver Bullets, they would be court-martialled, since the vehicles were too precious to be let sink. Make sure the submersibles come to the surface! said Lower, a calm, devout man as it turned out, an Anglo-Catholic. You are free to remain below and drown, he instructed them.

In that rough proving ground off Western Australia, disoriented men drove the Silver Bullets into the silt and came gasping up through murky water to the surface. How I wish one of them had been Leo! But solidarity with the Boss sustained him – even when he found, as he experimented on survival in opaque, churned water, testing the vessel's every gear, that he could get it to rise only by driving it backwards to the surface.

Doucette decided that Major Eddie Frampton, the engineer creator of the machines, must be their conducting officer, their representative on the submarine, the man who would arrange their delivery and pick-up. Frampton began work with the captain of the submarine *Orca*, a young officer rather strung out by the long war. When he found that Frampton's SB containers were incorrectly dimensioned to easily fit his mine tubes in the aft of *Orca*, and that when they were jettisoned they fouled against the roof of the compartment, he became very petulant and seemed to have decided that this is what happened once you got into the business of transporting raiding parties.

A lost commando from the abandoned Great Natuna plan also turned up at Garden Island. He was an English officer named Filmer, a member of an elite regiment, the Green Howards. Though a professional officer, a type usually suspect to Leo (apart from Doucette, of course), everyone seemed to like Filmer. He had the status of having been an actor in great events – he was one of the commandoes who went ashore by canoe during the night preceding D-Day to make gaps in the wire of the coastal defences. How could you leave a man like that out, especially if you were Doucette? Even though his arrival in Australia was due to absurd accidents and mixed signals between SOE and IRD, he became one of the party.

By the end of August they had boarded the sub, *Orca*, going north and largely living, officers and men, in the torpedo room. How does one exist on a submarine so severely overcrowded? How does a person sleep and keep one's energy in the cramped, hot, dim daytimes of a submarine? Mark Lydon gives a brief and superficial picture of their two-week journey to the island named NE1, Serapem. In the first days, within reach of Australian aircraft, they were permitted on deck at night for a quarter-hour of callisthenics while the bosun and messmen were preparing the evening meal. Apart from that, it was the torpedo compartment, where they hunched, did exercises in batches, slept in batches, and ate communally of the normal submarine diet of tinned herring, canned bacon and tomato, powdered eggs and *haricots musicales*, as the sailors called baked beans. The edgy Commander Moxham, had explained to Doucette that as much as he would have liked to entertain the other officers to his table, he could fit only Doucette himself at the wardroom table. Doucette decided, with appropriate thanks, he would be better to have meals with his own officers and men. That was, he said, the way it would be during the real part of the operation.

Mark Lydon and government documents tell us that the submarine got them to NE1, Serapem, east of Singapore, in a little over two weeks. Rufus and a sailor went ashore at night in a dinghy and stayed there throughout the next day. *Orca* had gone off into deeper water, but now returned in the dark to signal to the shore by lamp and so to pick Rufus and the sailor up. Coming aboard again, Rufus declared NE1 was perfect – a good landing beach to the east, a hill for watching and a swamp for concealment, and deserted except for a few structures on the west side.

During the rest of the night the Memerang group and the sailors of the watch transferred loads of supplies up through the forward hatches to the deck and onto a large inflatable raft which the Memerang men then rowed ashore. Well before dawn, canisters of food and equipment were safely concealed on the flanks of the island's hill and, as he always planned, Doucette left one officer at NE1, Serapem, to dig in the supplies and await the return of the raiding party for Singapore. The officer he had chosen was my cousin Captain Melbourne Duckworth, son of a devout admirer of that southern city.

Everyone else boarded *Orca* again and went hunting for a suitable junk. On the coast of Borneo, Moxham sighted a junk named *Nanjang*, and invited Doucette and Rufus to inspect it through the periscope. They both declared it perfect for their needs. When *Orca* surfaced, the Malay crew of the 40-ton junk thought them a Japanese submarine and so merely prepared for inspection. The junk was boarded and the fairly amiable crew were transferred to the submarine and made secure, taking the place of the Memerang men who were getting ready to board the *Nanjang*, with its rather spectacular feature of a Japanese flag painted across its stern. Over a frantic night, as a nervous Moxham fretted on his conning tower, all that was needed to raid Singapore with Silver Bullets and perform great warrior endeavours was loaded on the junk. The *Nanjang* crew would be delivered back to Western Australia and interned. *Orca* would then return to collect Doucette and his men.

At dawn, the submarine departed and submerged, leaving over twenty men on the junk, whose marine master was lantern-jawed Rufus Mortmain. The junk was turned for Singapore and the trades filled its lateen sails.

Throughout the rest of the winter of 1944, Dotty and I were still working and living in the communal flat. We had the comfort of knowing that Foxhill would tell us what was happening if he learned anything, since he'd done that in the case of Leo's father. I found it hard to discipline myself – not to call him every day, to check, especially since at the end of August Creed had whispered to Dotty in the office, Your husband's on his way.

We both had a date in mind as the longest we'd have to wait. It was December 10. Independently of each other, Rufus and Leo had told Dotty and me that by then at the latest they'd be back.

It was a rainy Melbourne winter and at night Dotty and I soothed ourselves with gin because it was hard to sleep. Dotty was writing a lot but was secretive about it all. I wrote a fair amount myself, but it was sporadic, it took many stages of concentration for me to get started. And often I'd be just started when Dotty would insist, as if our sanity depended on it and in a way it was hard to refuse, that we had to go out to the Albert Palais or one of the canteens to dance with soldiers. I thought she would be very selective about rank, being British, but while I sat on the balcony drinking a shandy, she proved that sergeants and corporals were not unworthy of her company. I could not have a good time on a dance floor, I decided. It was as if all my sensuality was bundled up with Leo, and was suspended pending his return. (Sometimes these days I fear it's been bundled up all my life. I hope my second husband got a return on his desire and devotion.)

Anyhow, we didn't analyse those things then – we acted them out, and as it was obvious that I was a sort of icy widow-for-the-duration on the balcony, it was obvious too that Dotty was available for comforting. Again, I didn't blame her. I envied her the distraction.

Every day I went off to the military transport office job I had, and deadened myself with routine work and small office filing confusions. The Melbourne football Grand Final came and went as a marker between seasons, and Foxhill could tell us nothing. We found this a bad sign because we believed that however confident he insisted on sounding, there was an edge of bemusement to him too. The weather turned warm, but it was an empty, anxious warmth to Dotty and me. Captain Foxhill organised for us to attend the Members Enclosure for that year's Melbourne Cup, and gin and expectation gave us a few hours' respite until a horse named Sirius galloped over the line and we tore our betting tickets up and the vacuum returned.

I remembered that Jesse Creed, the American, had been involved in some way too. But Dotty assured me she had heard nothing from him. Sometimes, she said, I get the impression they're all keeping some big secret. And I suppose the bastards are. But I think Jesse would tell me if he knew anything.

December arrived. When I felt hope it was feverish. Plain, flat, humid days set in, carrying no omens and dry of promise. Thunderstorms and dust swept down from the north onto the city. Foxhill and his wife visited us for a drink on December 2. I tried to gauge whether he knew anything he wasn't telling us, but he seemed just as uncertain as we were. He did not promise us quick news or mention dates. But he did say, When we hear, it will be sudden. Like a thunderclap.

Four days later, on the proposed date of their return, he was back with the news that they were missing. He stood bald-headed and genuinely saddened under the tatty, crepe Christmas streamers and Christmas bells we had hung in the flat. They're all military personnel, he assured us, so if captured they'd be POWs, every chance of survival.

At what point of things did they go missing? I asked.

I can't say, Foxhill claimed. I don't know myself.

But radio messages? asked Dotty. They would have sent a radio message if they were in trouble.

No, Foxhill insisted. They haven't. Look, for all we know they might have taken some native vessel and be on the way home as we speak.

Don't play us for fools, Dotty warned him, her eyes blazing.

But I was rather taken with Foxhill's scenario.

Of course, he said, he would tell us as soon as he got any more definite news. He invited us both to his place for a lunch, and I said how kind that was and that we would see if we were free, but when he left Dotty told me, with tears in her eyes, Bugger playing happy families! Did you sense this would happen? I could sense it. Bloody Rufus! I knew it!

We stayed in that night talking and comforting and sobbing and all the hopeless rest. I felt a mad urge to go out looking, as if he could be found in quiet streets running back from the Yarra. Next day we went to work, and kept our news secret. Dotty arrived home after me and cried out, To hell with staying in and moping. Let's just go out to the Windsor for dinner.

For some reason it seemed exactly the right thing. We dressed, and made ourselves up and called a taxi.

As we walked up the stairs of the hotel we could hear the festive buzz from within the dining room. The Windsor had that pleasant young woman in black who met us at the doorway of the restaurant and told us there that sadly there was no table available until a quarter to nine. Indeed the tables seemed all taken, by military men and well-dressed women. Dotty obviously felt a primal rage at this unknowing girl, because I felt the same. Dotty told her in a voice thin as a skewer to fetch the head waiter. She fled and got him. He sailed up, a tall man, with his forced smile on his lips, and asked dubiously whether he could help us.

Dotty said in the same thinned-out, furious voice which had compelled the young woman, Our husbands have just been reported missing in action. All we want is a meal. Just get us a table. And not one in a broom cupboard somewhere. A decent table. Otherwise we'll yell the roof in.

He looked at me for help, as the one with the less turbulent features.

We're fed up, I confirmed. Why aren't half these home front warriors missing in action, and not our husbands?

As I spoke I saw a change come over his face. No longer the bland bestower of tables, he nodded at me and a weariness of grief entered his own features. He too had been the receiver of frightful news. He had dead or lost children. He said he sympathised with us, and of course he would try to find us a table. Just give him a minute.

I thanked him. But I was not the same woman as before. I was unabashed by Dotty's act, and by my own. But it had taken a lot out of us. Dotty dealt with every suggestion of the elderly waiters with a high, clipped voice, whereas I wasn't sure what anyone was saying to me. Two British naval officers seated nearby were quick to move in and ask if they could join us. The wifely primness, if that was what it was, that had sustained me up to the point of knowing Leo was actually officially missing, not merely hiding somewhere in some archipelago, seemed to have simply run out. I could not be bothered telling them to go away, not in the face of Dotty's manic, serial-smoking, serial-drinking eagerness for the diversion they offered.

They were from a British cruiser presently in Melbourne, and the elder of the two did not seem to be able to believe his luck in finding a sparkling-eyed Dotty, full of a stored energy he hoped was sexual. He wasn't as good as the younger officer in sensing that there was really something demented about us. This time, I could tell, Dotty would find comfort in repelling and punishing him in the end. The younger one held junior rank to the other but possessed immensely more sensibility. It would count against his ever becoming an admiral, I suppose, though I doubt he ultimately wanted that anyhow. My young officer was so lacking in expectation that I was able to talk to him about real things, and it was pleasant.

And then we saw the Enrights. They came from a table at the back of the dining room to the dance floor. They began dancing with an easy, casual grace, Major Enright light on his feet. Mrs Enright had stayed in Melbourne with him and had won her battle and was in clear, quietly triumphal possession.

Excuse me, gentlemen, Dotty told our two officers. I've just seen the man who might have killed my husband.

This had the mouth-gaping effect on them that she wanted. She stood and advanced onto the dance floor. She could handle her drink well, Dotty, in fact she would later write a poem to gin. 'My constant lover and traducer,/ noble in promise, squalid in effect,/companion of verse and bedrooms . . .'

The Enrights' dance-floor connubiality was about to be dive-bombed, and I'm ashamed to say it was fascinating to watch. Dotty reached out and tapped Major Enright's shoulder playfully. He responded just as she wanted. He backed away from his wife, who still nonetheless carried a lacquered smile.

I could see Dotty ask him for a dance. How could a desk-born warrior respond when he had made the plans, as willingly as Rufus and Leo had gone along with them? He obviously wished this was not happening, but he turned to his wife and asked her to wait for him at their table.

In Enright's suddenly stiff hands, Dotty grew loose-haired and sinuous and eager. With the threat she might become shameless, she swung herself with a lover's confidence in his arms, fell back on his breast, twirled back to face him. She nibbled his ear, pulling languorously on the lobe. She cut off any impulse on his part to turn and explain to his wife that he was dealing with a mad woman; she whispered in his ear, hung her head back and laughed at the dance-floor lights, lowered her head onto his campaign ribbons, the strands of her hair becoming mixed in with the vivid flashes of his merit and service awards.

When the music stopped, Dotty kissed him fulsomely, and I looked to Mrs Enright's table, but she was gone. Our officers had sat through this display, but it convinced them that we were unreliable goods, and they were pleased to find a taxi for us soon after and send us home.

I didn't try to chastise Dotty. I'd lost the confidence for that. And I was too much in awe of her work. It had been a calamitous night, yet I delighted in her irrational vengeance on the safely wed, clad and housed Enrights. When we got out of the taxi at our block of flats, she sat on the brick wall in front of the building and looked up and down the empty street, as if at any moment Rufus and Leo and Doucette might roll by, yelling greetings to us.

I'm a bitch, she admitted. But I can't take this. I'm not as game as you. I'm going back to England. And then we'll see. Won't we, Gracie? We'll see.

# Eleven

It would turn out that Foxhill had been planning a rescue operation, Memexit. But it had not got support from others in IRD, who secretly believed the entire party were dead or captured by Christmas.

It was all distressingly vague, and the bereaved hate vagueness, especially if they don't know whether they're really the bereaved or not. Dotty and I spent a miserable Christmas together in the flat. My parents had invited me home, the Foxhills had invited us to their table. But we wanted to get it done with in our own company. I relieved my depression by writing the poem *To the Beloved Missing in Action*, but I didn't show it to Dotty, not then.

The New Year was a relief. Whether the war ended or not, it would be the year in which something more definite would emerge. The Germans surrendered as expected, but no surrender was predicted for the

Japanese. Dotty went out with Colonel Creed now and then, and I'd learn there was an affair. In a way, I envied her the option.

Dotty and I were both working the morning the fiery end to Japan's war came. Dotty called me and asked me to a party at Colonel Creed's office, where – I discovered when I arrived – the gin and Scotch flowed copiously, and everyone kissed and did the hokey-pokey, the latest brainless dance craze. Dotty and I were both edgy with hope and dread. We would soon hear of our loves missing in action, but we said nothing about it. That would have been to provoke the savage gods who, for some, hung over the coming of peace.

News did not come quickly. It was the Chinese driver of one of the Japanese judicial officers who told an investigating Australian that he had driven his master to the place where the executions took place, a nondescript field of weeds along Reformatory Road. He also said he had exchanged a brief conversation in Mandarin with one of the condemned men while they were still sitting and standing near the bus which had brought them, and told him to prepare himself for death, and that he should consider telling the others the same. No, said the condemned man – certainly Jockey Rubinsky – I know already and they more or less know. The condemned man was very brave, said the Chinese driver. They all were. When the truth became apparent there was no pleading, though a few of them retched from the smell of blood as they were led blindfolded to the edge of one of the three pits in which the earlier slaughtered lay. A month after the end of the war, the Australians found the rough graves. Six crosses had been put there – it seemed more as stage-dressing and for appeasing effect rather than from true respect.

The bodies were exhumed the next day. Two days later and I knew. Rufus was not among the dead there. Leo and my cousin Mel were. But another three days passed before a Malay led the British to where Rufus had perished, it seemed at first of wounds. I, half a week widowed myself, became the consoler then.

We could have kept the flat in Melbourne indefinitely, and we did stick on in that place booby-trapped by memory until October, when Dotty used her influence to get on one of the troopships returning to Britain after delivering Australian soldiers home. There was a not quite rational sense in which she was abandoning me, and although neither of us raised the idea, it would sometimes enter between us and make us awkward. I saw her off on her troopship from Port Melbourne, and then packed up quickly and went to Sydney, since it was to me a city unsullied by events.

I was lucky to find a small flat and there, before Christmas, I received a visit from a thin young officer named Captain Gabriel, a survivor of Japanese imprisonment who had now been given the duty of investigating the enemy's crimes against Leo's party.

At the time I was trying to be brave for Leo's sake – Leo's presence still so strongly abided that I would sometimes forget that I had joined that venerable category known as War Widow.

The first visit Captain Gabriel made was to tell me the Japanese court martial that condemned Leo and the others was specious, and investigations were afoot into its legality. The general responsible, Okimasa, had suicided, and others involved were under investigation for a number of crimes as well as the killing of Leo and the rest of his party. And I was nervous of Captain Gabriel, of how news he gave me, and questions he asked, would impose on me revised duties of grief and vengeance when I found it hard enough still to bear the initial grief and anger of discovering Leo had been executed. Gabriel himself remained earnest, dedicated and analytical, seeming more haunted than angry. I was outraged and consoled by one detail in particular. He told me that he had interviewed a man named Hidaka, an interpreter who seemed to have made friends with Leo and the others, and had brought them sweets and tobacco right up to the end. I could see them all sitting around, their jaws swollen with Chinese lollies Hidaka gave them, Amanetto, Yokan, Daifuku. This stood as a substantial item of mercy in opposition to the blades of the Japanese NCOs' swords.

As for the rest I had been stopped in place by the news of Leo's execution. The truth I was ashamed of was this: I did not want any minor and peripheral information about it all. What could adjust the fact? When I dared look at the idea of execution, I was dazzled and disabled by its vibrant blackness. Leo's body was irreparably violated. That reality lay in the supposed paths of healing like an unnegotiable boulder. My curiosity was paralysed, and there was something in me that feared new knowledge, even if this state of mind was a disgraceful thing in a widow.

Captain Gabriel visited me twice. The second time, in 1947, was to tell me the execution of Leo and other Memerang men would not be the subject of a war trial, but that various judicial officers, including the president of the court, Sakamone, had killed themselves, and the NCOs who did the work of execution, including the one who made a botch of Leo, Judicial Sergeant Shiro Abukara, were all in prison, Abukara for life, for other acts of cruelty in Outram Road prison in Singapore. What could a war crimes prosecution do about the mess the war had put us in? All this war crimes work, which Gabriel would end up spending three years on, and his superiors a half-dozen years or more, was to me nothing but the sort of pottering around the edge of a cauldron. Even two years after the war, the shameful truth was that I was happy to let it, *them*, all go. Since I was terrified that the more I heard, the more likely I was to find out some terrible, indigestible reality, I felt a bad wife.

I had been working as a secretary in the office of a hotel broker named Laurie Burden. The business was one his father had founded, and Laurie Burden had taken it over in early 1946, after he returned from England, where he had flown transport planes. He was a pensive young man, and rarely took a drink. I liked working for him. But I was aware of the entitlements of my widowhood, including the chance of a university education. I wanted to teach – it seemed that children, of whatever age, would totally absorb my time. Without Leo, I wanted a new self-definition. I felt that if I were stupefied and hypnotised in place by events, as had happened for the past two years, he would be posthumously displeased. Besides, I had a horror of being stuck without company on that island of widowhood – that description, War Widow, was so inadequate an explanation for the woman Leo had let me become.

Yet in another sense I suppose I unconsciously cultivated widowhood, writing verse about it, some of which Dotty got published in English literary mags. That poem of mine, *To the Beloved Missing in Action*, became a minor classic, much anthologised.

I did my degree and teacher training. Laurie Burden had remained my friend and attended the graduation. It was not until 1952 when I was teaching English to high school girls at North Sydney that we became lovers, not moving to each other with the certainty which had been the mark of my life with Leo, but more like two wounded creatures trying not to hurt each other. For Laurie, as he ultimately told me, had certain bewilderments too. He had toured Germany with his father in 1935, a busman's holiday during which they had visited all the leading hotels of Cologne, Munich and Frankfurt. Flying into those cities on transport missions, he had been appalled to find all the splendour reduced to such absolute rubble. Earlier in the war, he had had his own brush with heroes when he delivered members of the specially trained leadership groups whose job was to gather Maquis units into powerful garrisons in the countryside. The fortified positions were prematurely taken up and were reduced by the enemy with great slaughter, from which few survivors emerged. Laurie lacked the urge to march through Sydney with his former comrades on Anzac Day because he did not see how it would help or even enlarge the spirits of the doomed fellows he had delivered to France.

I had been at work as a teacher for a few months when a woman named Rhonda Garnish, an angel of great inconvenience, visited me. The dreary and deadly Korean War was still going, nuclear threat pressed down from the sky and challenged our innocence, and the past war, vividly recalled by millions of its victims, was nonetheless on its way to becoming historical, an item of study.

Mrs Rhonda Garnish descended on me from the Northern Rivers mail train. She had called me from the north coast, near Grafton, and said she needed to see me, and we made arrangements. I met her in Spit Road, Mosman, as she got down from the bus from town. She was a small woman, very pretty, with a plumpness which might take over in later years but which had a long way to go before it smudged her good looks. She managed her port tied up by two leather straps with a wiry strength, and when I shook hands with her, I could tell by the raspiness of her palm that she was a dairy farmer's daughter.

But she was smart.

Listen, Grace, she told me on the street, holding me by both wrists, don't let me talk you around. Just because I'm going to Canberra it doesn't mean you have to. This is the right time for me to go, that's all.

All right, I told her. We'll talk about it at home.

Hey, I saw that write-up of your book of poetry in the *Herald*. Crikey. They thought the world of you. It made me think twice before I wrote you a letter. There's another woman too, Mrs Danway.

I don't know her, I protested.

Rhonda said, Her husband was Hugo Danway. He wasn't on the first one, Cornflakes. He arrived over in Western Australia just in time to join them on the second trip.

Danway. Yes, I recognised the name.

He was one of the group, I said.

Yes, the Japanese beheaded him too. I'm going to visit her, but don't let me drag you along. As my husband says, I'm a bossy cow.

I took her home to my little flat – I had not yet married Laurie and the proprieties were observed. I'd made a cake for her, and she ate heartily, and drank her tea strong and black and with three sugars.

You see, what happened, she told me, was I was engaged to Pat Bantry. Did your husband ever mention him?

Yes, I lied.

I had a crush on him since I was thirteen. I'd be getting ready for school and I'd see Pat drive the old Bantry Hupmobile full-pelt down our hill and over the wooden bridge, and all the timbers of the bridge would slam together in protest. I can't hear that sound to this day without my heart missing a go.

My hands were sweating. What did she want, this young wife from the Northern Rivers, who had a perfectly good husband at home in Aldavilla, and had left him to cook his own meals and patiently keep her bed warm, and all to chase ghosts? I had let her into my house for Leo's sake, for the sake of his honour, for which as a good widow I was supposed to be hungry. Rhonda Garnish went on extolling Pat Bantry as the ultimate cow-cocky and bushman. The corn up on the Clarence River grew eighteen feet tall, she said, but Pat harvested the Bantry crop as well as Rhonda's father's. She and her brother had helped him when he offered to rebuild the floodgate on Sawpit Creek, and he brought along a picnic in a sugar bag – he must have looted the Bantrys' kitchen pantry.

Pat would often go bush, cutting tea-tree, and he'd cart it in for Mr Bantry's distilling plant. Mr Bantry was from Ireland, she told me, and knew all about distilling, but he was a great admirer of tea-tree oil, which he called 'The Australian Panacea', and sold at agricultural fairs up and down the Northern Rivers.

Bantry seemed the ultimate Australian, even though he'd been born in Ireland and come here as a child. On top of all else, he'd gone cutting sleepers and bridge-bearing timbers with Rhonda's uncle, who said he was the most cheerful of company in the bush camp, and never swore but had as much wit as most swearers. Furthermore, this bush paragon had broken in a small team of steers and used them to snig a fence strainer, thus becoming an invaluable friend to every farmer on Sawpit Creek. And when the war brought petrol rationing, Pat had easily converted the Hupmobile into a kerosene burner.

These were the polished feats which had enchanted the young Rhonda. Everyone, Rhonda included, had been astonished when Pat volunteered early in the war. There was a story that a recruiting sergeant managed to get abstemious Pat full of bombo in Grafton (Leo's home town, by the way). It might have been a version Pat wanted spread, since old Mr Bantry was not a lover of the British Empire in itself. When Pat vanished to North Africa, Rhonda hung on news of him. He was a member of the Sixth Divvy, that fabled division. After defeating the Italians, they moved up to Syria and beat the Vichy French, before returning to Libya to face Rommel.

Home on leave in early 1943, like a god descending, he proposed to Rhonda. Her parents didn't like Catholics but they liked Pat, who was still robustly teetotal and non-swearing. She began taking instruction in the Catholic religion from the local parish priest. She was willing to cross any barrier and bridge any gap to be his mate. He became a weapons instructor at the Canungra jungle training school, and so was safe from battle, and Rhonda could not overcome her astonishment that, all that time, he had watched and admired her. She was disappointed when he did not want to settle in the instructor's job. She was aware of and a bit frightened by a restlessness in him. Like the blokes who came back from World War I, her father said. They were the only blokes who could understand themselves.

They intended to get married in January 1945. But of course . . . her trousseau waited until 1949, when a man named Ron Garnish came back from serving in the army occupying Japan, started a tyre business in town, began by taking her out and then asked for her hand.

She had been married a year or so, and had a miscarriage, very sad, but the doctor up in Grafton reckoned there was no reason she wouldn't bear healthy children. And then she had opened the door of her little house one morning and Pat Bantry was standing there, looking just a bit dazed. Where's the reward, Rhonda? he asked her, and then he was gone. She knew he was dead, of course, but she would have known anyhow, because he was talking with great effort over a great distance. She said she knew she should have been embarrassed to say she had seen and heard from the deceased, except that would be to deny the effort she believed Pat had made to speak to her. She told her husband as early as lunchtime that day. We don't hide things from each other, she said. In any case there were still mothers and wives all over the Clarence River who had confusing visits from the war's dead sons and husbands. Mrs Bantry was rumoured to have had a visitation from Sergeant Bantry too.

Ron Garnish proved such a tolerant and understanding fellow that he took her seriously. Many husbands wouldn't have, would have talked about old flames and so on. She assured her husband of her full loyalty to him, but she hoped he would not stop her from seeing the Minister of Defence about a reward for Pat Bantry, who could have been safe in Queensland for the duration if he hadn't been such a convinced man of action. She didn't speak to the aging Bantrys, who were still inconsolable about their son. (Indeed, they sounded more or less like me, in terror of more information than could be accommodated.) It was up to her, as Pat's former fiancée, to put the matter to rest. What if we went as a delegation? she suggested. You and me and Mrs Danway, if she'd be in it? The Minister couldn't refuse to receive the spokeswomen for three heroes. Especially since one of them had written a famous poem about a lost husband.

I knew, of course, I had to go. I had had so many dreams myself that I was in no position to laugh at the idea of Pat Bantry's spirit turning up thirsty for merit at Rhonda's door. She told me one of the support troops, the Beta men who worked on getting the expedition away from Western Australia, had told her after the war that Pat always kept her picture upright on his boot box, and when some of the other men began talking about their adventures with women, he would say, This isn't for your ears, dear, and turn her picture face down. The more she talked about it, the more I thought it was this tale, as much as the appearance of Bantry's ghost, which had her by the throat.

She'd gone to the trouble of looking up the train timetable for us, Sydney to Canberra, and the names of Canberra boarding houses. I told her about the Kurrajong, where I used to stay. They knew me there.

How could I refuse to get on a train to Canberra when Leo had walked under his own power onto that murderous weed-bed at Reformatory Road?

We weren't able to see Mrs Danway until the following Saturday afternoon. Laurie had a vehicle and would have happily taken Rhonda and me across the city to Kogarah, where Mrs Danway lived in a flat. But I did not want that. My affection for him was still not of the kind that looked to acquire debts of kindness, not yet, and as he would say later, even after five years I hadn't cleared my slate of the war. Indeed, there were a lot of people like me, a whole sub-class of women in the world, invisible except to each other, who were making their dazed way amongst a society obsessed with housing shortages and electricity strikes, with horse-racing and football, and who were being told against their own instincts that the war was over and suddenly remote, and the dead to be referred to only at ceremonial moments.

When these women visited each other, they usually travelled by ferry, bus and train, as did Rhonda and I. They had generally been left short of the means to hire taxis, or buy a car. Mrs Danway met us at Kogarah station and walked with us back to her little flat. She was a thin woman, older than Rhonda and me by as much as five years. I was a little ashamed I had not sought her out earlier. It seemed now the most obvious thing I should have done. I should have contacted all of them. I told her I was sorry we hadn't met previously.

Oh, she said, as if it forgave me, Hugo was a late inclusion.

She told us at some stage that afternoon that she had lost Lieutenant Danway's child after the men disappeared to

Western Australia, so that between her and Rhonda there were two lost children. She told us Danway loved the training camp over in the west. Doucette had taken him on rather late in the process, so that he had to endure long training sessions to catch up with the others. She showed us a letter he had written. Rufus had him climbing hills and canoeing by the mile from eight thirty in the morning till two the next afternoon. On that coastline, the tent accommodation was very cold at night, said Lieutenant Danway. But it was the same for everyone, he said, and Doucette had infused everyone with a wonderful sense of unity. Everyone pitched in, officers and men, all equals in Doucette's eyes, and so all very energetic and in an inventive frame of mind. She raised her eyes as she read that, as if it showed some kind of innocence, which it did. Doucette is a particular kind of Englishman, Danway said. The other Poms aren't like him at all.

Hugo Danway had been a great canoeist, Mrs Danway said, attributing it to his Islander blood – his mother had been a woman from the Marianas Islands, and his father an Australian missionary. And yet his whole leave time he would spend with her, with Sherry Danway, on the block of land he'd bought by the harbour. He had made drawings of the house he intended to raise there after the war.

We didn't have to ask. Rhonda and I knew that she had had to sell the land. With it and what he had put in his building account she had bought this little flat, she said. I keep busy, she claimed, and then she raised her stricken eyes. Isn't it heartbreaking, she asked, when a fellow is so young and full of life and hope and skill, and then the axe? An obscene death for very little purpose.

Those words, *very little purpose*, hung nakedly in the air. I did not like their presence. Dotty Mortmain had been very angry with Rufus for not reappearing by the New Year of 1945, but she said it was due to his desire to keep Doucette out of trouble by following him into it. That axiom or mantra – or whatever you'd call it – took up a solid residence in my mind too, but applied to Leo instead of Rufus. But the words *very little purpose* threatened to reopen the issue and to revisit the flimsy story I consoled myself with.

They were brave men, Rhonda insisted.

But what for? asked Sherry Danway. After all? What for?

Rhonda said, Men believe they're born to be brave, and you see hollow men walking round who've never had a chance to try it. Or else they failed. But your husband . . . braver than MacArthur for a start. Braver than any politician. Braver than that old soak Blamey.

And I thought there was something to that, too. To men of a certain kind, not to all men, but to some men in certain circumstances and under the force of certain ideas, bravery was its own end. That comforted me a little when put up against *very little purpose*. The purpose was to be brave, the purpose was even to be doomed.

Mrs Danway said, I don't think I want to go to Canberra. I'm sorry. The truth is, I couldn't care two bob whether they give my husband a medal or not. It has no effect on me or my memory of my husband. It's certainly not worth risking going to Canberra to hear his name rolled round the mouth of some shitty old official.

She was very firm about that, and I felt embarrassed that I didn't know my own mind, that I had been shamed into going with Rhonda. Rhonda gave up and said to me, The train into Central's due in twenty minutes, Grace. We ought to start out.

In fact, the station was in sight when Sherry Danway came running after us. I'll go, she called to Rhonda. What time should I meet you at Central?

Rhonda yelled the details as we sprinted for the train. I'll see you there, she cried, and I asked myself, Who elected you leader? Sherry Danway and I had lost husbands. Rhonda was a wilful, married woman dragging two reluctant widows into a confrontation they didn't want to have.

The following Tuesday we all met precisely where Rhonda had decided, the country-train indicator board at Central. Rhonda and I had got quite friendly by now. On Sunday, we'd shared a picnic at Bradleys Head. On Monday, Laurie Burden took us to a five o'clock session of *The Third Man* at the Regent Cinema. It was a wonderful tale of complexity arising from the war, and was strangely comforting, since it implied we were still stuck in that same territory too, in a land of shadows. I was convinced by then that Rhonda was indeed a splendid woman. I reassured myself she would not let her grief for Pat Bantry trample on my own decisions about grief, or complicate it all for me.

I remember my view of myself in those days with some amusement and with a sense of loss as well. I was at thirty-one considered almost too old to bear a first child. I saw Sherry Danway and myself as already middle-aged, already bowed by history, and as unentitled to girlishness. It was as a coven of senior women that we met by the huge indicator board at Central, and took our reserved seats in a carriage with pictures of the Blue Mountains above the upholstery, and a cut-glass water bottle above our heads, clinking in its brass retainer. We were all nervous and had brought plenty of reading matter of one kind and another. I was reading Evelyn Waugh, his world remote from my experience, and thus a good one to lose myself in.

When we arrived in Canberra, there was no snow on the Brindabellas out to the west, and the town seemed ominously vacant, still mainly populated by eucalyptus foliage, as if everyone who had an answer for us had fled. We caught a taxi to our boarding house, and despite inquiries about buses, were forced to take another cab to the Department of Defence in its bark-strewn parkland. Though Parliament was not in session, the minister had agreed to see us here. Mr Philip McBride had been a regular member of the cabinet of Prime Minister Menzies. I had seen his face in the press and on newsreels. His office at the department was a plain big room with a massive desk, for which one or two native cedar trees must have been plundered. The office was heartened with pictures of fighter planes and bombers, an aircraft carrier and a cruiser. The planes in the pictures were at ease with the sky. The ships had the sea where they wanted it.

We three were already seated in there when Mr McBride entered with a young man who carried a number of files. Don't get up, ladies, said the minister, as he made his way around the desk. We did half stand in honour of his political gravity, but we were not as innocent as we had once been, so did not overdo it.

The minister settled in his chair and the young man sat on a harder one by the corner of the business end of the desk. Mr McBride began briefing himself on who we were from the notes on his desk.

Rhonda said, Perhaps you remember? We're the women calling on you about the Memerang men.

Ah yes, ah yes, said Mr McBride. Brave men.

He looked up at us, and caught our eyes. Every one of them, he assured us.

Rhonda explained, I was merely the fiancée of Sergeant Bantry. Mrs Waterhouse and Mrs Danway were married to the officers of those names.

Mr McBride asked, The men were . . .?

His secretary muttered something. Oh yes, said Mr McBride, dolorously. Terrible, terrible. Members of the enemy were never charged over it, I've been told, but I believe that most of the people involved were caught for war crimes of another stripe.

Rhonda sat back to allow Mrs Danway and myself to take up the running. We were both guiltily reluctant, but at last I said, We are all concerned that none of the men have been honoured for that last operation.

Mrs Danway stepped in, anxious to emphasise she knew it was no substitute for a husbandly presence. Not that it will bring them home, sir. But they did something very adventurous, and it seemed that no one gave them a lot of credit for it.

Mr McBride turned to his secretary. Was it normal for men to be honoured for secret operations? he asked. Were other IRD men honoured?

The young man looked up from his files. Not normally, sir, he told his master. Only in special circumstances.

I said, My husband, Captain Waterhouse, was awarded the DSO for an earlier mission.

The young man rose and whispered further to Mr McBride. The cabinet minister knotted his broad brow as the whispers entered his ear. At last he said, Ah yes, Mrs Waterhouse, that was for Cornflakes.

He shook his head. These names, he said, chuckling a little. But that was exceptional.

Pat Bantry got the Military Medal, Rhonda said. In North Africa. But Singapore was where he gave everything. And yet there is nothing at all for that.

Mr McBride said, I'm sure it was given every consideration at the time. His secretary was passing another file to him which he quickly read. Oh yes, the policy was reinforced in 1943 after the Cornflakes expedition.

But he read further into the file, squinting his eyes up into a frown now and then. You see, he explained, on

Cornflakes they all came back. So they were all witnesses to each other's valour. Sadly, there were no witnesses left after Memerang, and hence no military awards.

He looked up. I know it's harsh, but it is apparently the rule.

I believe we all became simultaneously annoyed at this pettifogging. Mrs Danway said, But there are enough witnesses now. *We* know what happened, don't we? From witnesses. From the records.

I said, Captain Gabriel told me even the enemy thought they were brave.

And they gave more than most people ever did, said Sherry Danway with an edge. More than any general ever gave.

The minister let a painful smile cross over his face, left to right. Well, you're probably right about that, he admitted. Of course they had cyanide pills . . . Did you know that? All such operatives were issued with them.

I hadn't known. Though I'd heard rumours about it, mainly from Dotty, no one had told us that officially. We took a while to absorb it.

I can't imagine Leo taking a suicide pill, I told McBride. And I don't think he should have been expected to.

Hugo would never have taken his, said Sherry. It was against his religion.

Would you give them a medal if they all took their suicide pills? asked Rhonda.

No . . . The minister knew he had made a tasteless mistake and was back-pedalling. No, suicide is contrary to my principles too.

Though I had sustained myself to this point as well as I could, I wanted the meeting to be over. I wanted it to end in Mr McBride's reasonable surrender. Now that we'd done our duty, I wanted him to say, Of course! What an oversight! I'll take it up immediately and achieve justice for these men.

Then I wanted to gallop down the stairs without the burden of any further knowledge. If you had asked me what I was scared of I wouldn't have been able to tell you. Poor Leo deserved a more valiant wife. But then I thought, What are Dotty or Minette doing? They were fussy women. Though Dotty wrote to me and kept me informed of Minette, she had never mentioned their trying to make a fuss about the men in Whitehall.

So I summed up the feelings of my sisters in grievance. It seems strange to me, I said, that they were decorated for Cornflakes, which didn't kill them, and not for Memerang, which did.

Well, said McBride, it was considered at that time by a thoroughgoing military commission, young lady, and there are no grounds on which I could reverse their decision. Anyhow, look how often the story of Doucette's raiding parties are told in the press. The Memerang people will always be honoured and known to future generations. I really think you'll have to be content with that.

I doubt very much that Sergeant Bantry is happy to let it go at that, Rhonda told the minister.

McBride smiled at her with a sort of heavily tested tolerance.

We're sadly in no position to know that, young lady.

I prayed she would not admit to having seen the ghost, which of course would enable him to end the meeting very promptly. He took this moment of confusion to break away from the mid-desk seat and go to lean over his male secretary for yet another muttered conference. The secretary pointed out paragraphs in files he handed to his superior. McBride scanned them before putting them down again on the desk with a Yes, yes.

Through this, Sherry Danway's eyes remained fixed on his vacated chair. She was pale but – like me – was sticking it out. As the minister returned to his seat, she said suddenly and in a near shout, I think if we tell the newspapers . . . I think they'll find it all pretty strange like we do.

This did upset the minister a little. Look, they can't make any judgement on this matter. At least I am operating on full information. Besides, why now? There is another war raging. Perhaps you should have come forward earlier.

That idea struck us hard – that we'd delayed. In fact, all Sherry Danway and I could do was look at each other, surrendering the advantage to the minister. But Rhonda went on fighting for us. Come on, you have to be fair, Mr McBride, she protested. In those days it was hard for these women to say anything. Memerang were missing. Then every month they learned something new, and it was never good news. They were as scared as billy-o of what they'd hear next. And in any case, they're here now.

The minister nodded, conceding all this. Look, he said, I sincerely urge you all to leave this issue where it stands. I could tell you some committee or other would return to it. But that would be a lie. The matter is finally settled. I wish you'd take my word on that. So, for your own sakes . . .

Our only power, I could sense, was that he was worried we might weep, scream or do some of the other things that made men his age lose their natural colour and close one eye and wince at the messiness of the world. And we could not leave. We didn't know whether his advice was kindness or a lie. He turned to his secretary.

Would you like to talk about this, Mr Henley?

A man unleashed, Mr Henley was happy to. But McBride had a sudden doubt. He held his hand up. Ladies, why not just accept my word on this and go away from here certain of the bravery of your husbands, your . . . men.

Rhonda leaned forward to check our faces. She said, We can't all go away now, Mr McBride. You've raised a mystery.

All right, then, he said, and nodded to Henley. Henley told us that the Memerang men had been considered for awards and decorations. But, he said, there was a further problem than lack of witnesses. As part of the operation, the group had been trained to use a new and very valuable submersible craft. This craft was of such revolutionary design that it allowed operatives to approach enemy ships without being seen. During their training the men learned to handle these craft, and it was impressed on them that if intercepted they were to destroy these vessels and say nothing to the enemy about them. When things did go wrong, they destroyed the vessels. But fragments were retrieved by the Japanese from a shallow sea floor, and presented with these fragments, a number of the Memerang personnel were betrayed into giving information . . . I stress they were probably tricked. Your husband was one, Mrs Waterhouse, and yours another, Mrs Danway. I'm afraid SOE in London, who had ownership of the craft, were very angry about it. And it certainly vitiated any chance of awards and honours.

At this news I felt my consciousness departing and leaned forward in my chair, letting out a great Oh!

McBride said, It doesn't matter at all. They were still heroes, and no one's going to bring out the matter of the submersibles publicly. It would need to come out, of course, only if you made public accusations that we were niggardly towards those men. Are you all right, Mrs Waterhouse?

He was rising in his seat. I felt heeled-over, hanging at a disastrous angle, and when I tried to correct that I stumbled off my chair. I certainly could not speak. There was a flurry of people entering the office and bringing water, but that made me angry for some reason, and with normal irritation, I returned to myself.

Does it mean they were tortured? I asked. I meant, tortured about the submersibles.

For the first time the minister showed some unease. He mumbled, I think it was more a matter of deception and feint –

I stood up. I said, I can't bear it if they were tortured!

My ears were ringing. I knew I was failing Leo, not up

to his strength. I have no clear memory from that point until Rhonda and Sherry were taking me down the stairs and assuring various women staff that I was fine now and that we didn't need tea. It would have been impossible for us to drink in McBride's shadow. I couldn't have borne it.

We were fortunate that in the vacant parkland beyond the front door, a cab was discharging a passenger. Rhonda ran and captured it, and we all got in without a word. The only things said during the journey were by Rhonda. I probably shouldn't have pushed this trip on you, she told us wanly. Neither Sherry Danway nor myself was speaking.

We arrived at the boarding house, and Mrs Danway got out immediately and hurried inside, still without saying anything. Since Rhonda insisted on paying the first fare, I applied my confused mind to paying this one. Then we caught up with Sherry – she was in the lobby asking the girl for her key. Rhonda took her by the arm and said something about hoping she was not too upset. She did not get an answer. Well meaningly, she followed Sherry to the stairs. Don't go up to your room, Sherry. Let's have a cup of tea and all cheer up. Why should we give a damn about these submersible boats? If it saved any of them from getting beaten up, all the better!

Sherry Danway said, I wish I'd never seen you. You'll go home to your husband. Nothing's lost to you. Grace and I go home knowing our husbands are blamed, and the blame will always be there, in some file. I thought I was as lonely as a person could be. But you've managed to make it worse. I have a different picture of Hugo I have to live with now.

She covered her eyes with a web of fingers. Poor bloody Danway, she said. Wanting to build his house. Poor helpless big bugger!

I went up to her and held her, and began to feel her inner collapse and the release of tears. It was as if the impact of the original news of execution had occurred all over again. It was exactly as Sherry had said. The minister had given us a new dimension to the version of their deaths we had become accustomed to and managed to live on with. We both doubted we had the strength to absorb new versions.

Rhonda moved to join us in our mourning, but I dissuaded her with a severe look. I felt Sherry Danway's crazy, unstoppable anger too.

Rhonda's face filled with colour. You blame me for this? she asked. Do you?

Yes, I admitted. Don't worry. We can't help it. But it was never your business!

On the way back to Sydney on the train, we all read and moped. Rhonda knew that whatever she said it could call up a fury in us. I went especially to get a cup of tea with her in the buffet car, and I was able to summon the grace to say to her again, Don't worry. It's not your fault.

If I were married to Bantry, she said, I wouldn't blame him for anything he gave away.

Do you really think we blame our husbands? Of course we bloody well don't.

I felt a desire to hurt her badly – even with a blow. But it had to be suppressed. I warned her though. You're in no position to understand it or be impatient with us.

She sighed and looked out the window. She was a good woman, slow to take offence.

I realise I shouldn't have come, she said, only partly in chagrin.

# Twelve

It was not easy of course, but I adjusted to the new terms of Leo's death because people do that, changing the course of their thinking even while believing it can't be done. In some ways I didn't want to examine too closely, the new version of Leo, once painfully digested, made it easier for me to enter a new phase. I married Laurie Burden in 1953, and – in defiance of doctors and nurses who considered me an 'elderly primapara', a first time mother of advanced age, an opinion they expressed in terms such as my making 'a *late* run' or 'leaving things a bit late' – I gave birth to a healthy boy, Alexander. Alexander was one of those children who carry an air not of being a stranger visiting the earth but of having the ways of the world worked out. He was what we sometimes called a happy warrior, perpetually engaged in cricket, rugby and surfing, an adequate scholar but not to an extent that interfered with his social life. His father considered him not adequately serious. I blessed the balmy star under which he'd been born.

We were suddenly a sanguine and fortunate family, living above Balmoral Beach, sailing every second Saturday on Laurie's boat, opening up Laurie's house and garden to a tide of visitors, contacts of Laurie's, many of whom I found myself liking.

Occasionally a Memerang story would surface without warning in the press – brave Doucette, brave everyone, the gallant Captain Leo Waterhouse. A tale of confrontation, escape, betrayal and tragedy, etc. I knew by some instinct I had not heard the last of any of it.

In the 1960s, Memerang came to a head again through the researches of a young man named Mark Lydon. He was one of those Australian journalists who heavily populated the British press in the days when Fleet Street was a name synonymous with newspapers. A handsome, mannerly young fellow whose clothes had the appropriate scuffed look of a graduate student, he worked for the *Observer* in England and was contemplating a book on the history of Memerang. From the way he carried himself when he came to see me on a journey home to Sydney, I noticed in him a doggedness which might raise awkward questions all around. The Beatles had just become big, and I wished his mind was set on them rather than the 1940s. But he was easy to talk to, and I did enjoy revisiting such subjects as what an extraordinary pair Dotty and Rufus were.

The submarine? he asked me at last. You know, it came back late to the meeting place, this NE1, Serapem. But

Moxham did come back in the end. And Eddie Frampton, their conducting officer, landed there but decided they weren't there to be picked up. He landed once. And that was it.

I said, He landed *once*? To look for them?

Yes, I regret that's the situation.

For the moment, I felt impaled.

Look, that's all it seems from the documents I have.

But if you want to pick men up, you have to look more than once.

When I go back to England, said Mark Lydon, I've got to try to see Frampton. He invented the Silver Bullets, you know. But why did he land on the pick-up island just once?

He certainly had a hunger to question Major Frampton. Look, I said, I'm sure he did all he could. I was almost tempted to say, Leave Eddie Frampton in peace.

Is it possible, I asked myself, for the dead to appoint their archivist? For Lydon was as relentless and painstaking as a brother. Maybe more so.

A year or so later I received a letter from Dotty, and enclosed in it a suicide letter from Eddie Frampton addressed to Dotty and Minette and none of the rest of us. Eddie Frampton had been found dead in his car at Doncaster station.

This applies to you as much as it does to myself and Minette, wrote Dotty. In fact, more so. I think Frampton meant we'd send it on to other involved parties, and though I hate to subject you to this stuff, Grace, I also feel it would be criminal not to.

The letter was written on the stationery of Frampton Engineering, Single Girder, Double Girder, Torsion Girder with Cantilever, Gantry Portal Cranes, and Traverser Cranes. It was an excruciating document, occasionally falling away into self-pity, but ruthless as well.

*February 20, 1966*

*NOT TO BE SHOWN TO MY FAMILY*

*To be sent under CONFIDENTIALITY instead to Mrs Minette Doucette, England; Mrs Dotty Mortmain, London.*

*Dear Ladies,*

*This is told you in confidence. A simple rough letter full of the blunt sentiments of a man who's dying, and if I offend you with that you'll just have to forgive it. I have to let you know straight what I can't tell my wife, and beg you in decency not to disturb her or visit her.*

*I've been questioned by this Mark Lydon fellow, and I always knew it would happen. If I'd stayed on at SOE in Baker Street and not gone gallivanting off to the Indian and Pacific, I could have had an honoured career. Everyone knows the letters SOE these days. Books coming out. Special Operations Executive. The letters are an adequate explanation of a life to those chaps in bars who still ask what you did in those days. And who were you with, old chap? SOE does the trick. Sworn to discretion. They imagine parachute drops and explosions and being bound not to reveal anything.*

*Mr Frampton? This author, Lydon, asks me by phone. He's an Aussie, a Fleet Street bugger works for the* Observer. *Trying to write an account of Doucette's two great missions to Singapore. He has a British publisher. He mentions the name and it's a publisher I recognise.*

*I thought I'd better see this writer then, but I've had no peace of mind from that day. Sleepless nights. Isabel saying exasperated, Come to bed, love, and similar, making me tea I put Scotch into.*

*I fought my way through a number of meetings with Lydon, but it was all hopeless. Did you ever nearly piss in your pants, I wanted to ask him, like I did when Private Stapler and I landed at Serapem and saw that Jap walk past down Hammock Hill with his little dog? But the reason I write this is because I have no excuse to offer, so I'd better stop offering one.*

*Private Stapler wanted to capture the man. He said he'd shoot me. Rather shoot a Pommy than an enemy of the Crown, he said. Pommy poofter! he said. He put the barrel of his Sten against my cheek. We could know everything that happened if you'd let me capture that Nip! he said.*

*And what would we do? I asked this berserk colonial boy. With ten hours before dark? What would we do with him after?*

*Anyhow, as we Framptons drink tea with this chap the author, Isabel said to him, I hope you appreciate the problem it is for Eddie. He's got enough problems running the factory and serving on the County Council, you know?*

*I do appreciate it, said the young man. I saw him nod all right, but could tell he was bloody ruthless. He'd read too much. He'd been into the records and he'd read my report on visiting*

*NE1, and Lieutenant-Commander Moxham's – who's a bloody admiral these days. He'd read Stapler's report too, he told me, which I think should have been destroyed in the interests of decency.*

*I wondered, asked this colonial, how Commander Moxham could have so misread the orders . . .? I mean, the orders for picking up Doucette's men on time? As I understand it, he was to bring you to NE1 for the rendezvous every night for a month, starting on October 20 1944?*

*Yes, I admitted. But subject to the safety of the submarine.*

*The smell of Orca came back to me, and I felt I wanted to be sick in a new sense.*

*Well, he didn't get you there till sixteen days after the agreed time.*

*I feel you deserve the answer I gave the boy. Moxham got a fixation and insisted on staying out and using his fifteen torpedoes. I told Moxham we had to move along to NE1, Doucette's crowd would be waiting. I didn't like Moxham's stubbornness any more than anyone else. But the simple truth was these sub commanders hated picking up operatives. They didn't get much credit amongst their peers for that.*

*As the baby author pointed out, we now know the Memerang operatives I was meant to pick up were on NE1 at the appointed time. And by the time I got there were still hiding on another island by day and paddling across to the Hammock Hill site on NE1 by night. My report showed I visited the Hammock Hill only once and in the day.*

*It's true that when I got back to the sub, Moxham said he couldn't land me there again. Water's too shallow in that archipelago, he said. I mean,* Orca *had been tracked that day by a Japanese anti-submarine plane. They were on to us, you understand. Only a matter of time . . .*

*I ask your pardon. I had been, however, eighty days there, on that sub* Orca*, conducting them up there to Serapem, then back to Fremantle so the Malay crew of the junk could be interviewed by intelligence. Then off again to fetch the party. I had only three days ashore in Western Australia in all that time. By the time we got to NE1, I had no muscle tone left. I was physically done. I could barely stand, scarcely use an oar, and even found walking difficult.*

*Lack of muscle tone isn't an excuse. I never got over it, any more than you have. After the war I swore off sophisticated engineering, and became a plain old steelwright who liked putting together big transoms of steel for ordinary purposes. Deliberately went from little cunning devices to big plain structures – to get over what I think was a kind of crack-up, though a fellow couldn't tell anyone that then. I never said so to anyone.*

*I should have insisted on going back to Hammock Hill on Serapem the next night, and the night after, and if that hadn't worked, should have insisted we capture the locals and ask them what they knew of my lost brethren. There were still so many of the Memerang boys living and hiding out on NEs and NCs at that stage. Not only did Mark Lydon know that I should have done all that, should have been an enterprising officer like Doucette, who always consulted locals. But he also knew that I* knew *I should have done it, and that my failure was eating my vitals and that I dreaded all the stuff he had to tell me.*

*Right now, Mr Fleet Street is waiting at home for me, Isabel telling him, He'll be here in a moment, something must have come up at the works. I remember when I met her her family didn't use the word* the *in sentences and she's had to learn.* Soomthin coom oop at works, *she would have said once. Dear Isabel.*

*The Independent Reconnaissance Department was so fussy in some ways, but also incompetent in others, and never asked me for my glass-coated death pill back. I kept it in my kit. I kept it in my office desk as a sort of insurance against anything becoming intolerable – cancer or bankruptcy or such. Bakelite and glass coating to stop accidental usage.*

*I am the last victim of Operation Memerang, and I suppose I can't blame you for thinking I'm its last war criminal.*

*I would be obliged if you and your sisters in loss forgave me my neglect, and I seek that favour from you.*

*I'll soon be walking the shadows with your brave fellows.*

(MAJOR) EDDIE FRAMPTON

# Thirteen

But of course, time does erode betrayals and further subtleties of loss. You absorb it all, no matter how terrible. I never thought either that Eddie Frampton deserved the death penalty, though I could see the sense of his last act, and I never wrote his widow a condolence letter. I was helped by the fact that I loved my job. By the mid 1980s, I was and had been for two decades head of English at North Sydney Girls' High, teaching bright and receptive girls, and fortunate to be liked and respected by them. I was aging and was spoken of by other teachers as 'an institution'. Though I had accepted that my education as a widow would never cease, I was a happy woman, a reader, a savourer of gardens, with a companionable husband. Laurie and I were frequently visited by our son, Alex, a structural engineer, a man who relished life and had an acute sense of its value. Though he lacked a few of the literary bones which I would like to have given him, his wife was a first-class conversationalist, an athletic, intelligent woman who sometimes reminded me of Dotty. And of course I had those visits from my post-modernist, gender-studies granddaughter Rachel. We sparked off each other.

I knew from letters from Dotty, now about to retire as a senior editor in a so-called 'hot' publishing firm, that she was as harried as I was by an increasing number of Memerang hobbyists and even serious researchers. The chief of them was still the journalist and author Mark Lydon, whose interviews with Major Frampton had triggered the latter's suicide. Lydon had been shattered for a time by Frampton's swallowing of his death pill, but after a number of psychiatrists assured him that Frampton's suicide had been Frampton's choice and could not have been foreseen, Mark returned to his book, ultimately publishing a fairly flattering version of Memerang entitled *The Sea Otters*, in which he extolled Doucette and Rufus and Leo and the others and was, no doubt inhibited by the publishers' legal advisers, mildly critical of Frampton and Moxham.

After *The Sea Otters* Mark, who could be seen as conscientious to a fault, became a lifelong devotee of Doucette's story, and others joined him or competed with him in businesslike pursuit of new information. In the end they found out everything that could be known, every little squalor, every little move. About the rest they had hypotheses on such subjects as what Leo Waterhouse really felt like in the bus from Outram Road prison to

Reformatory Road, what mixture of terror and exhilaration – for everyone mentions the evidence of exhilaration! People spoke during the French Revolution about a shining serenity on the faces of some enemies of the state as they travelled in the tumbrel to the blade. As if the guillotine were such a total cancellation of the world that it solved many of the victim's smaller daily anxieties. They no longer travelled in uncertainty.

But I couldn't bear to discuss that sort of thing with Lydon or any other outsider. It might just encourage them. As it was, they rushed to tell me new information as if I hungered for it. Between these flurries of research by others I felt content, engrossed in my only grandchild, my son's daughter, a child I felt was very like I had been but thankfully less burdened with painful bush politeness than I was. By now I had seen the sad decline of both my parents, who died with the uncomplaining demeanour of their type, but my world was nonetheless enlivened by Rachel and her capacity from childhood to ambush me with unexpected questions.

Meanwhile, about 1985, Mark Lydon successfully tracked down the Japanese interpreter Hidaka, who had worked on Leo and others. Hidaka had assumed a false name for some decades, precisely because of what befell his Memerang charges, and Lydon found the man through his disgruntled wife, a former nightclub dancer. Lydon took Hidaka's photograph outside his broken-down steak-house in Yokohama, with a red banner advertising Suntory at the door and a murk beyond the door to match the mysteries behind his edgy smile. For like all of us Hidaka had not even told himself everything! Everyone, from Mark Lydon to poor old Hidaka, the former interpreter for the Japanese in Singapore, with his evasions and boasts about a special relationship with Leo and the others.

*I stayed away that day because I could not bear to see what was done with them.*

That's one of his claims.

*I brought them books. I bought them sweetmeats.*

But you did not save them, nor could you, nor did you at a profound level dissent from what was done to them. So you're no use to me.

And your superiors also valued you for the way the men trusted you and told you things, and you took that credit too!

So to what extent was Hidaka a man of sentimental fraternity, and to what extent a cunning operative?

Every new, well-meaning interviewer and Memerang hobbyist puts the stress-mark between these two possibilities in a different place and then, visiting Hidaka, most of them want to call me up and tell me exactly what they think the formula for Hidaka's supposed generosity to Leo and the others was. As if *that*'s a question on which I would still be working, adjusting still my balance of hatred or gratitude when it comes to Hidaka and the Japanese military code.

Some of the researchers are starting to be true scholars now, even a doctoral student, a captain in the army. They either examine Hidaka's record or go to Japan to interview him. This raises in me the old fear that something new might emerge which must be borne, something dangerous to the honour of Leo's ghost and something perilous to me. More than the human frame could carry.

The young doctoral army captain thinks that Hidaka might have been lucky not to be prosecuted by the War Crimes Commission. After all, he did the interpreting for a number of Kempei Tai interrogations. But then, says the captain, dozens of more senior military men were let off too, through lack of personnel to investigate them or because of the war-weariness of the victors. I am a terminally polite old woman, but inwardly I flinch and there's a trace of acid in my response. Thank you, captain, for your fascinating assessment.

The young captain completed his doctoral thesis, *Planning and Operational Shortcomings of Operation Memerang*, graciously sent me a copy, and disappeared from my life.

One enthusiast has told me it rained at 1300 hours as Leo and the others made their way in through the gate of Raffles College to appear before the sitting of the Military Court of the Seventh Area Army. He had also kindly taken a photograph of the college motto above the gate: *Auspicium Melioris Aevi*, Hope for a Better Age.

Just a photograph to him, but I am thereby locked into the journey Leo made that day of his trial, and become raddled with the mad wish that I had been there to argue with the judges and offer my head for Leo's. Over decades, Laurie, a man of great generosity of spirit, learned to read my moods, which were profound but not always very visible, and accommodated himself to them in the days after I'd been visited by the enthusiasts, when I felt myself hurtling down in a pocket of free air between two ages and two marriages.

Anyhow, on the day of Leo's trial, when the accused parties dismounted from their Mitsubishi truck, guards took Leo and Filmer and the others in amidst the dripping shrubberies of the college garden, the leaves already steaming as the afternoon sun failed to decide whether it intended a cool afternoon or not. The prisoners entered a lecture hall with leadlight windows. I imagine sudden, renewed rain on the roof.

The presiding judge was a Colonel Sakamone of garrison headquarters, but the judge with the greatest experience in the inquisitorial Japanese system, which – as the researchers tell me – is based on the Code Napoleon, was one Major Torosei. A third major filled out the trinity of judges.

Hidaka the interpreter would later tell Lydon that his own senior officer, Colonel Tomonaga, had declined to serve as judge. He had made it clear to Hidaka he thought the men should simply be put in Changi as POWs. But Colonel Sakamone, a former policeman, disagreed. He was a fanatic, said Hidaka, even though fanaticism was getting less popular with officers as the war went on. Sakamone had said at dinner one night that he believed the war would begin only when the Japanese mainland was invaded, and he was looking forward to that cataclysm. Everything up to now had apparently been mere prelude. The war would be won on ancestral land, he said. Sakamone had taken the job which Hidaka's colonel refused.

The prosecutor or attorney-judicial, a man the judges had already met with to decide the shape of the trial, was a professional lawyer, Major Minatoya. What did Minatoya think as he prepared his papers? Tokyo burning to ash, the home islands falling, even if the great nuclear secret had a month to go before it would be revealed. Singapore gravid fruit hanging on the empire's tree. Yet at such times of uncertainty men cling to the certainty of routine duty.

Next to Minatoya the prosecutor sat the young Hidaka, Leo's friend, in his white civilian suit. Hidaka had a slightly spiv-ish reputation amongst the officers for having once worked as a bookkeeper and greeter of foreigners in a Tokyo nightclub before the war, but he was always a meek figure, and the enthusiasts and hobbyists tell me he was not above soliciting women for officers. He was in love with a Tokyo nightclub dancer whom he'd marry after the war.

The supreme figure of the trial sat in the gallery at the rear of the courtroom, above the double-leafed doorway of the lecture hall. Major-General Okimasa, head of the judicial apparatus for the Seventh Area Army, wanted to see the process through. He must have had a glimmering, given all his robust activities in Saigon and Singapore, that his own future might contain a suicide by blade, or else a scaffold. In Indochina and Malaya he had been a monster for his gods. I would like to think his foreshadowings of fear were unmanning him even then, but I do not believe they did. He certainly seemed to feel a kind of administrative urgency to get this trial settled.

Each of the prisoners was asked to state, one by one, his birthplace, his unit, rank, name and age. To what extent the not yet identified Stockholm syndrome was at work in Leo and the others, I have no idea. They were human, after all. That growth of solidarity between captor and captive, particularly when exalted by the solemn ritual of a trial and the prospect of a formal execution, probably works even on heroes. Was Leo still looking for, grateful for, signs of humanity even in Sakamone the presiding judge or in Minatoya the prosecutor, or perhaps even from the real presiding presence of the general in the gallery?

Lydon later told me that the Japanese came to trial only when they felt the case was eminently provable against the accused. Their inquisitorial process was begun that afternoon, and to match the prosecutor, Minatoya, there was no corresponding defence counsel.

Minatoya, I also knew from briefings by Mark Lydon, had set out to prove the men were both perfidious and heroic – that was always Hidaka's claim, anyhow. The 'stratagem' of which they were guilty was that, except for a few commissioned officers, the party willingly refrained from wearing badges or caps to show their ranks, so that they could not be recognised as fighting members of the armed forces to which they belonged. They had used camouflage dye on exposed skin surfaces. Doucette and

Leo and six other members had worn sarongs! A Japanese national flag was flown by them, and a further Japanese flag was painted on the stern of *Nanjang*.

On October 10 of the previous year, the party under Lieutenant-Colonel Doucette had launched a sudden and heavy fusillade at a Kaso Island police boat containing five Malay policemen. Four of the crew of the police boat were killed. By December 1944, the time of apprehension of all the accused persons standing before the court, they had confronted Japanese garrisons on a number of islands and killed Captain Matsukata, Lieutenant Hiroshi, along with some fifty-five other army personnel. Thus they had engaged in hostile activities without wearing uniforms, and had also used the vessel as a stratagem of offence and penetration.

The second charge was espionage, the accusation that various of the party had collected intelligence to take back to Australia, information on the strength of garrisons, movement of shipping, docking arrangements at Bintan and Bukum, bauxite mining at Lingga Island, etc, etc. While waiting for the party to return to NE1, my cousin Mel Duckworth had made notes on the passage, frequency of military aircraft, anti-aircraft defences and shipping. Now they brought these forward and questioned the Englishman Filmer, the man who had landed on D-Day but then blundered into Memerang.

The prosecutor held up one Japanese flag, one notebook, one sketchbook, one camera, seventeen negatives. Yes, all that property belonged to Memerang, said Filmer. The flag had been waved, the photographs taken.

In lonely years I would complain savagely to myself about Filmer. I had thought him a dupe – he reminded me of the British commander at Singapore, Percival, who was foxed into surrendering by the Tiger of Malaya, Yamashita, even though many officers under him wanted to fight on. The pattern, I believed, was repeated in a modest but terrible way by Filmer. My thesis had been that Filmer, the professional officer, blinded by fatuous codes of military behaviour – or, to invoke it again, the Stockholm syndrome – failed to attack the charges head on. In a strange way the fool felt honoured by them. Combine this with the fact that he was probably the one who opened fire on the Malay police boat off Kaso, and thus gave their presence away, and you have the reason why, whenever I've encountered Major Filmer in dreams, I've torn the flesh from him and flayed him with bitter Australian insult. Basically, my grievance against him was that he was the first to accept the Japanese charges, and he laid down the pattern for the other men to do the same. Major Minatoya asked him, Did you commit these crimes?, and Filmer said yes without qualification. When he was asked how long his group had plotted their attack, he said he only knew the details of it a few days before he left Australia, a statement which shows that compared to Leo he was one of those ring-ins Doucette had a weakness for, that he was brought along by Doucette on impulse, or because he pleaded. And yet here he was talking on behalf of the whole party, and impervious to the wrongness of that, as only a professional officer could be. He agreed with Minatoya that rank should always be worn, so that the enemy could identify officers. That was an asinine thing to say, as our side had little training in *their* badges of rank, and I bet their side had little training in ours.

Did Leo resent him giving it all away like this, or was he resigned, or was he stuck by now in some grotesque officer code of honour too? Had all the Bushido nonsense got to both of them, so that they were competing for honour with the Japanese? I don't want to mock that, since they were willing to die for it. But men become dupes for codes of honour which any sensible woman could see through in a second. Yes, said Filmer, they had a Japanese flag on the junk and were thus sailing under false colours. But no, they had not themselves painted the Japanese flag on the stern of the junk. It had already been put there by the Malay owner. At least five silenced automatic weapons on the junk opened up on the patrol boat at Kaso, he admitted. He didn't mention it was almost certainly he who first pulled the trigger. He began shooting because others did, he said. As the police vessel approached, everyone thought it was Japanese, he said, not Malay police, and they yelled, Patroller, patroller! They did not know it was an unarmed vessel. No, no British or Australian flag was hoisted on the junk before they opened fire. There was barely time. Doucette did not directly order them to open fire.

The affidavit of the surviving Malay policeman from the patrol boat was read to Filmer. Poor fellow, a local mixed up between two powers, seeing his fellows on the launch cut to pieces, and then himself diving, bleeding copiously, into the water. But it strikes me that, abstracting from race, Leo and all the other Australians had a lot in common with that Malay cop. Like the policeman on the patrol boat who was a servant of the Japanese, they were also caught up in other people's imperial dream, doing for Churchill what Churchill never did for us, with all his talk of Australians being of bad stock and bound to cave in to the Japanese anyhow.

Leo was the next brought forward before the court, and he accepted the charges just as Filmer had. He offered the information that Doucette had worn his badge of rank while on the junk but he himself had not. He had shot at the patrol boat, and had also resisted the landing by the army at Serapem, but he was not sure if he had killed any Japanese soldier. He admitted he had sketched and photographed islands and shipping, and made notes. That is all that's in the record – no pleading, no mention of a young wife and of her hopes and rights and expectations. In that regard, I suppose, he had nothing exceptional to plead. He had worn commando grease to colour his face and had stopped wearing a beret after they all got on the junk.

In turn, each of the other men admitted the same, in their peculiar and grievous honour.

The afternoon showers stopped, Hidaka told Lydon, and the sun came out with its afternoon intensity, and then yielded to shadows from the foliage of the Raffles College garden. The cocktail hour. All the accused were asked to stand. Each one was asked did he have anything to say in his defence. The judge urged each of them to point out anything in their evidence which was to their advantage. None of them said anything. The silence of honour locked the tongues of Leo, Hugo Danway, Jockey Rubinsky, Chesty Blinkhorn, Sergeant Bantry, the naval rating Skeeter Moss, Mel Duckworth, Major Filmer. Each of the accused was asked if he had any objection to the statement of any other member of the party. One by one they said they didn't. You can imagine a robust fellow like Chesty Blinkhorn thinking, Wouldn't give the bastards the satisfaction. Each was asked if he wanted to alter any part of his statement to the Suijo Kempei Tai or the prosecuting attorney, and they all said no. Thus, bridges burned, they all turned their inner eye to the sword's edge.

Hidaka, in his white suit, hung his head. Prosecutor Minatoya then went into his fancy arguments as the air thickened around the heads of the accused. The Haig Convention 1907 required that all ships other than warships, entering an attack, must affix to themselves a true representation of their nationality. Hostilities conducted under false or no colours were a crime under international law. The junk flew a Japanese flag, and hence no British flag was flown, and commando dye and sarongs were deliberately used to make the junk look civilian. They should also have worn badges of rank or unit to identify them as belligerents. The fact that they were wearing Australian jungle fabric, very much like that which the Japanese used, was no adequate warning that they would attack the patrol boat.

Minatoya then argued with less legal validity that military personnel lose their right to be treated as prisoners of war if they disguise themselves. The green military shirts most of the men wore were not enough. Then, tying himself in a knot, he further claimed that international law in any case gave way to the law of the capturing country, and so whether under international convention or Japanese occupation law, the men were doomed. The occupation law involved, he said, was the Martial Law of Japanese Southern Expeditionary Force, Section 2, Clause 1, Paragraph 1 (iv).

Minatoya made mention of the poison they carried, the capsules which would come as a surprise to us women when we first heard of them from Mr McBride on our visit to Canberra. Their possession of such poison demonstrated that they could countenance death with composure (a supreme virtue in his eyes), just like the sailors involved in the Japanese midget submarine attack on the *Chicago* in Sydney Harbour three years past. The Australians had treated those heroes with full honours, and now it was the chance of the Japanese to treat Australian heroes with equivalent honour.

Have you ever heard such utter horse-feathers? the aging Dotty had asked me in a letter. With one sentence he says they've violated international law, and with the next he deifies the poor sods. For Lydon had sent her the transcript too, including the peroration of Minatoya's address to the court. It went this way, or was later doctored to go this way: These men struck out from their native home,

Australia, with the most ineffable patriotism blazing in their souls, and with the expectations of all the people of their country upon their shoulders. They battled most sublimely to attack and evade. The last moments of such lives as theirs must be sublime and appropriate to their past history. For heroes are extremely jealous of their popular regard, the way their memory will stand amongst their people. This is a feeling the Japanese people know and respect. And so we must glorify the last moments of these heroes as they expect and as they deserve, and by doing so, the names of these men will be invoked for all eternity, in Australia and in Britain, as those of truest heroes.

This *Let's give 'em the send-off they deserve* argument included the rider *Even if it kills them*. As Dotty said, utter horse-feathers. And before sentencing, as sudden darkness closed the day, that fool Filmer thanked Minatoya for saying his bravery was likely to be remembered in Britain and Australia. He did at least make the point that at the time they captured the junk, flew the flag and attacked the patrol vessel, he had not believed he and his fellow soldiers were engaged in any unfair or illegal combat. At the time he and the others had not realised, he confessed, that these were such grave crimes. Now he was willing to face the punishment that was due.

Some of the hobbyists and researchers think Hidaka was later given the job not only of translating the trial into English but of prettifying it as well – if any of it could be called pretty. That his job was to make it all seem less a show trial, something decided before Leo and the others even entered the court. Some researchers have told me too that the Memerang men were tried and liquidated entirely for the sake of the Oriental value of *face*, and that they were to die not for their efforts in Memerang but for the earlier success of Cornflakes. After that previous raid, it turns out that the Japanese brought into Singapore from Saigon a special investigative unit of the Kempei Tai, the Japanese equivalent of the Gestapo, to investigate the blowing up of the port's tonnage.

The Kempei Tai were convinced that the ships destroyed in Singapore by Doucette's Cornflakes in 1943 had been targeted not by raiders but by local saboteurs working with some influential civilian prisoners of war at Changi, whom they accused of being in communication with the Allies by radio. They arrested former executives of British oil companies, wealthy Chinese they suspected of belonging to sabotage cells, and humbler Chinese – a woman who ran a soup stall at Keppel Docks. Many of the people arrested were killed. The arrests also extended to Malays, twenty of whom were still in prison that afternoon Leo's trial began. They were under sentence of death for their nonexistent roles in the sabotage really created by Cornflakes. As Mark Lydon says in his book, 'Hidaka would early let Leo Waterhouse's group know that other men were under the death sentence for a supposed part in Cornflakes, and that seems to have influenced the way the Memerang men behaved at their trial.' Now the Kempei Tai *knew* who the culprits were, since they had captured Rufus's diary, and they thus found out that all the questioning and torture, water treatment, beatings and electrodes on the genitals of last year's local captives had produced false confessions and unjust executions.

On the question of face, General Okimasa and Court President Sakamone and the Kempei Tai officers asked themselves with a fractured but potent logic: how could the twenty Malays, men in their prime, fathers of families, a humorist here, a balladist there, a sketcher here, a teller of profane jokes there, be under death sentence, and the ten Memerang men not? But it meant, as the hobbyists and researchers have frequently assured me, that for some periods of time during their capture, the limitations of torture having been proven the year before, Leo and the others had it easier than the locals, Chinese, Malay and Britons, who had been arrested.

So I had assimilated all that, and stowed it away within me the way people do. The rivers of our blood flow and flow, and grind down into smoothness into a sort of habitable geology, what is too sharp to be known. I knew the details of the trial from the late 1960s on. I had the English language transcript provided to me by Lydon, and from then until the present it lay in my desk drawer at home, where I would frequently encounter it and flinch, a duty of pain I felt I owed it. I was familiar with the names of Okimasa, Sakamone the fanatic, Minatoya the prosecutor, and above all with that of Hidaka.

The severest test occurred in the early 1990s, when Hidaka, reconciled to having been discovered, was brought to Australia by the now middle-aged Mark Lydon and by an Australian film producer who wanted to have his technical advice for a proposed film. Lydon called us and said Hidaka would very much like to pay his respects to me. I shouldn't have gone along with it – what could the meeting mean and how could I balance his part in the trial and execution, and his undoubted kindnesses into one feasible greeting and one safe little discourse? But then how could I ignore the half-century of transformation, which made us fortunate participants in the business of our region, which made Japan 'our major trading partner'. After discussing it with Laurie, I suggested to Mark Lydon he bring Hidaka to our place for afternoon tea.

I was still full of that terror which had lasted nearly fifty years. Every time I approached Leo's death I was repelled by the temperature of the event itself and saw refracted through its heat a new version to which I had somehow to adjust. I remembered Doucette's guilt about his inadequate rejoicing at news of Minette's survival, which was paralleled by my sense that I had never adequately mourned. Now that Mark Lydon was bringing Hidaka to my house, the whole file was open again, nothing was settled, I might hear anything. The fear that there were limitless versions of the thing to absorb was, despite what I thought of as my good sense, acute and like a form of madness. Combined with that, I suspected that a good, brave wife would have sought Hidaka out years since, would have been frantic to meet him earlier.

Laurie was wonderful at such times. He had not yet suffered his stroke, and he attended to everything, meeting the guests at the door, making the tea. As Hidaka came into the living room, nodding, bowing to Laurie, not yet daring to smile, he proved to be a lean old man of average height whose mouth was beginning to slacken with age. He seemed to have a respiratory disease, and I noticed his fingers were nicotine stained and his nails blue-ish from lack of oxygen. I could tell at once that he and I were both playing this for Lydon, Hidaka playing along with Mark who had set up his air ticket from Tokyo to Sydney. At a moment like this one, I was sure, Hidaka was asking himself whether he should have taken the trip, despite the honour he received in the Australian tabloids under the film-company generated headlines such as 'JAPANESE TRANSLATOR BEFRIENDED DOOMED AUSSIES'.

Under Laurie's understated stage management, we sat down to drink tea, and began to talk about Hidaka's flight and whether he was able to rest properly here. And yet in no time the matter of the trial came up as if by its own force. I don't even remember the sequence of sentences, but there it was, amongst us. Like a slaughtered beast on the carpet, it demanded comment, and I could see Mark Lydon sitting forward, eager to assess what Hidaka and I would say in each other's company.

My superiors order me to dress immaculately, the old man told us, with his chronic wheeze.

This was the most important and portentous trial he had ever seen, but he was not required as a translator – a translator of military rank sat with the judges. He wondered what his superiors would think when the prisoners who were brought in winked at him and smiled at his posh suit.

And the prisoners did, one of them, Sergeant Bantry, unleashing a little sharp, almost inaudible whistle.

As Laurie made unconscious affirmative and comforting sounds deep in his throat, at Lydon's request Hidaka went through the order they stood in. It is engraved on my soul, said Hidaka.

That was a sentiment I believed, and I heard my husband Laurie also give his accepting growl. At the end of the line, on the left, No 10, was Jockey Rubinsky, twenty years old. Big Chesty Blinkhorn beside him, same age. Sergeant Bantry, the non-swearer. No 5 was Private Appin who survived Doucette's last stand. No 6 was the young naval rating Moss, and then a much-beaten and sickly army officer named Dinny Bilson. Lieutenant Danway stood at No 4 in the line. At the other end, Nos 3, 2 and 1 from the left, were Melbourne Duckworth, Leo and Major Filmer. They all wore Japanese army boots, and their hair was close-cropped. I try to imagine Leo thus, very thin, with cropped hair.

And General Okimasa was there the whole time, wasn't he? Lydon asked Hidaka, as if I did not know that.

All the time, Hidaka confirmed. He did not leave for a minute. So it was . . . the important trial.

Lydon loves all this straight-from-the-horse's-mouth stuff. The order in which people stood, and so on. Did Okimasa sit on a rattan chair or an armchair? The reason Memerang's supposed crime under Japanese military law was translated by him as 'perfidy', an old-fashioned and stately word, is that Mr Hidaka had learned his English from Shakespeare, Tennyson and PG Wodehouse.

But I could see old Hidaka was gasping, even after such a short time, and so, secretly, was I.

I smiled and said to Lydon, Listen here, Mark, curb your enthusiasm. I think Mr Hidaka is tired.

Of course, Mark admitted. One thing though. Mr Hidaka saw them while they were waiting for the verdict. To paraphrase him, without putting him to the trouble of telling it all again . . .

As the afternoon-long trial ended, said Lydon, the accused were taken away by their guards, to wait in half-darkness on benches in the garden. Hidaka had not been stopped from visiting them. Their spirits were high, and they spoke quite loudly and in lively terms, and Hidaka had organised cigarettes to be handed round.

Thank you, Mr Hidaka, I said, as earnestly as I could.

But I knew there must have been a secret fever in each man. They must have muttered to each other reassurances about some coming invasion of Singapore by the Allies. The Seventh Area Army had grown soft in its occupation of Malaya and Singapore, and was on the verge of losing Saigon. Having condemned them, the court might in any case simply let them stay in Outram Road Gaol or in Changi.

I would ultimately get more information on what was said amongst them too. They were pleased none of them had begged – I would ultimately find that out. Because Jockey Rubinsky, world traveller, conceived in Harbin, Manchuria, born in Shanghai, raised in Sydney, came up to Leo and said, as if naming the central issue, 'We didn't beg. The bastards didn't hear us beg!'

How do I know that? Well, that resulted from the Hidaka visit too.

We had drunk our tea and I could see that Hidaka was as pleased as I was that the visit had got this far without too much discomfort. Before they left, Lydon said, he would like to show Hidaka the garden and the view from it. Laurie jumped up, happy to show him around, and Lydon and I followed. Hidaka was impressed by our jacaranda, by the roses, by the nectar-producing grevilleas which attracted rainbow lorikeets. We were on the gravel path, looking over Middle Harbour, the acres of blue water surging in through Sydney Heads. The day was warm, and it was humid too, though nothing like Singapore. Hidaka, saying, 'Very beautiful', was suddenly gone, vanished from my eyeline. I turned to see him lying flat out on the path, and Laurie and Mark Lydon kneeling to attend to him. As soon as Lydon saw him stir, he lifted the little man in his arms and propped him on the seat of the garden bench.

My husband went and got some iced water, and Hidaka revived with a rasping dollop of breath, but kept his eyes down as if he had shamed himself in front of us. Maybe to his generation a collapse in front of others from heat or the vagaries of blood pressure was a cause of disgrace. We got him into the house and laid him on the sofa. Mark took Hidaka's shoes off. Laurie suggested we send for our friend the local GP, who even in these days would make a call to the house if he was needed. Lydon relayed the offer to the clenched-eyed Hidaka. The old man shook his bony head. Driven by his frank human friability, I made him green tea, and he sipped it, then he joined his hands, opened his eyes, rose to a sitting position and bowed to me. Then he muttered to Lydon, and Mark turned to us.

He wants to visit you again, Mark said. And he apologises one more time. But he has something to give you.

His eyes lowered, the old man declared, It is not a long visit. I wish to give you something.

Maybe it was another doll. Lydon had brought me one back, a bland, ageless, child-woman doll in the kimono style of some region of Honshu. Its smirk was the smirk of Salome. I had it in a cupboard somewhere. I could not say I wanted to see Hidaka again. The answer caught in my throat, so at last my husband, just out of politeness, said, Of course. When would you like to call in, Mr Hidaka?

I felt angry at my husband, who couldn't have said anything else in any case. My widowhood had grown primal again, and I just wanted Hidaka to go. But it was organised Lydon would bring him back the following afternoon. This was done with very little more input from me than nods and choked assent.

From early the next day I was gripped by dread. It seemed to me that people required a repeated disinterment of Doucette's men, Leo not permitted his quiet grave, and I deprived of a fixed and stable widowhood. I always feared that if I confessed this to Laurie, he would despise me. Or if he didn't, he would know too much about me. He knew repeated reference to Leo hurt me in some way that he was willing to take account of and honour, but he probably thought my secret reactions were nobler than the squalid panic I felt. He never complained of the mystification I brought to the whole business.

In the afternoon, Laurie dutifully put the china out again. He visited a patisserie in Mosman and brought home cakes and petit fours – all just in case anyone had an appetite. When they rang the bell at three, I watched from the living room as Laurie opened the door to them. They both looked strangely hangdog, Mark Lydon as well as Hidaka, whose head was down like a penitent's. From the hallway, Lydon said to Laurie, and over Laurie's shoulder to me, Mr Hidaka does not wish to stay for long. I hope you haven't gone to any trouble, Laurie.

No, said my husband. No, Mark . . . always a pleasure.

Mr Hidaka wishes to apologise, Lydon explained.

Please, said Laurie. Come into the living room.

It was only with a lot of nudging from Lydon that Hidaka came into the core of the house. He bowed deeply to me and I stood up, and before I could invite everyone to sit again, I saw he had an aged folder in his hands and held it out to me. I'm very sorry, Mrs Waterhouse, he told me carefully.

Lydon said, He showed me this last night – I swear it was the first time I knew it existed.

Still stooped, Hidaka opened the manila folder and held it two-handed, like a dish he was offering me with the most sincere apologies of the house. It contained a series of brown, square slabs of paper connected up at their top left hand corners with a ring of twine.

Hidaka said, Captain Waterhouse asked me to give.

Mark Lydon explained, It's a journal Captain Waterhouse wrote in pencil on slabs of toilet paper. You see, if it was in danger of being discovered, he could just dump it in the nearest waste bucket or latrine.

Hidaka bowed even lower, like a man inviting punishment.

This is the diary Captain Waterhouse asked me to give you. I was shamed by it and I did not give it until now.

He's had it for some years, Lydon told us. I think it's psychologically understandable . . . Now, he has emphysema and wants you to have it.

Hidaka closed the folder and pressed it more insistently on me. I took it. I saw his suppliant shoulders. I began howling and punching him on both shoulders. His deep bowing to me was too easy a gesture, and I wanted to show him that. If he was a man, I thought, like some bigot I would normally have hated to meet, he would look me in the eye now. I was punishing him both for having retained the grubby squares of pages for so long, and for presenting them to me now, years after I hoped everything had been settled.

Until stopped by Laurie, I went on beating the neatly made Japanese man in a raw-boned, tall Caledonian Australian fury. Arthritic problems which normally inhibited the proper making of a fist were not an issue now.

Anger made me a harridan. My husband moved in and clasped me by the elbows. I realised I had no breath, but it returned as I settled.

Get him out, I ordered Lydon, and don't bother me again. Get him out. I'm sick of witnesses. I'm sick of new evidence. Everyone who comes to me is self-interested!

Mark Lydon's face had gone a terrible, abashed red. I assure you, Grace, I didn't know it would cause you . . . I have your best interests –

I cut him off. Best interests? Best interests of the Memerang men? They're all dead. I bet you looked through the file as soon as he gave it to you.

No, said Mark. No, Grace. I won't say I wasn't tempted. But it wouldn't have been right.

Just take him back to his hotel! I roared.

Mark and Laurie tended to the old man, whose face was covered with tears and who needed to be restored with water. Given Hidaka's weakness he and Lydon went very briskly, and I felt the deepest shame I could, knowing Leo would not have approved of my behaviour. As they turned to leave, Laurie called, I'll be in contact, Mark. Grace is understandably upset.

He saw Lydon and Hidaka to the door, and muttered something conciliatory I wouldn't have approved of to them as they went. Then he came to where I stood shaking frantically in rage and shame, and he embraced me.

Now I'll have to apologise to Mark and Hidaka, I said.

Laurie kissed my forehead. No, he said, let it slide. They understand well enough.

It was from these pages written in pencil on Japanese toilet paper that I ultimately learned that while they waited in the garden for the sentence, Jockey Rubinsky said to Leo, The bastards didn't hear us beg!

# Fourteen

From the Outram Road prison journal of Captain Waterhouse:

*When it happened, it was a bloody calamity. It was the last afternoon, and we were at a fever pitch and ready to go. Very ready to go. The Boss had already sent two of the blokes ahead to watch Singapore from NC1. When we got there, they'd be able to brief us on the day's shipping news and naval movements. From the junk* Nanjang *we could see through the binoculars a lot of naval shenanigans way out in the Phillip Channel to the east of Singapore – Rufus reckoned it looked like exercises. He said we'd better stick close in to shore. The bow waves of destroyers could just about sink an old junk like this.*

*There'd just been one of those Sumatras – blinding rain. But now the sun had come out, and we were between two hummocky islands, Kaso and Sambu.*

*The Japanese had this Malay auxiliary police force – we hadn't heard of them before. They called them the Hei-ho. We had three hours before dark and this Malay police chief notices our junk and comes out from shore in his little launch to look at us. Of all the junks in those oceans. The watch saw him coming and started yelling, 'Patroller, Patroller!' We thought it was some bush-week little navy launch. I was on deck under the shade of our tarpaulin, and I found my Sten gun and got down under the gunnels. It changes the world, once you take up arms. The light looks different. Right or wrong, everything that went before that moment doesn't count. All your memories get reduced to this pulse in your ears. Doucette was calling from the wheelhouse, Steady! Steady!*

*I don't know who started firing. I know it wasn't me. I think it might have been a certain British officer we took aboard because he'd been at D-Day and came from the Green Howards and wanted an adventure. And now of course we joined in the firing – there were at least five Sten guns and one Bren, all silenced. We saw a man jump over the side of the launch. It was raddled with the holes we made. I think there were dead and wounded on her, but I did not want to look directly at that.*

*And it turns out they weren't Japanese, they were these Malay Hei-ho. Pity they didn't have a Japanese officer with them. Sad for all parties. After all our stealth, on the last afternoon we'd let ourselves make too much noise. If the firing hadn't started we could have let them land on us and then taken them prisoner. That's what we discussed as long ago as Melbourne. The junk stank of cordite, a smell we'd hoped to avoid.*

*We were appalled – that doesn't begin to speak the truth. We knew we'd made ourselves visible. Ashore, the policemen's colleagues were probably on the phone to the Japanese naval base at Bintan.*

*The Boss came out of the wheelhouse. He was the very soul of calm. Rufus Mortmain came up from below, his Sten in his hands. He looked more sad than angry. But the young blokes were really angry, yelling at each other, asking each other who started the calamity. Was it you, Skeeter? Was it you, Chesty? They were eliminating each other loudly like that because they were trying to shame the culprit into confessing. Even Jockey and Blinkhorn and others were saying frankly they'd seen Filmer open fire, and the name, the way they said it, dripped with contempt.*

*I was half ready, I have to say, to turn my gun on the poor fellow myself. And what a mistake that would have been. Because we couldn't have got on in prison and at the trial without him. I think Filmer was about to confess too. But the Boss suddenly said it didn't matter who did it, it didn't change anything, and he forbade them to talk about it and point fingers. It had happened. The measure of all of us would be what we did as a result of it happening. All the rest was academic. More rain came up, and gloomy rain clouds. It would help us get away, but had it come five minutes earlier we would have got past Kaso in the murk.*

Of course I already knew the outline of what had happened to them. But I put the pages Hidaka had given me into the desk drawer with the transcript. They would need to be faced, but not yet. After a week, Laurie, aware of the influence they had on my composure and my moods, asked me tentatively whether I wanted him to read them, and he could then tell me whether I needed to bother myself with them or not.

That won't be necessary, I told him starchily.

Well, he suggested, whatever's there, you have nothing to reproach yourself with. You've been a good widow to Leo.

Please don't discuss that, I told him unkindly.

It was for his sake that I knew I had to approach the rough diary Leo had written and Hidaka had delivered fifty years late. After three weeks of tension, I went to the drawer and took up the pages. I knew about the attack on the police, but not of the subtleties of that afternoon. The details of their behaviour, like so much else in Leo's diary pencilled dimly on yellowish-brown squares of harsh paper, were new to me.

Throughout it all, as we know from the trial documents, the wounded policeman, Sidek Bin Safar, was hanging on to the stern of the launch, bleeding into the water and too terrified to move. It was clear that Doucette reacted to the calamity with the admirable calm and decisiveness of a leader at the peak of his judgement and adaptability. He declared the junk must be sunk with its Silver Bullets, the submersibles, so they were to bring up the folboats for launching and load the rubber raft with their supplies. Using the marspikes designed by Major Enright, Leo and Rufus attached limpet mines on short timers around the inner hull of the junk. Sadly there were not too many fathoms under the junk's keel, but Eddie Frampton's elegant machines would at least be torn to fragments. All the effort, all the mastery that went into learning to drive them, was for nothing.

As the men prepared their packs and took to their folboats, Charlie Doucette was back with what he really liked – the pure human mechanics of the folboat, and reliance on his own sturdy little body.

The Boss had two men watching Singapore from an island named Subar, or NC11, which he used himself to keep watch on the port the year before. They had their folboat with them but would need to be collected. His, Mortmain's and one other folboat crew would go and get them. Leo was given the secondary job – he had to take a flotilla of six folboats back to Serapem, NE1, the base where Mel Duckworth waited. And I learned for the first time from Leo's slabs of toilet paper that Doucette had his reasons to abandon Leo and, if things went wrong, to court death.

Leo writes, *The Boss was shouting orders from folboat to folboat, and Jockey and I had a complete set of nine mines, and you can imagine how I felt, being told to back away from Singapore. I felt like that fellow Cherry Apsley-Garrard when Scott told him he wasn't going to the Pole. I knew in my water that once the Boss got to Subar he'd go on into Singapore overnight, or the next night, and mine some ships. The Boss rowed up close in his folboat and said, Get rid of your mines. Because you have to look after them all, Leo. Filmer hasn't got the skills for it. I'm sending you away because I don't want you to run the risk of being captured with me. I can't be taken alive, you see, otherwise they'll use Minette and the boy to get at me.*

*I said, Boss, why don't we all just come back to NE1?*

*After I've collected the team from Subar, he said.*

*I said, like a kid, You're coming back though, aren't you? And he said, Certainly. But jettison your mines too, for speed.*

*His group rowed off, pulling the inflatable raft behind them. It was packed with ammunition and explosives. Passing us in his folboat, Rufus told me he had the two Japanese flags with him, in case they were able to pirate another junk. So, whichever way one looks at it, I was to have the lesser part. Yet it was a comfort to be back at sea in the old folboat with Jockey and my other fifteen blokes around, and I knew how important each one was to people back in Australia.*

Leo seemed to sense the Boss had become an angel of self-destruction, he was not an angel of return. In the meantime, Leo's world was contained in his folboat's storage places fore and aft – their weapons, their iron rations, their camouflage, the walkie-talkies, malaria tablets. Suicide pills might have been left aboard in some cases. They were not a high priority. Leo and the others, still wearing the camouflage grease they called *commando*, could not see each other's faces as dark came on.

*We dispersed quickly in that late-afternoon sea. I'd say we were pretty confident at that moment – somehow everything had been resolved, we were pretty much in a state where we'd forgotten the question of whoever had shot first.*

*When the junk went with two separate explosions, we were a mile distant and nearly out of sight of the Boss and Rufus. We felt the end through the canvas and through the sea itself, our junk going to pieces, and our fine unused SBs, the submersibles. I spent so long trying to fight a sense of drowning and learn to handle the controls of those machines. The helmet over the head was very claustrophobic, the mask, pushing the controls down took some doing at first, with green water everywhere, and you couldn't be sure what was up and down. I got on top of the things, we all did for the sake of not being drummed out. And they were gone now. We were awed, the paddlers in the folboats around us stopped for a few seconds, to let the successive jolts rock them. I called out then in the after-silence, All right, gents. Now we just wait for the sub home. Fremantle's Esplanade Hotel awaits us!*

*It's the sort of thing an officer's supposed to say – judging by the war pictures I'd seen. And we all took up paddling again.*

Michael Casselaine, Doucette's stepson, would later write to me declaring how proud he was of the fact that after the crisis with the junk, his father and seven others, including Rufus, stayed around in the centre of the great archipelago south of Singapore. People consoled themselves for losses in various ways, and Michael Casselaine may well be right. He points to three unidentified large wrecks in Singapore Harbour the Japanese did not have time to label on their maps before the war ended. Or more accurately – and, according to Lydon, Hidaka is willing to go along with this hypothesis, the poor fellow would go along with anything for the sake of peace – they did not identify them because they were ashamed they had occurred. Michael Casselaine presumes these wrecks were the work of a last fling by Doucette, and Mark Lydon, with whom I had reconciled, tends to agree.

I did not say to Michael, Shouldn't your stepfather have stayed with the bulk of his troops? Though it might have changed nothing.

There is a long, low, coconut-groved reef island named C5 on Memerang maps, though others call it Pangkill. It was the sort of island that had a village whose chief task was coconut harvesting for the owner, generally a Malay nobleman or entrepreneur.

Whatever the Boss and his party had done in the Singapore roads, they were still towing the rubber boat with all of its equipment, including limpets, as if they were not finished with their brave acts, when they got to that island, Pangkill. Leo and his men were far to the east, and could now be considered safe by the Boss. There were two villages on Pangkill Island. Rufus took three men and went and spoke to the head man of the south-western one, who accepted their offer of cigarettes, and Doucette similarly visited the village on the northern end, and had a meal of fish and rice with the head man there. This head man, Rajah Buja, was their betrayer, but they couldn't have known, for he was genial towards them. And I am sure he was genial, and wished them little personal harm. But they were complicating his world. The Japanese recruited their informers throughout the islands with the not-to-be-sneered-at prize of a sack of rice per month, a few hundred rupiah for special pieces of information. And beyond that, many informants were pressed into service more by fear for their family's safety than by lust for reward. Rajah Buja knew the Japanese were paranoid about a fifth column, were willing to torture and hang head men who did not pass on news of untoward contacts, and bayonet and burn villages. After the war, Buja could say to the investigators, and no doubt did, that he was simply trying to save his people.

Doucette and Mortmain would have presumed innocently that a natural alliance and nostalgia for the old British times would have given the head man an automatic feeling of fraternity and warmth towards them. If imperial powers have one naive trait, it is a total bewilderment about why outsiders might resent them. Not all Doucette's familiarity with and love of Malay culture would have altered the betrayal. Not that Doucette had any other choice than to make human contact, show his face. For it was harder to betray a known face.

After their visits to the villages, they made a camp and slept overnight there, but their view of the Japanese anchorages off Bintan was blocked by a mole of a hill on a neighbouring little island. So Doucette and three of his party paddled over there to CE7A to keep an eye on any Japanese movement. Banana trees, lily bushes and tussocks of tall grass trees grew amongst the coconut palms. It all made a good hide. Back on Pangkill, C5, Mortmain remained with his partner. Early the next morning, a Malay turned up and told Mortmain that Rajah Buja had taken a motorised fishing boat west to Pandjang Island to report the presence of the Memerang men to the district police chief and thus, to the Kempei Tai. Mortmain immediately paddled across to lush CE7A to warn Doucette.

One Indonesian family were living on CE7A, a coconut grove attendant who worked for the little island's owner, and his name was Ahmed Dulib. He had with him his wife and one young child. His chief job was to cut down coconuts and extract the oil from them. He had a boiler, whose fire he fed with husks, going continuously. He had already spotted Doucette's party, each with Sten gun and pistol, in green and khaki, and a badge – the Rising Sun Australian army badge – on their caps. (He would thus have made a good witness for the defence at the trial, except there would be no defence.) In passing, Doucette asked young Mr Ahmed to cut down some green coconuts for them, and so they enjoyed the milk, and then they had Ahmed split open the fruit, and savoured the meat.

On the afternoon of that same day, while boiling down the coconut oil near their hut, Ahmed and his wife saw two Japanese landing barges approaching their beach. They were Kempei Tai troops, who landed and came running up the beach and into the hinterland towards the hut. The Japanese had a Malay interpreter who found Ahmed and asked him about white men. Had he seen any on this island?

Ahmed, for whatever reason of resistance against the occupiers, or for the sake of a peaceful life, said he had not seen any. Whatever it was, this coconut oil man and island supervisor kept denying any sight of the fugitives, and became stuck with his first denial and had to play it boldly, and did so, poor fellow. A detachment took him back to the landing barge, while the others began searching the little tropic mole. From his encampment below the island's slight hill, Doucette had also heard the noisy arrival of the landing craft. He organised his party of five around some trees and a clump of coral-like stones on the east side of the island. They saw the Kempei Tai coming and opened fire on them with their silenced weapons. It was as if a silent wind had pushed down the leading soldiers in the Kempei Tai advance. The Japanese were terrified, disoriented.

We are told the initial gun battle lasted two hours, before the Kempei Tai troops retreated to the clearing around Ahmed Dulib's hut, where they laid down their dead and wounded. At some stage in that two-hour battle, however, Rufus Mortmain had felt the impact of a sniper's bullet in his chest. By the time the Japanese pulled back amidst the palm trees, Rufus must have felt cold taking over his extremities, and a terrible uncertainty of breath. I find it hard to think of his death without tears, because his vanities were such boyish ones, he lolloped like a large, lithe dog around the bonfire, and now felt the reality of being devoured by flames. An awareness of his own death would obviously have settled on him.

Poor Ahmed Dulib was taken away on the barge by the Kempei Tai, but somehow his young wife, Mrs Dulib, who had been hiding from the Japanese with her baby, came out with her little girl and visited Doucette's group. She bent over to feed water to the gasping Rufus Mortmain. One of the soldiers in the Memerang group, Private Meggitt, had a severe but less serious shoulder wound. Doucette spoke urgently to the young woman, telling her to take her little girl and get away, for the Japanese would be back in greater force. She seemed to accept what had happened calmly, which I think astonishing and in the truest sense heroic. By which I mean, in part, innocent and short-sighted as well.

If one wanted to be cruel, and I frequently and shamefully did in Doucette's case, one could say Doucette now chose his own death rather than his duty to Leo and the others, when Leo had chosen him over me. I have to be frank that I'd always had this argument to wage with Leo, except he could not be reached for questioning.

Anyhow, for Doucette, things had gone messy beyond belief, the grand Memerang plan was in tatters, and thus he chose irresponsibly to orphan Leo and the others. In the last hour of light, he and the two men still standing with him gave Rufus a dose of morphine to dope him up for the journey, loaded him and Private Meggitt into a folboat, gave Meggitt a paddle to use one-handed and told them to head for NC2, six miles south. Somehow, Meggitt completed the paddle to NC2. What athletes these young men were. But Doucette's decision was crazy. Rufus was dying anyhow but to give him a meaningless six-mile start, Doucette threw his own life away.

Or so it seemed to me until Leo's pencillings made things clearer.

On NC2, Rufus and Meggitt sheltered in rocks over which palm trees cast a shade. They were fouled with blood, but Meggitt administered his last shot of morphine to himself and Rufus, which helped their wounds to stop bleeding. The next day, the Japanese found them sitting dead but still warm on a jungle rock ledge. Though the Allies would hide the fact from Dotty, though Lydon would not say it until the second edition of his book, glass was in their mouths – they had taken their suicide pills for fear of what they might say under torture.

Still on CE7A, Doucette took a new position and planned his fields of fire for the return of the Japanese. He put a tall young man named Private Appin, a prominent Victorian cricketer with a powerful throwing arm, in a limestone ditch to the right, with a large supply of hand grenades. He and Sub-Lieutenant Lower, the submersible instructor, chose perches in *ru* trees with clear views along the avenues of palms. He planned to lay down enfilading fire with the silenced Stens. Doucette rested then, and waited until the afternoon, when they heard the noise of landing and patrol craft.

The garrison troops on board were commanded by a particular Major Ninasu. He was, Hidaka told Lydon, a tough nut, a veteran of China and all its horrors, some of which he had himself been guilty of.

Major Ninasu's men penetrated the island in good order, sending scouts ahead, using the available cover to creep forward. There was no suicidal charge. But when the Japanese moved within range, Private Appin began throwing his grenades. In the midst of all the sudden flame and chaos, Doucette and the young naval officer and their silent Stens did lethal work, though in short bursts so that the flashes did not give away their location. Ahmed Dulib, who had been brought back on the barge and stood under guard in his clearing, saw the Japanese wounded returning, being laid on the beach and attended to by medical orderlies. He would tell the war crimes investigators there were an astounding number early – sixty of them.

As darkness came on, Ninasu sent forward some experienced scouts to draw fire from Doucette, and thus to discover where the Stens were in the darkness. There was by now too much blood around these groves of coconuts for any soldiers to proceed too calmly, but one of them got to within grenade range and blew Doucette out of his tree, after which the assassin was quickly shot to pieces by Sub-Lieutenant Lower who himself, at the end of firing a long burst, was shot dead. Private Appin was still there somewhere, alive, but there was no triumphant charge to obliterate him, since there was a belief amongst the attackers that they had silenced only a portion of the fire which had done them so much damage.

Some fifteen miles to the east, Leo and his men, who were and would remain ignorant of what befell Doucette and Rufus, had already come ashore at NE1 and met up with Mel Duckworth, the caretaker of that island, dropped earlier by the submarine. Shaped like a wine glass painted by Salvador Dali, the island had a hill, Hammock Hill, not very high at all, from where they kept watch and searched the sea for omens, expecting to see Doucette at any time. It would have seemed astonishing to Leo, and it sometimes seems so to me, that a little bit of chemical could bring the living intentions of Rufus Mortmain to a halt so easily and promptly, or that Doucette's huge intentions could be reduced to fragments of flesh by any weapon.

I know from Mark Lydon how unlucky Leo and his men on Serapem, NE1, now were. Lydon, in his study of the Japanese war files, discovered that a Japanese pilot flying a light aircraft from North Borneo to Singapore experienced a sudden alarm sound in the cockpit caused by lack of oil pressure. The pilot was carrying a naval officer and the Japanese manager of a bauxite mine in North Borneo, and the pilot told them he would need to make an emergency landing at the airfield on Bintan Island. He brought the plane in safely, and began to inspect it. There seemed to be a hole in the engine casing, which might have been caused by gunfire. The army in Singapore took no risks. They sent out troops to look for enemy agents and infiltrators on the islands to the east of the emergency landing, a task which would bring them ultimately to NE1. They sent a captain and a full company of men.

When the Japanese arrived, they landed on the west of Serapem, where Malay fishermen had a few huts. As his men unloaded weapons and ammunition from the barges, the captain, Captain Matsukata, another China veteran, issued a severe beating to one of the fishermen, and when that rendered him no extra information, moved inland from the beach.

*We were making lunch at the normal place under the hill – mixing up the usual big stew of compo rations. Our life was very ordered – we spent time on watch, and we had dug a lot of supplies into the caches on the lower ground below Hammock Hill. Poor old Mel Duckworth, darling Grace's cousin, who had been here alone since we went off on the junk, had been so pleased to see us.*

*I took Mel aside. I asked him what shape his Bolton radio was in. It's good, he said. I've been cleaning the valves.*

*Let's signal IRD to get that sub here.*

*Mel looked wistful. The problem is the Boss has the code page with him. You see, the code's based on a page from* Robbery Under Arms *– IRD's got their page, and the Boss has ours.*

*I wondered whether the Boss had remembered to fetch it from the* Nanjang *before it blew to pieces.*

*We couldn't transmit in plain. The Japanese would come straight to us.*

*Well, I decided in my own head, this isn't a tragedy, Leo. The sub will come. But there was all the more reason to miss the Boss, and daily we expected him. And there are a lot of empty hours when you're hiding on a tropic island. That lunchtime, I was with the cooking group. Hearing the engines of the landing barges, we killed the fire, left the stew, and all grubbed our way up the little knoll at Hammock Hill. About four of the blokes were still missing – they had been excavating a new supply of rations Mel had hidden in the swamp. I sent Chesty off to fetch them. They came back in ones and twos, whispering, holding their weapons.*

*I made a line of my fellows below the ridge, and put three men down to the right to enfilade with a silenced Bren, and similarly three down to the left with their Stens. We looked out from amongst the volcanic rocks and foliage on the slope, and we could see the Japanese landing on the wide-open rocky, shingly beach, on the side where the coconut plantation grew wild, and they were exposed to anyone with weapons. A few seemed to have started a casual approach, but without any urgency, and I said to everyone, These jokers aren't a danger. They're ambling along. If we just hold fire and lie low.*

*Because we had pandanus and cactus palm and wild sago, as well as papayas and betel nut and broad leaf banana trees to hide behind, we could re-position ourselves better than they could. We watched the troops come walking in an orderly way over the volcanic rocks of the beach and into the coconut groves. They were still highly visible. They looked strange and innocent, spread out that way, as if you shouldn't take advantage of them. They didn't expect anything to happen. That was it. They looked like they might slope back to their barges at any stage.*

*Could we be struck twice by the same curse? It seems we could. The sort of thing that happens amongst recruits, but I suppose fear and excitement made all of us recruits. Someone slipped his safety catch while his finger was on the trigger of his Sten – everyone knows you shouldn't do that. But the Sten fired silently, with a little hiss. It wouldn't have mattered had no target been struck. The Japanese might have heard a sound like a few hard pellets of rain, that's all. Except the bullets killed the captain that was leading, and his batman at his side. The Japanese looked at the two of them, pole-axed, not knowing where this damage came from. The rest of us began to fire and made a pitiful shambles of the advancing men. Then some of them became soldiers and hugged the ground, and others dragged their dead captain and their wounded into shelter. Even we could see that some were shattered, nearly cut in two, and their blood seemed to stain everyone near them. It was shocking what silenced Stens could do.*

*Another younger officer came up to take the captain's place. He showed himself to be pretty competent. He kept his troops down and told them to direct fire to the hill, he'd worked out we were there. Full marks to him. He decided to stay low, and we could hear shouted and relayed orders. The afternoon thunderstorm rained on them and us both, clearing away the memory of their dead captain. Out on the beach, we could see the Japanese flogging some Malays into carrying the captain's body to the barge. They beat the poor natives all the way across the stones, with half an eye on the hill all the time, worried about us, worried about our silent weapons.*

*I took a roll-call and two of our fellows, I discovered, hadn't made it back through the jungle to us. They were a young army private, Kelly, and an English fellow I hadn't got to know so well because he had a quiet nature and seemed to choose chiefly to talk to his fellow Pom, Rufus. His name was Lieutenant Carlaw, and he had been assistant to Lower in teaching us how to ride the SBs. I hoped Kelly and Carlaw would join us on the hill once night fell. Then we could all slip away to one of the other islands, maybe Proma NE3, and we could hide there and creep back over here at night and wait for the rendezvous with the sub. I could see Proma from our position. Across the water it looked good to me– even thicker cover than NE1. But it seemed to lack a beach, at least on this side. Well, we'd just have to presume one existed on the blind-side.*

*When it was dark, Filmer and I sent the others off over the hill to fetch their folboats and drag them down to the beach on the east side of NE1. We were conscious that if the Japanese had landed there, we would have needed to fight for them. Leaving, the fellows moved as Rufus had taught them, flitting like ghosts. We saw a patrol boat circling the island, but Jockey timed it and it appeared off the eastern beach only every few hours. I went down to send all but one folboat away. In the acute dark, we had been able to find only seven of the vessels, not enough for all. We had been trained how to handle this. Two of the boats would need to tow a passenger, and we used the stratagem in each case of a pair of trousers stuffed with coconut husks, the passenger floating in the Y and holding on as he was dragged through the water. Jockey and I were leaving last so we weren't burdened in this way. We went back to Hammock Hill after the first six boats got off and waited till the last hour and minute, three forty-five am, for Kelly and Carlaw to turn up. It was such a little, intimate island. We had to presume they'd been killed or captured. Otherwise, we reckoned, they'd easily be able to find their way back to our hill.*

*At the last we smashed the Bolton radio we weren't able to use because the code had been sunk in the junk or was with the Boss. But we all had walkie-talkies in our boats for contacting the Orca when it turned up. We had packed the folboat so tight with supplies, there wasn't really room for my legs, so I paddled kneeling.*

*Pushing off the beach with Jockey, I felt a real dingo. Lieutenant Carlaw was apparently an Oxford graduate in Middle Eastern studies. Kelly was only twenty years, and an athlete, and a handsome kid, a bright one too. We made a very nice little beach on the west side of NE3 – Proma – half an hour before dawn.*

# *Fifteen*

*By morning, we were on NE3 and had all our folboats under cover and were making a dump for our gear. We made a camp on the crest amongst cactus palms and pandanus and undergrowth netted by creepers. But from it we could see anyone coming from any direction. We drew breath and we hoped, and were more tired than we'd ever been from such a short paddle. Some slept – it was the fight and the sleepless night that had worn them out.*

*But I watched everything that was happening on NE1. Soon the daylight woke everyone and I was joined in that exercise of watching. I think we felt like people whose house, Serapem, had been taken over and we didn't approve of what the new owners were doing.*

*Then we saw one of the worst things I've ever seen. We saw Lieutenant Carlaw running down out of the thick cover on the hill on NE1, sprinting south into scattered palm trees with just a pistol in his hand. There was no sign of Private Kelly. The first thing I thought was, I hardly know him well enough. I heard Jockey groaning, Jesus, Jesus! Poor bastard!*

*The enemy were all over our hill over there, that's where Carlaw was running from, down into the clearing, amongst the papayas and coconut trees, but wide open, a clear target amongst the volcanic rocks. He was making for the sea. He could run, that boy, a beautiful runner, and he could probably swim strongly too, and intended to reach another island. We saw him weaving. You could hear them firing at him, and by the rocks on the edge of the sea he turned. We saw him twice take clear aim and fire, and the Japanese were coming close to him not only down the ridge from the hill but from the place where their barges were too. And now he was out of shots, so he threw his pistol away, and he just stood there and blessed himself – I hadn't even known he was a Tyke, in fact, because he was English I believed he wasn't – and a number of shots lifted him and threw him down the last decline to the sea. And everyone on our new place NE3 was groaning, Poor bastard, poor bastard! And then there was a second of mercy, when one of the Malay fishermen came up and took Carlaw in his arms and looked down in his eyes, but the Japs ended that with blows of their rifle butts.*

*Despite all they'd seen, two of my men vomited.*

*We watched them make the Malays dig a grave for Carlaw. We watched them all the time for three days, but on the morning the sub was due, the barges pulled away, leaving a section of soldiers and a few Malay Hei-ho, but taking the Malay fishermen with them. The Englishman Filmer was very troubled and came to me. He had written the fishermen a reference, saying they should take it to the British in Singapore after the war. He was sweating that the Japanese wouldn't find it. All at once it seemed very difficult to do good in this world.*

*Slowly, as we settled in, we became aware of things we'd left behind in the confusion of the dark. I'd left my camera. It had pictures in it. Filmer had left his sketchbook journal. Damned awful not to be able to vent oneself on paper, he told me. I was getting to forgive him for what happened on the junk and to think, Maybe it could have happened to anyone.*

*We watched for the Boss and Rufus, and Lower too. If they landed on Serapem and saw we'd been jumped there, they would quite naturally come here. We were getting used to the idea they might have been caught.*

*Two of us always rowed over to NE1 every night from then, landed on the east side, climbed up Hammock Hill to the lookout tree. We listened and called for the sub every night on our walkie-talkies, but it did not respond. If it had broken the surface, our eagerness would have picked it out in the darkness. At first we hallucinated: there it is! Half a dozen times an hour. Then we got more critical with ourselves. It didn't appear the first night. We told ourselves it was coming – even if late, or even if we'd missed it, for it was to return every night for a month if necessary. But it didn't come at all. God knows what happened to it.*

*On one of our visits to NE1, Jockey and I had found another intact folboat, and towed it back to our hiding place. We might all need to row to Australia.*

*To fill in the days, everyone told stories of their lives. Sergeant Bantry told us a great one. About an old man up in the bush near Grafton who was given a farm in Australia in return for giving testimony against some of the Irish gunmen. As he got older, he became convinced that the Irish were coming for him, so he holed up in his outhouse in the back of the homestead with a rifle and waited for them. He ended up wounding the dunny man coming with a new can. A silly enough tale, but we laughed at it and repeated it. You need to make what you can of that sort of stuff to spin time out when you're waiting.*

*Lance-Corporal Dignam, who I barely knew till now, was a useful member of the group that way. He was a hard, coiled little man. He had been a merchant seaman from Melbourne who got stuck in Marseilles, he says, in bad company, and on an impulse joined the French Foreign Legion. He had served in Algeria and Syria for six years. Many of his stories dealt with Arab and French prostitutes, but others with Algerian rebels and the filigree work of Damascus. I asked him whether the training for the Foreign Legion had been harder than the training for Memerang. Much harder, he said. Memerang's nothing. In his company they'd bury you alive in a pine coffin for three hours or more before digging you up to see how you'd dealt with it.*

*Jockey said that was bulldust, and Dignam said, Maybe it was only two hours, but it felt like three.*

*Major Filmer told us about holidays with his two alcoholic aunts in a house in Scotland, and with an uncle in Dublin who spent all his time in the mountains of Wicklow looking for prehistoric graves. There when he was a boy, he met Lawrence of Arabia, wearing plus-fours, who happened to have studied archaeology with the uncle.*

*Stories like that stopped the onset of the horrors. But after thirty days had passed – and they went quickly in retrospect, with two of us every night on Serapem, and hope starting with the dark and failing only with dawn – no submarine had come, no Doucette had appeared. It must have been sunk. Poor Eddie Frampton, everyone said.*

*December 7, I told them we had to start south, no choice to it. We would be out of rations if we didn't begin paddling for Bengku Island, eighty miles away, where we knew the Allies had placed a depot for operatives and downed airmen. On the journey we lay up for part of one day on a tiny, unpopulated place, and I noticed the men had begun to suffer with leg ulcers from the constant salt and the plain rations. But we didn't rest for long, and paddled throughout the afternoon, the folboats scattered but all on the same bearing and hard to see on dazzling water, and then into the night.*

*So we came to Bengku and found in a clearing the mounded cache left there by some other members of IRD. We rested for a day here – I got a shave from Dignam, and we prepared a sort of farewell feast, to which Hugo Danway, a very handy spear-fisherman, added the catch he had taken at dusk. The reason I call it a farewell feast – it was a good luck ceremony as well – was because I had to split us up into three or four groups from now on, all travelling south on a different bearing, to ensure we couldn't all be taken in one gulp. I repeated IRD's dictum that if captured, each of us should hold out for a day under interrogation, to give the others time. I heard someone say, Bugger that, Dig. I'm going to hold out for a month just to spite the bastards.*

*We all took to the sea. Now everyone had a folboat to ride in, and we travelled in groups of two canoes. Making for Australia. No reason why we shouldn't get there. We tried to hide by day and travelled by night, in and out amongst the pagar, the stilts of fish traps. By day we avoided Malay or Indonesian villages, and sometimes that meant sitting out in the mangrove swamps through the heat of the day. But a person just had to endure and promise himself night would come, and be quiet too. Jockey got a bout of fever, and was a passenger for two nights, raving away in Yiddish in the rear compartment. My only worry was that he'd throw himself in the sea at some stage, and I mightn't notice. I thought, I'll put him in the forward cockpit tomorrow night.*

*We knew you'd all be worried about us – I remember I told you, Grace, to expect me about December 6. It was nearly Christmas when Jockey and myself, big Chesty Blinkhorn and Pat Bantry – both of the latter at various stages Rufus's partners and pretty fretful about what could have happened to Rufus – were all cooking a meal in the bush in a coconut grove on some little place marked NE27 on our maps. We had paddled across the equator some days earlier and it had given us a boost to think we were now well into the hemisphere of home. And then Filmer and his crewman stumbled ashore. I wouldn't have been certain he had such a long paddle in him. And then Mel Duckworth and his bowman. Four boatloads in the one place at the one time, because of accidents of current or bad map-reading –*

*there was no time to hold an inquest to find out why. There were too many of them in one place. But what a comfort it was to see them. They looked dark and greasy and like skeletons, and I was pretty sure I looked no better.*

*I told half of them at least to disperse to the other side of the island, and soon after I saw through the dazzle of the sun a landing barge enter the lagoon through the hole in the reef and come into our beach, with another standing off the beach. We were down to a few magazines now, and were concealed in a piled-up clump of volcanic stones the patient seasonal workers of this coconut grove had made as a means of leaving the avenues between trees free. The landing troops looked more awesome and professional to us than any of the others we'd met. They came inland at the run, and saw us and began firing at us. We made a stand with our silenced Stens and our loud pistols. Chesty Blinkhorn was wounded and cried out to me, some advice I could not hear. Bantry and Jockey helped a hobbled Chesty away, and then the rest of us went running too towards the far side of the island. We would soon discover there wasn't much hope in that direction. The second barge had landed there and its troops had already captured Filmer and Mel Duckworth and, I regret to say, were beating them hard.*

*We four hid on a small volcanic hill. The Japanese did not pursue us. Mel's bowman had tried to swim for it, and late that night his body came washing back up, before the Japanese had even removed Filmer and Mel and taken them away by launch. It happened they were taken to a prison on a large island named Singkep Island, off Sumatra, and the base for the Japanese who'd attacked us.*

*Jockey and I, wounded Chesty and Pat Bantry – we all managed to find our folboats lying in the mangroves on the southern end of NE27. We took to the water but we were suddenly out of steam. We made little more than eight miles before dawn, when we put into the island of Selajar, and we dragged ourselves ashore. We were sheltering in an abandoned native hut when we heard the barges land and the shouts of Japanese officers. I could hear them coming in the undergrowth, and I had my loaded pistol, but I remembered Lieutenant Carlaw, and it struck me all at once to ask, What would any of it mean if I shot them and they shot me? Was that cowardice? The question didn't even worry me. I didn't even think of my poison. Poison had never been stressed anyhow. I have to say – it's no excuse – but I had some of Jockey's fever by then, so they entered the hut and I stood there stupidly with my pistol pointed, and a tall NCO came to me and knocked me down with a rifle butt. There was a bit more beating on the beach, before we too were put on a barge and came in the darkness to the stone cells in the old Dutch prison at Dabo. We were each put in a separate cell, except Chesty, who'd been taken to hospital. Filmer and Mel were already there. We were able to yell to each other, cell to cell. It was a comfort. We rested in the end. There was a ratty thin floor mattress in each of our cells.*

*Bantry and Skeeter Moss were soon brought in too, and each placed in his separate cell. There was a comforting feeling in that whatever was to happen to us would happen to all of us.*

I've been through those islands on a liner. I've left the cooled interior of the *QEII* and walked out on the rather narrow decks, designed more for the Atlantic than Pacific, and felt the sun like a blow on the neck and the shoulders. To spend a day in mangrove swamps under that sun would bring on madness if not fever. I know Indonesian civilisation is ancient, but it feels out there on deck as if all that is impossible, as if morality and culture are called off or driven out of the blood by the ferocity of heat. The joggers and walkers on the deck greet me, getting their aerobics over before the full muscle of the sun makes it impossible. And I flee inside, ashamed at choosing to be a pallid woman, stricken by that misery my husband Laurie can sense and wants to assuage and can't understand, since I was the one who talked him into this voyage. Always failing the young hero, always missing him, always enraged.

On one of the islands, Bintan, Leo was tortured and sodomised with a baton.

*We were thrown like fence posts into the bottom of one of their patrol boats and moved to a gaol on Bintan Island. This was a worse place, a Kempei Tai compound. It was bad. For a start, Blinkhorn now had malaria as well as his thigh wound and we could hear him calling to us and talking about such things as getting the cows milked and hay-baling, urgent things that he brought from his life on the family farm. Bantry, a cow-cocky himself, would sometimes answer him to soothe him down. Chesty was still raving when I was taken out of my cell to the interrogation room for questioning, and was sat down on a chair on that hosed cement floor.*

*I was soon kneeling on a piece of wood, and then somehow I was spread-eagled by the wall. So I must tell you this. Some dreadful thing happened there, with an NCO of the Kempei Tai. I don't mind being beaten, I'm sure we do the same. But this was . . . Yes, this was a violation. I hate to tell you but I have to. They pushed a baton into my body. Damn him to the pit, that's all I can say. And I'm telling you – I don't know why – because it's necessary for you to know that I've lived through that and that I'm still Leo.*

*Straight afterwards I felt all the shame was on me, but I've got to a stage now where I know the shame's on the mongrel who did it. Since you're a wise girl, you'd expect something like that might have happened, and you might have thought that it haunted me – well, it does, but it doesn't. It doesn't weigh on me. The Kempei Tai. Bastards.*

*The rest was beating and making me kneel on a piece of wood and one awful bloody session when they put a hosepipe down my throat and just pumped water in. I gave them nothing. I certainly didn't mention the SBs. As far as I know all the others gave them nothing. I think we were as surprised as anyone. The sort of pain they put us in just made us angry. Even the drowning torture. That should have got us talking as soon as we got our breath back. The only thing was they already seemed to know a lot about us.*

*One day they put Jockey and me and Chesty, who was somehow recovering, pure bush vigour, on a Kempei Tai launch at the wharf at Bintan – we just lay on the deck under the sun, roped together, sweating and done for, no more stories to tell each other, and not fit to hear them if there were. It was Christmas Eve but we didn't know it. The launch set sail and we came into the Singapore docks proper. We landed so close to Kempei Tai headquarters that they walked us there along Tandjung Pagar. I think the first Singapore laugh we had was when we saw that the place had been the Chinese YMCA – it said so over the door. Young Men's Christian Association. We all said it aloud, and we all hooted, and our guards belted us. But it's funny how kind of immune you get to being belted. One of those hitting us was a Malay Hei-ho, another one was Chinese, and the other two were Japanese Kempei Tai soldiers. Having a joke was more important than their authority.*

*On the way in through the lobby, I saw Hidaka the first time. I didn't know his name then. I couldn't have told him from the other officers that were around, except that he was wearing a white suit with no insignia.*

When Leo saw Hidaka, the interpreter was on his way to a meeting. He had told Lydon and others, reliably or not, that at that meeting at Water Kempei Tai headquarters it was decided by his superiors that in general torture wasn't going to work. They'd already tried it at Bintan, and they'd tried it on Private Appin, the cricketer, who'd been captured and taken to Surabaya where they beat him senseless, and no doubt subjected him to the repertoire of torture, and they had got nothing from him. I hope such a conference as Hidaka claimed did take place, and that it *was* now decided to go softer on everyone at the YMCA in Tandjung Pagar.

Tandjung Pagar these days – you can't see it for Singapore's thrusting buildings and shopping precincts, and the little Chinese YMCA, with all its screams still unresolved inside it, has been pulled down to make way for something appropriate to the new Singapore. The new architecture, the Capital Building and the Fountains, are more assertive than the memory of Leo's bravery and the bravery of the others.

After the conference Hidaka alludes to, those first three YMCA prisoners were brought into an interrogation room and paraded for the Water Kempei Tai officers and Hidaka. Hidaka would tell Lydon it was plain how exhausted they were. They'd been running for three months, since October, and they had not shaven and their clothes had turned solid with salt and then picked up the mud of mangrove swamps in which they'd hidden. It was at that stage that a Kempei Tai lieutenant, Sunitono, announced to them that they would have time for a bath and a shave. He also announced that he would not question them until after Christmas, given that he knew Christmas was so important to them.

*We know the bugger was softening us up, but you've got to take what mercies there are. We were happy for the moment but uneasy for the future. We could tell it might be a Kempei stunt. But we had to take what came, punches or privileges.*

*After Christmas, they began questioning us again. We played dumb about other members of the party. But they mixed up their act on us. Sometimes they would offer us one of their cigarettes, but another time they would get in an NCO to punch us again and again. Sometimes they'd just make us kneel on a sharp piece of dowling or bamboo, while the NCO burned us with cigarette ends. And one day they poured the water not only down my throat but pumped it into my rectum. Hidaka would be there. But to be fair to him, he didn't like any of it. Everyone could tell that. Them and us.*

*We had a reason not to tell them about the blokes still on the loose. Hugo Danway was out in the Lingga Archipelago, probably trying to capture a junk. The idea of us stalling the Japanese while the others got away was at the forefront of our minds. Long sessions. But it was milder than what happened on Bintan. We kept saying the junk carried folboats and limpets, because they knew that already.*

I remember old Mr McBride, the Minister of Defence who more than forty years ago gave us a miserable day in Canberra. I refuse to quote directly what Leo says in case this little memoir addressed to no one but my granddaughter should by evil chance, however remote, become public and the McBrides of this earth seize on it. Hidaka and Lieutenant Sunitono knew the prisoners were hiding something, for there were references in both Filmer's captured journal, and in Rufus's, to something named SBs.

This is the story Hidaka told Lydon. It had been noticed that Jockey tried to talk in Mandarin to one of the Chinese orderlies. The orderly was authorised by Lieutenant Sunitono to pass on the details of the deaths of Doucette and Rufus – Sunitono guessed it would put Leo and the others in a depressed and less guarded state of mind.

*Jockey's been talking to this Chinese orderly who takes us back to our cells. He told Jockey the Boss was killed by grenades and is buried on one of the islands.*

*The Chinese guard wouldn't risk telling us if it's not so, and a pall is over us. I'm certain the Boss let himself be killed so there'd be no retaliation against his wife and stepson. We knew something must have happened to him and Rufus, but to get the final news . . .*

So the next day, Sunitono told Hidaka to ask Leo, What about these SBs? It was shallow where you sank the junk. And so our divers have found the wreckage of them. They're no secret anymore, Captain Waterhouse.

That's the lie Leo fell for. And if he fell for it gratefully, who would not gratefully fall for it? But it meant that fat sleek men who never knew danger would forever refuse him posthumous honour.

The next day, as a further grace note, Hidaka told Leo and the others that there were twenty Malays under death sentence for the Cornflakes explosion. Leo spoke to the other veterans of Cornflakes, and they offered to make a joint confession to Hidaka, to which they appended an appeal for the release of the Malays.

Hugo Danway and a sickly, shrunken officer named Dinny Bilson also turned up at the YMCA now. Bilson was sadly depleted and had only a few tufts of his fair hair left.

They had tried to capture a Chinese *prahu* but the crew had sold them to the Japanese. They reported that Private Appin, who had hurled grenades for Doucette, had been captured too, but was very ill when they saw him in the gaol at Surabaya.

There were two left, including Dignam, the old Foreign Legion veteran, out there heading south-east for Australia.

There had been one small success for Memerang. A particular Japanese naval officer who had failed to have any success interrogating Hugo and the others sat down in a Surabaya restaurant and blew his brains out. But they would never know that.

So Memerang were interrogated and, when the naval prosecution considered its evidence was complete, they were moved to Outram Road Gaol, a huge old British prison which would not have been out of place architecturally in the Home Counties of Britain. And they were tried, and condemned, and came back to Outram Road, which they called the Grand Hotel because there the torture was at least random, not structured.

# Sixteen

*You wouldn't believe, Grace, how calm I am now, here in Outram Road. The way I see things, I've got two people to be thankful to. One's Hidaka and the other's mad old Filmer. He's such a character. I've got to say it's just as well we've got him here. Hidaka's brought Filmer some books from the Raffles College Library, and they're PG Wodehouse stories which Filmer reads us at night in all the right Pommy accents and gets us laughing. Could have been an actor, Filmer, and he might be, he says, if he gets out of here. He says he knows some fellows in the Royal Marines that have got connections at the BBC. He also says that he's related through his mother to one of Bernard Shaw's Irish brothers. Filmer says they were all drunks, except George Bernard Shaw, who was a vegetarian, but he was just as mad as them without taking to drink. Filmer can do all the accents in Shaw too, this book of plays,* Plays for Puritans, *Hidaka gave him.* The Devil's Disciple *is the best one of the three plays for us, because it's like our situation, men under sentence, etc. In fact we've started calling ourselves the DD's – the Devil's Disciples. We like the chief character's gumption. None of us are really keen on* Caesar and Cleopatra, *but* Captain Brassbound's Conversion *has a whole range of accents in it.*

*They've given us a mess room, and during meal times Filmer organises us into parts and goes through our lines with us, and then after lock-up we've got Blinkhorn, who has got better quicker than we could have hoped, doing Cockney from one cell and Hugo Danway doing the Yankee Captain Kearney from another, and Filmer doing Lady Cecily from a third, and prompting us, and it's all great for our spirits. I'm doing a couple of Captain Brassbound's sidekicks at the moment, but I'm going to take over the role of Brassbound from Jockey in a week or so. Jockey can do an English gentleman's accent, you wouldn't believe it. I really take back everything I ever might have said about Filmer.*

*There's a heavy-lidded guard we call Sleepy. He lets us make a fair bit of noise. It must be okay with his superiors. He looks like a fellow who's in the army by mistake, shows a lot of patience, but when his temper goes, he's frightful. We saw him beat a poor Dutchman dreadfully a week back. As the fellow stood outside his cell. He must have smiled or something – Sleepy can do that to you, sadder than a donkey in a cartoon one moment and the angel of death the next. I took a risk one day with him – he was putting Mel and Filmer in the same cell, as usual, and I knew they had something gnawing between them, so I said, No, not him, pointing to Mel.* Him.

*And I pointed to Jockey. And to my surprise he let me nominate who went in with who, so everyone gets variety, a good thing for them and me, and it's easy for us to pass on messages. Sleepy must know that, but I suppose he knows too we've got nowhere to go and no more harm to do. And that added to the play rehearsals – we were able to rehearse each other's lines very closely – I suppose we're getting a bit obsessed with it all. I almost got to consider I want to be an actor instead of a lawyer.*

*As for Hidaka, he brings us bags of these little Chinese lollies, and they're delicious – it's amazing how much like heaven sugar is when you haven't had any for a long time.*

*The DD's, the Devil's Disciples. If we have to face the penalty, old GBS has shown us how it can be done with as much style as possible. We're determined to have style like Richard Dudgeon, the central figure in the play.*

*Filmer's talked to Hidaka about how the prison boss Matsasuta ought to let us do a performance of* The Devil's Disciple, *with your dear husband in the starring role of Richard Dudgeon, and Filmer himself playing General Gentleman Johnny Burgoyne, and Jockey Rubinsky playing the clergyman Anderson.*

*Hidaka said to him, But the play concerns a great defeat for the British.*

*And Filmer said, like a true Pom, Yes, like Singapore. It can happen in the best of empires.*

*I think we've got Buckley's of the Japs letting us put it on, but rehearsing it is great work, and so is just reading the parts at night, from cell to cell. We get away with it!*

*There's another thing I ought to tell you about Filmer, so you don't blame him for anything. He's been pretty happy just as theatrical director. He has left the command of the blokes to me. You are Doucette's successor, he tells me, and, he says, You know how to handle Aussies. It isn't an art everyone has.*

*I always assumed he was a fairly toffee-nosed character, but you can't judge the Poms as easily as that. And I tell you what, I wish he'd been my English teacher at school ...*

I had thought that Leo's journal was the last item I would need to adapt to. Yet there was one side of me that quite correctly believed that Leo's story would only be settled by my own death.

Now my husband Laurie had a stroke which cruelly paralysed his left side and made it difficult for him to speak. The poor fellow was embarrassed by the impact his deadened lips had on his diction. He now lived in a home, quite an elegant one, but in permanent care, where I visited him daily. He was not disgruntled – he has always had a positive frame of mind, and the stroke, instead of souring him, seemed to have confirmed him in his best temperamental habits. Our son took him out for drives and to concerts at the Opera House in a wheelchair. Except he didn't want too many of his old friends to see him like this.

I visited Laurie every afternoon and read to him, and I thought that was the way his and my life would go, with no surprises but the expected ones of deterioration and sudden, perhaps fatal crisis for both of us. To extend our lives I read long books, like *Great Expectations* and *Quiet Flows the Don*, because I'd read somewhere that having a book to finish actually helped keep people alive.

Yet even as the century ended, I got an unexpected call from California, from a heroically aged Jesse Creed, the American who used to hang around the boys and whom Dotty worked for. Doucette had always been contemptuous of him, though I had found him very urbane and sensible. But I was rather surprised to hear he was still alive. He was coming to Sydney with his wife and wanted to see me. I'm ninety-two years, he admitted, and I had to get all manner of medical clearance to do this trip. Finding travel insurance was a hell of a business. But it seems my vascular system is that of a forty-year-old. And I have a wife to help me round – she's barely seventy.

I asked him why he wanted to come back. Well, he said, the claim of memory. And in any case he remembered and thought often about Doucette and Mortmain and Leo – in fact, of all the wars he had since been involved in, he said, he remembered Doucette, such a character, and still felt uneasy about him.

I did not like to hear phrases like that. They possessed all the danger signs. Hidaka had felt uneasy too, and been full of surprises.

Why uneasy? I asked. Dotty doesn't blame you. She blames Doucette fair and square.

I'd like to come and discuss that with you, Grace, he said.

You're very welcome to come, I told him. But is there anything more to be said?

I hoped there was not, but I felt the same fear I'd had before Hidaka visited me.

There are a few things, he assured me.

Damn him.

Bring your wife with you, I suggested. Safety in numbers, I thought.

Well maybe, Grace. We'll see.

I agreed to talk to him, of course, for Leo's sake. Because I visited the retirement home in the afternoons, I asked him to call in one morning at ten. I gave him the address and directions but he told me not to bother with those – he would have a local driver, he said.

The old man who presented himself at my door ten days later was indeed on his own, and wearing slacks and a fawn jacket. Despite his age, he still possessed those ruby-cheeked boyish features rather reminiscent of President Reagan's face, a particular sort of glow Americans retain through tennis, golf and watchful dieting. I had expected him to bring his wife. When I said so, he told me that she was still jet-lagged and had begged off. She gets jet lag real bad – always has.

He laughed benignly.

And the poor old thing doesn't have the stamina she once possessed.

Something told me that was just his story, and he had not wanted her here. We sat a while swapping life histories. He had married twice, been widowed once, had an abundance of children and grandchildren and great-grandchildren. He sometimes got breathless and they'd shipped extra oxygen aboard the plane in case he became short of breath, but he hadn't needed it – he'd known beforehand he wouldn't, but you couldn't convince wives and doctors.

I could see he was not utterly at ease telling me this, and so I was not utterly at ease hearing it. I created detours in the conversation. I asked him when he'd retired from the army. He'd hung on a long time, he said – until the late 1970s. He told me that he'd ended up his military career a major-general – a prince of the Pentagon. You know the saying about how behind every great fortune there's a crime? he asked. The same could be said of high military rank.

After retirement he served on the board of a staff college and took two quarters a year as an adjunct professor teaching politics at the University of California, Santa Barbara.

Underlying all we said, I think, was the awareness in both of us that he was the blessed warrior, always marked by himself and others for survival amidst the reckless. That was something I refused to blame him for, but even such a reasonable attitude called up its opposite, a little cloud of possible widowly rancour in the room. We were therefore happy when we found ourselves talking about Dotty. He'd read her half-dozen novels. She was very British, you know, he told me. I don't think all that postwar British squalor she wrote about is as interesting to Americans. The Brits go for squalor, but we try to ignore it.

I told him a bit shortly I thought squalor was inescapable for war widows, and inevitably influenced Dotty's novels.

I suppose that's true, he conceded, with careful grace.

But she had never remarried, which rather surprised him. She was a lusty girl, Jesse Creed said fondly. I imagine you've heard I was in a position to know. We had an affair, as the rumours said.

Before or after Rufus vanished? I asked.

Creed said, Both, I'm afraid. I don't expect you'd approve. To an extent I took advantage of her loneliness. So there, I can't be franker.

That's Dotty's business, I told him sharply. I've got other things to live with.

I hoped nonetheless that this was the chief of his old man confessions.

He said, When she had anything to do with other men, it was always really to do with Mortmain anyhow, that crazy monocle-wearing Limey.

Dotty also seemed to have remade her life. I got letters from her. About 1948 she had published a brilliant novel on East End women. It had been made into an angry little film everyone considered a classic. She was poetry editor of two magazines, and a literary figure, and she was tossing up whether to join a new publishing company as senior editor.

Dotty had been moderately successful with her novels, and her poetry was anthologised. She was a bit of a cult feminist writer, and had made her mark in London until emphysema and diabetes in combination had brought her down suddenly in the early 1990s.

What about Mrs Doucette? Creed asked. Do you ever hear?

Indeed, I could fill him in on Minette, and the scandal of the way Minette was forced to live.

Last I contacted her, said Creed, before I could answer, she was living with Doucette's mother, Lady Doucette.

I told him that was right. After the war, Minette and Michael were liberated, hungry but unharmed, from their convent-camp in the hills. She had nowhere to go – she did not want to return widowed to Macau, and she did not come to Australia, though I think a new world would have been her redemption. She made perhaps the worst choice, joining Lady Doucette in her family house in Wiltshire. Since her elder brother had died, Lady Doucette had become the chatelaine of the place. I wrote to Minette a number of times and got back plain letters about life in the countryside and walks she took Michael on along a nearby Roman road cut in a hill of chalk. It was Dotty's letters that told me of the full impotence of Minette's life. During her years under Lady Doucette's thumb, Dotty told me once, Minette and her son took their meals in the kitchen like servants, and soon discovered why Doucette had so feared his mother and flourished in the East, away from her oppressive presence. Dotty said a lot of the fight had been taken out of Minette by her imprisonment by the Japanese. Now Minette suffered the indignity of being the poor relative acquired through an ill-advised marriage, though the old dragon did send Michael Doucette to Eton, where his stepfather had gone.

A local landowner fell in love with the by-then middle-aged Minette and rescued her from the witch's castle.

I paused in my recital. Then I decided, Let him hear this, even at third hand, what Dotty told me Minette had experienced. I told him, While she was still at the house in Wiltshire, one day in the kitchen garden, Doucette appeared to her and said, I always wanted to give you something better.

Oh dear God, Creed murmured, and put his hand to his forehead. He said, A lot of ghosts after that war, weren't there?

It seems so. Leo had the decency never to trouble me.

We were drinking our tea by now. I steered him to that old standby topic of where else he was going while he was at this end of the earth. The winter sun was on his face and enhanced the sense he exuded of a life well lived, and a mind still active.

Oh, I've already been some places, I've just visited Melbourne again, he told me. It's changed, but it's still Melbourne. I always liked that place. It had a lot of character. And before then, we were up in Cairns. That's changed too since we were there, but you only have to scratch the surface to see the old town, the houses on stilts. There's something about that coast that won't let it be turned into a total Florida. The mountains behind, I suppose.

And this is your last call? I asked.

Yes. I don't expect ever to see lovely Sydney again. The truth is, Grace, I discouraged my wife from visiting today. I really wanted to see you alone. To talk about Leo and the others. To clear my slate.

I really didn't like that sentence.

Yes, I said, feeling that peculiar flinch. I appreciate that, Jesse. But there's my slate, too. What condition will you leave that in?

I'll try to be careful, he assured me. I know nothing about Leo but what reflects glory on him.

I was pleased to hear it.

He paused. He said, I remember a meeting I had up in Cairns one day with Doucette and Leo and Dotty's husband. I should tell you I was certainly trying to make a bridge with the guy – Doucette, I mean. Dotty's husband was fine. And nothing had happened between me and Dotty at that stage. But I wanted to work with Doucette because I could tell he was a special kind of man, and I could see he and his expedition could be an important business and might get lost in the wash-up. With our help it could be something special. That's what I believed anyhow. But he had a lot of contempt for Americans, that guy. He thought we were fools, an idea easier to argue now than it was then. But even if we *were* fools, we were the fools that were running the game, and everyone else, even Mountbatten, a fool enough in his own right, had to come to terms with us. Doucette thought I was being sent to clip his wings or spy on him and take his project off him. In fact I was genuinely concerned about him.

Why? I asked.

Because he was a terrier dog. And without our help, he should never have been encouraged to go again, you know. I'm sorry to say that, it must be painful for you. Cornflakes didn't prove that the thing could be done again. It proved that the thing could be done once.

It seems you were right about that, I told him.

A silence grew and although I understood that the longer it went the more we'd be landed back with the business of cleaning his slate, I could not think of a word to utter.

Suddenly, he said, My superiors, General Willoughby, General MacArthur. They believed Doucette's attempt to go back to Singapore was an imperial gesture, to set up a British claim for the place after the war. I know that from the standpoint of the present, their attitude might seem hypocrisy, but we Americans were genuinely all in favour of the Malays getting their self-determination, and Churchill and Mountbatten wanted back that which was theirs.

None of that mattered to Leo, I said. He just wanted to smite the Amalachites. He would have gone anywhere.

I know that, he conceded. But I was aware of one big problem I couldn't tell Doucette about. That was, if he kept Memerang to its timetable, it would coincide with General MacArthur's invasion of the Philippines. And the Philippines would take up all our attention. And that's exactly what happened, Grace.

Creed seemed to have been parched by a few minutes' conversation and drained his tea to moisten his tongue.

I was still in Melbourne in late October 1944, he said. I hadn't been moved forward to the Philippines because I was fielding all the interceptions of Japanese radio traffic. You must know by now that early in the war we'd captured Ultra, the Japanese code, and we'd been intercepting all major signals and orders since mid 1942 onwards. These intercepts were absolute gold, Grace. Ultra. The absolute standard. And we needed to be careful how we reacted to the messages we intercepted. We couldn't react, for example, in a manner that showed we had the code. Because we needed them to go on using it. So we could afford to take actions that looked to the enemy like skilled guesswork or good luck, but we couldn't take action which indicated foreknowledge. You understand that?

Of course I understand that, I told him, but my jaw was set, like the jaw of an unbreakable instead of a friable woman.

Okay, he said. The recital of this triumph of intelligence now, decades after, seemed to cause him as much melancholy as it did me.

So every day, he continued, as you might imagine, the Ultra intercepts were argued about, and as a mere lieutenant-colonel I had an advisory role in that. Some intercepts had to be ignored – we could have swooped in and saved this or that endangered officer, say, but that would have shown foreknowledge. That was the point, the intercepts dealt sometimes with local matters, with the movement of prisoners, say. Then at other times with considerable tactical issues, and then the entire strategic plans of the Japanese.

Look, I said. I've read the appropriate spy books. I'm up on my le Carré. None of this astonishes me, Jesse.

He looked me in the eye and spoke flatly. By way of Ultra intercepts, he told me, I knew by late October that Memerang was in trouble.

I felt that prickling sensation, like the soul breaking out in hives.

You're saying you knew, Jesse?

There was an intercept from the Seventh Area Army in Singapore that more than twenty Caucasian people had been engaged in a defensive stand on a junk in the northern part of the Riau Archipelago. The message said they had dispersed using sampans and canoes, and had infiltrated many islands of the archipelago. Even though the Kempei Tai hoped for cooperation from its network of agents, strict watch was to be maintained. And as we sat round the table in Melbourne, orders came from the Philippines, from General Willoughby's office, to say nothing to IRD yet.

It meant they could have signalled the submarine to pick them up at once.

You were sleeping with Dotty . . . and you wouldn't save Rufus.

The old general covered his eyes with his hands.

I was tempted to call Foxhill, but I was also inhibited . . . Next day or so we intercepted a Seventh Area Army message that four of Doucette's people were dead in combat and the others being hunted. Now I know what should have happened in an ideal world – we ought to have made up our mind to release the information to IRD so they could get a signal to the British submarine, that character Moxham, to move into the pick-up island with all speed. But there were risks in warning IRD. So we were coming to a decision. We didn't have any idea then that Moxham would dawdle criminally round the South China

Sea trying to find targets, or that he'd only visit the pick-up island once . . .

I could guess everything he was going to tell me. That their plight had been known. That they had been written off. Someone as precious and complex as Leo written off by people in temperate, secure Melbourne, just for policy's sake. I stood up. All the blood had raced to my brain. I could feel the inner pressure against the bone of my skull. The room swayed promisingly. So I'll die, I thought. I won't have to listen.

I am sorry, said Jesse Creed.

He stood too. He wanted to hold my shoulders but I backed away.

That's been a weight on me for years, he said.

He was distressed, sure enough, but now he implied he had transferred the weight. When I could think again, I found that for reasons I couldn't understand I did not want him to claim too much responsibility in front of me. I wanted to curse him after he'd gone. It was as if the normal denunciations just weren't adequate for dealing with him.

Well, you said you had a merely advisory role, I told him through my teeth, as if it was my job to comfort him.

No, not exactly, he said, refusing to be silent. I had the power to change decisions. With some danger to Ultra, sure. But of a very low order. I was asked my opinion. I felt I could have persuaded the committee. I believe I could have. But at the moment I should have spoken, I remembered Doucette, and all I felt was annoyance at him for getting himself in this mess. If you'll excuse me, I thought, let that

British bastard stew in his juice. He'd sneered at every gesture of friendship and cooperation I'd made. He'd pushed ahead with his Gilbert and Sullivan, tally-ho trapeze act. To hell with him! To hell with him! Then by the time I'd got over my rancour, I thought, Jesus, you have to raise it again tomorrow. But by then there was another flood of Ultra intercepts which kept me up all the following night, and it would have looked strange for me to revisit yesterday's business when thousands of men were dying in the Philippines. Basically, I lacked the moral courage to do it. I consider it the great dishonour of my career.

*His* dishonour. He might boast of that, but he still retained his remarkably robust face, and any torment he felt had not halted him from dressing his old bones in a camel-hair jacket and golf shirt and cream slacks and loafers. I felt my newly calm anger working along with my old familiar bewilderment, and a sense of being stung into brutality. Who did he think he was to make this confession to me? But fortunately I now lacked the physical endurance to beat him with fists, just as he lacked the endurance to receive such a beating. I felt affronted though, and this might have been the greater part of my anger, that I was being made party to nothing more than some sort of spiritual bookkeeping on Creed's part. And I felt for him too some of Leo's anger for the desk soldier, the ones who drew up plans for jungle forays, or supplied the gear of champions.

The thing is, I told him, you weren't condemning Doucette. You were condemning Leo. Doucette had chosen to throw himself on the first bonfire he found.

He made a concession with his hands. Remember Foxhill? he asked me. In the tartan pants? He was organising a group to go in by sub and fetch the survivors. Well, by that stage we knew it wasn't much use. They were all dead or captives by Christmas, except two, and we thought they'd probably drowned.

And you were wrong about that too.

Maybe. Anyhow, telling Foxhill to call off Memexit didn't involve any chance of jeopardising Ultra, and so I let him know.

Jesse Creed spread his hands further. He seemed to be expecting something more from me now. He was lucky that I did not know which viper of a sentence to sting him with first. *The great dishonour of my career*. How sad for you, that you discovered you were a bastard! It didn't stop you breathing, progressing, mating, breeding and aging and finding travel insurance at the age of ninety-two. I certainly didn't intend to absolve him, and I itched to attack him as I had Hidaka. And then it struck me. As I was ready to curse and whack him, I thought, You poor old bitch! What are you about? Doing what you could, and inadequate to Leo. But they all were inadequate to Leo. Foxhill, Doucette, Rufus. All of them. Eddie Frampton, Captain Moxham, Jesse Creed. At eighty-four, why not just let yourself go in peace? The ghost is satisfied, the ghost has had its explanations, the ghost has departed the scene. Just ease up now, you foolish crone. And be Leo's widow from this point only in honourable name.

Never mind, I suddenly told him, conceding nothing, dismissing him. I had scorn, too. All the stuff you try to lay at my door, you'll have to take all that with you when you leave. I'm going to get a bottle of gin. You and I will drink a health to the men you let down. Then you can go off in your car and make of it whatever you want. I'm not here to help you feel easy about 1944. You can go to hell for all I care.

He nodded. That's a good Australian curse, he said. And I deserve it.

When I brought the gin, he sat because I told him to. With the drink in front of him he looked so much like an aged lost boy. He laughed. I'm not supposed to have this. Ruinous to a guy's blood pressure.

I think you'll get through to tomorrow, Jesse. You always have.

He shook his head. He looked eroded now, and I was pleased it had gnawed at him, the same thing that had eaten at me. And at a calm level I acknowledged that after the century I had lived through, I wasn't nearly as surprised that day as I would have been had he told me in 1945.

Here's to Leo, I said. He abashed me by beginning to weep. Tears made his handsome, aging face look more squalid and rheumy. Ah, I thought, good. He should know some indignity.

Don't think of sending me a Christmas card, I told him.

He said, I don't think there'll be any more Christmases.

*As if they know they're feeding important theatricals, since the trial the rations have got better – some fish with our rice. Then one day little Hidaka smuggled in a dozen egg tarts in his valise. Succulent. We were groaning with joy like a pack of old ladies. He said, Steamed buns next time. But they haven't turned up yet.*

*Yesterday, a week from the trial, we suddenly got called up by Sleepy and told to get our mattresses and mess tins. We were sweating a bit because we didn't know whether it was the final walk, but Jockey talked to a Chinese orderly again and found it was routine after all. Naturally enough, we're hoping to wait the war out. Anyhow, as Sleepy led us to another wing we could hear some poor wretch being beaten somewhere on the lower floor. His screams were bouncing from gallery to gallery. In the end, we found ourselves at a cage, in a corner of the gaol, bars three sides and brick the other. There were bunks in there, some bed-rolls too, and so we were all going to be together till the finish, whatever the finish is. And crazy old Filmer looked at the cell and bed-rolls and said, Well now, chaps, we can really perform the play.*

Leo and the others must have read George Bernard Shaw's preface to the play, *The Devil's Disciple*. It's GBS at his most tendentious and engaging.

I read *The Devil's Disciple* with an appetite for its hidden magic over Leo. I found an unread edition of George Bernard Shaw's *Three Plays For Puritans* on our bookshelves, a 1962 Penguin edition. When I opened it, I found the outer rims of the pages browned with time – it was as if the book had lain close to a fire, but it was the dull plod of second after second which had done this. I can see why the other two plays did not closely interest Leo and Filmer and the men. In *Caesar and Cleopatra* and in *Captain Brassbound's Conversion*, a melodrama set on the coast of Morocco, there isn't the same focus as in *The Devil's Disciple* – the focus there being provided by Dick Dudgeon's embrace of execution in the place of another man, the Reverend Anderson, in New Hampshire in 1777.

From my Sunday school days, the phrase 'devil's disciple' still carries with it a whiff of brimstone. In what sense was Dick Dudgeon the devil's disciple? (asked the old English mistress in me). And how did Leo and the others see themselves under that banner too? Sergeant Bantry was a Catholic, and Jockey Rubinsky Jewish. In what sense were they devil's disciples?

I studied the issue. It wasn't an abstract matter for me. Even though George Bernard Shaw was playing with ideas in his safe study, or else his summer garden in Surrey, and did not have to face the blade himself, there is cogency for me and for Leo in what he wrote. As an introduction to the play, Shaw wrote an essay called *On Diabolonian Ethics*, and in it he complained that while he was away from London, a theatrical director interpreted *The Devil's Disciple*'s willingness to save the life of Reverend Anderson by dying in his place as motivated by his love for young Mrs Anderson. That was to miss the entire point of the play, said Shaw. A glorious thing, the thing by which the Devil's Disciple transcended Sydney Carton in *A Tale of Two Cities*, was to die for a man you didn't know, for a man who had a wife you didn't know, and whose features were unknown to you.

Shaw wrote: 'But then, said the critics, where is the motive? *Why* did Dick save Anderson? . . . The saving of life at the risk of the saver's own is not a common thing; but populations are so vast that even the most uncommon things are recorded once a week or oftener. Not one of my critics but has seen a thousand times in his paper how some policeman or fireman or nursemaid has received a medal, or the compliments of a magistrate, or perhaps a public funeral, for risking his or her life for another's. Has he ever seen it added that the saved was the husband of the woman the saver loved, or was that woman herself, or was ever known to the saver as much as by sight? Never. When we want to read of the deeds that are done for love, whither do we turn? To the murder columns; and there we are rarely disappointed.'

I'm sure the twenty condemned Malays for whose lives Leo and others of the Cornflakes gang had petitioned the Japanese were never far from the consciousness of Leo and the other Memerangs as they rehearsed the play. I prefer to believe that it was for those men that Leo was ready to die rather than for some flatulent concept of military honour. That he died neither for some bankrupt British officer code nor for the bankrupt code of his jailors.

I imagine the play under way in their communal cage, with Leo enacting his part, and Essie the servant girl asks him why he lets them call him the Devil's disciple? And Richard replies, 'Because it's true. I was brought up in the other service; but I knew from the first that the Devil was my natural master and captain and friend. I saw that he was in the right, and that the world cringed to his conqueror only through fear . . .'

I can imagine Filmer, who had been to Oxford, explaining the meaning if any of the group were theologically timid – that Richard Dudgeon is not really speaking of the Devil, he is speaking of the God of Purposeful Love, a deity unhonoured in the Dudgeon household in the play but honoured by Richard.

It is touching to think that under Filmer's direction, Leo played the scene in Act II in which he speaks at length with Mrs Anderson, played by Jockey Rubinsky (seriously it seems, and not for the easy laughs that derive from young men playing women). There is something almost consoling about that, the earnestness of two young men who would never touch a woman again, enacting sexual attraction.

I must curse GBS because he taught them how to do it, to be Devil's Disciples. I must thank him for reinforcing the necessity of the path they were treading, so that they went with a certainty that transcended flags and empires and all that weary dross.

*The reward for a good rehearsal is that Filmer reads us a Jeeves story by Wodehouse. You see behind the men's faces that the more they enjoy that, the more they think: Maybe they'll let us and the Malays live on too. But no one could say it, of course, because that would be a deadly bad omen.*

*When we read the whole play in our communal cell, Englishmen and Dutch and Chinese we had never seen applauded from their cells. Because by now Memerang fellows knew each other's stories, the play was like the new conversation we had with each other. We were grateful. If George Bernard Shaw had walked along the gallery on the third level of Outram Road Gaol and appeared in front of our cage, we would have cheered him to the echo. So would the poor buggers in all the cells.*

# Seventeen

*Hidaka's brought a huge bag of Amanetto sweets, which he knows are my favourites. He did not want to stay though and looked evasive. I wonder is something about to happen.*

*There are possibilities other than the worst. They might even take us over to Changi, to the general military camp.*

*Just in case though, I put down all the love I can find in this sentence. For you, Grace. It'll be wonderful if we meet again. It'll be a wonderful life.*

*Hidaka's sworn he'll get this to you if I can't.*

In a tiny *kolek* or fishing boat, two private soldiers, including Dignam the Foreign Legionnaire, were still at large in January 1945. They would call at villages but then move on before they could be betrayed. They had travelled 1900 miles through enemy territory, and at Ramang Island off Timor were only 137 miles from an air force pick-up island, and only five hundred from Darwin. By now, however, they needed to rest for days, and a village head man told the Japanese that they were there. They were taken to Dili in Timor where their torture was horrifying, and both, left alone in their cells at last, died of their injuries.

Then, in Singapore, on the morning appointed by the authorities, some four weeks before the war would end, guards came to the large communal cell at Outram Road prison and tethered the arms of all the Memerang men behind their backs. Sentries went screaming along the galleries telling prisoners, Don't look, Don't look! So there is no record of anyone having seen Leo and his men descend to the ground floor. They were dressed only in their shirts and shorts, and their feet were bare. It might be a move to another prison – they could partly quell their fever of expectation with that idea. But they hadn't been told to bring their mess kits. They probably all noticed that fact. By the time they were put in a small bus with painted-out windows, Jockey probably knew. Did he tell Leo? Did he bespeak death with total clarity? The orderly says no. But surely he'd tell Leo, they were so close. Japanese documents say they behaved coolly, and with the example of Richard Dudgeon before their minds, it was quite possibly so. As well as that, Jockey Rubinsky's attitude of not giving malign forces the satisfaction of showing obvious and reasonable fear was no doubt at play amongst all of them.

Not a lifetime of ambitious imagining, dreams, obsession and terror has managed to recreate that journey definitively for me. Hidaka says he heard from the guards that the men sang. Not hymns. They just sang. Studiedly casual songs. *There's a track winding back to an old fashioned shack . . .* or *Coming in on a wing and a prayer*, a hit of the time – I know Leo liked that. *Though we've one engine gone/we can still carry on/coming in on a wing and a prayer.*

The guards got them off their bus, and they stood on waste ground, and since they were not blindfolded they must have been able to see other burial mounds around the place, and certainly would have seen three freshly dug pits. So, their deaths became established in their minds. There was a considerable crowd of Japanese officers and men there, General Okimasa and at least two of the judges. The prison governor of Outram Road told them in English that they were to be beheaded. According to Hidaka, he himself was not there, he had hidden by the cars on the road, but he claimed he saw through the stunted trees that Leo and the others had now been released from their bonds and were smoking cigarettes, and shaking hands. I hope he's telling the truth.

He probably is, because even Hidaka doesn't pretend it was nice. He came close to the site, he fled, he came back again. Three at a time, the men were made to kneel, one at each pit. They were offered blindfolds, but some did not take it.

It is all very well for men to strut with swords and invoke Bushido, as it is all very well for mass-murdering generals to invoke chivalry amongst the shrapnel and napalm. But Bushido, like chivalry, required purity of heart and was beyond the reach of most narrow men. The NCOs of Judicial Section might each have owned a sword, but they had debased its meaning and its edge by beating and executing too many prisoners, and following that with too epicene a life, good Singapore food, blunting drafts of liquor. Had they been true warriors of ascetic and muscular leaning, the beheadings would not have been botched. Even Hidaka says it took half an hour, with breaks in between, while the fat judicial sergeants recovered their stability and their breath, and again took up their lean swords in their thick and inefficient hands. When the thing was done, the body of my beloved lay gracelessly and headless in its pit. Having been promised a death fit for heroes he was given a death barely fit for oxen. I know it. After the executions, Korean witnesses told the war crimes investigators, the NCOs in the squad room at Outram Road teased Judicial Sergeant Abukara about his messy work during the beheadings. Abukara would later suicide, impaling himself on his sword to avoid punishment for his Outram Road brutalities.

But enough. Enough now.

I sit where I like to sit in the mornings, having crossed the minefield of carpet edges and chair legs which is my living room to reach the sunroom and look out my window through the august North Head to the Pacific which connects us to all peoples and all cultures. There is an absolute purity out there that transcends the slogans: King and Country, Banzai, Blood and Fatherland, Semper Fidelis, Who Dares Wins. These are the mere trellises upon which men uncertain about their weakness grow their peculiar and imperfect intentions. Doucette and Rufus and the incompetent NCOs who struck the head from my husband's body were all in the same game. The truth is, heroism and its codes take you only so far, as it took Eddie Frampton only so far, and then he bit the capsule.

I didn't want a hero. A person is never married to a hero – the heroic pose is not designed for ultimate domesticity. Ulysses on his return found not a wife to charm but suitors to fight. Nothing is learned, and everything is learned.

*And at last Abukara gets it right and my eyes fly like rockets to the sun.*

*And look there.*